Ms Marie La
Apt 3
66 Kennedy
Somerset, M

A Love to Come Home To

A Time of Grace
Book Three

For Marie ☺

Alicia G. Ruggieri

Alicia G. Ruggieri

Books by Alicia G. Ruggieri

A Time of Grace Trilogy:

The Fragrance of Geraniums

All Our Empty Places

A Love to Come Home To

The House of Mercy (stand-alone novel)

THE REGENCY ADVENTURES OF JEMIMA SUDBURY (series):

The Mystery of the Missing Cufflinks

ISBN: 1534622047
ISBN-13: 978-1534622043

For Londie and for Bekki:
"I could never love anyone as I love my sisters."
(Louisa May Alcott)

"Hereby perceive we the love of God, because He laid down His life for us: and we ought to lay down our lives for the brethren."

1 John 3:16

CHAPTER ONE

Spring, 1937 – Massachusetts

"Them cards is fixed."

The low growl crawled across the makeshift table, slithering through the clouds of cheap cigarette smoke puffed through three sets of nostrils. The accusation made Ben's heart shiver. But he kept his face impassive, knowing that Aldo watched closely, alert to the smallest tinge of fear Ben might show. *Don't let him know you're nervous!* Raising his eyes to the level of the cards he held tightly near his face, Ben met Aldo's gaze. "You wanna say that again?" He made sure to use the same cement tone as his *friend* had.

Never let 'em know you're frightened, boy. Papa's admonition from a decade-and-a-half ago slunk through Ben's brain, firmed up his jaw, and hardened his gaze into ice. Guys like Aldo would take advantage of a man's fear. Like overgrown schoolboys, they'd use it to twist your arm up behind your back 'til you cried, "Uncle!" at the top of your voice.

Nobody's twistin' my arm. Ain't never gonna let 'em. He raised his chin a notch. "Hm?" he urged Aldo, letting the edge of his threat show as he clenched his free hand into a calloused fist. "Say it again, why don't ya?"

From his seat across the barrel table, Aldo's eyes narrowed into green slits, like a backwoods fisher cat when it thinks it might have at last met an enemy it can't beat. A huff emerged from his fattened lips, still bearing the shine of grease from his fried bologna supper. "Never mind."

"Ya sure?" Ben pressed past his fast-beating heart. If it came to it, could he beat Aldo in a fight, fair-and-square? *Gotta show him who's boss.* "Sure ya don't wanna say it again?" he egged on. The more he demonstrated his fearlessness, the less likely Aldo would be to take him up on his offer. For all his brawn, the Italian kid was lily-livered. "Cuz I think ya were accusin' me of cheatin'? That right, Aldy?"

Aldo glanced at the third guy playing with them, Pretty Joe, who twisted his own cards with the nervousness of a jacked-up racehorse. The younger man – really just a boy playing a man's part – skittered his wide eyes to the straw-strewn floor of the empty stall they occupied. Ben smirked. *Old Aldo won't get no support there.*

Even if he was right: the cards *were* fixed. Ben had made sure of that.

Finally, Aldo grumbled, "Aw, stop beating ya gums. I'm just pullin' ya leg, buddy. Ya got luck on ya side, I guess."

Ben felt his heart slide back into its normal rhythm. "Yeah," he stated after a minute. "I guess I do." He breathed deeply, the scent of fresh hay and horse-hair filling his nostrils, and prepared to play on.

Much later, in the early morning hours, Ben gathered up his winnings, as well as an i.o.u. from Aldo for nineteen dollars and twenty-five cents. Satisfaction warmed his chest as he swept the ratty bills and limey nickels off the battered surface. The coins clinked against one another in his pocket. Enough there to put away for the future. He wasn't going to be a loser like Aldo and Pretty Joe all his life. Or like Papa'd been. *Long may he rot in hell.* He would make something of himself, like the man he worked for, the politician Gerald Bousquet.

Ben didn't care much for the political part, but he'd take the racing-horse-owner bit. *That's where the money starts.* And money would make him happy. The lack of it had been the bane of his and his family's lives always, hadn't it? If he'd risen faster in the world, Mama wouldn't have had to go crawling to her old boyfriend to marry her. She'd have been able to rely on her eldest son to get her outta the mess Papa'd left her in.

Doctor Samuel Giorgi. The name of Mama's new husband left an acrid residue in his mind. During Ben's last visit, the Doc had permitted no question that he – not Ben – ran the Picoletti family now. *Even Grace is on his side.* Ben twisted away from the memory of his kid sister telling him to turn away from his sin, to turn to some kind of personal Jesus. *Sin? What sin?* What he'd been doin' – trying to get by in life, have a tolerable time of it – wasn't that just living? Wasn't that what a guy had to do? Unless you were rich enough – like the Doc – to do otherwise. *Nobody's gonna give you a hand up unless you pull them down and make them.*

Ben's fingers brushed through the bills in his pocket, mixing with the grit of crumbs. A smile flavored with bitterness pulled at his mouth as he watched Aldo and Pretty Joe shuffle out of the stall. Aldo mumbled curses under his breath. Ben chuckled silently. Much good that'd do his friend. If Aldo wanted to win, he'd have to fight for it, just like the racehorses in whose service the three of them slaved.

A few more decent card games and maybe Ben could buy his way into the boss' favor – maybe he'd become head groom, makin' bigger money. He was good enough at his job, wasn't he? *I'll be the master for sure.*

And then maybe Mama and Grace and all the rest of 'em will look to me to save 'em, rather than that goon who threw her over once before.

Ben blinked. Where had that thought come from? Hadn't he left all his family behind him, almost two years ago? The last time he'd seen the rest of the Picolettis, they'd been happily installed as members of a new family: the Giorgi family. *And they didn't want nothin' to do with me.* Resentment bit into his heart, though his mind told him that what he claimed wasn't really true. *They did want ya to stay. Ya chose to leave. Of your own free will.*

He shook his head violently and switched off the single bare bulb hanging down. The stall – the entire barn – plunged into darkness, save for the moonlight streaming through its windows. *They wanted me to stay if I'd change. They didn't want me – just their own version of me. They wanted to control me. Put their religious leash on me. They couldn't accept me the way I am. And I can't help the way I am.*

The horses nickered softly as Ben made his way down the moonlit barn corridor. Coming to the stall of his favorite filly, a beautiful bay with a feisty temper, he paused a moment. She put her velvety nose over the door. "Hey, there, Wild Girl," he greeted the horse with his own name for her. "You don't like bein' told what to do either, huh?"

She put her head down low, a sure sign that she wanted a scratch. "Ah, takin' advantage of my being awake?" He shook his head in mock dismay. "Well, alright, I guess a couple of minutes won't hurt." Not late as it was already.

Ben's fingers found their way to the spot just beneath the filly's forelock. He scratched for a long while, the back-and-forth motion acting with soothing monotony on his mind, driving all thought from it except for the pleasure of the scent and sight of the horse before him and the joy that his action brought such a wonderful creature. Pity all of life couldn't be like that: full of simple beauty and selfless giving. "But it's a dog-eat-dog world, sweet girl," Ben muttered to the horse. He felt no remorse for cheating his card-playing buddies, Aldo and Pretty Joe. They'd do the same to him… if they'd thought they could pull one over on him. He smirked. *Which they never could.*

Good thing, too, 'cause Ben had seen the murderous look on Aldo's mug as the dark-haired kid had stalked out of the stall after the game had finished. *Gotta keep my eyes sharp and my wits ready with him around.* Pretty Joe's passive company and innocent baby-face were much to be preferred.

An immense yawn overtook Ben's lungs. He gave the filly a last scratch between her perfectly-formed ears. "This is your last year, Wild Girl. Last one, and then you'll go out to breed. Get fat and have lotsa pretty babies, huh?" He laughed, and she sighed back, as if in happy agreement. The young horse was a fairly successful three-year-old, and Bousquet had already told Ben that he didn't plan to race her after this season. Ben slapped her neck gently. "Get some beauty rest, okay? Time for me to hit the hay, too."

Precious few hours remained to the night when his feet finally shuffled their way to his own flimsy bed, a rickety cot crouching in an empty stall.

~ ~ ~

Gladstone Conservatory — Crocksville, New York

When had she come to dread the sight of the postman? *It's not right, Grace.* Biting her lip, Grace let the thin lace curtain fall back across the glass. Better to face it now than to wait for the inevitable, the dread seeping through her bones all morning long during her theory and music history classes.

A glance toward the other twin bed told Grace that Elaine still slept. Silently, lest she disturb her roommate's rest, Grace tossed a cashmere sweater over her shoulders and pulled a thick, soft scarf off the back of the dorm-room door, wrapping it around her throat. Crocksville teetered right near the Canadian border, just off Lake Champlain, and May mornings still nipped with cold. Professor Baldacci would not be a happy camper if she arrived hoarse at her private voice lesson with him. *"Thoughtless,"* the sparrow-boned musician would mutter, shaking his head with the solemnity of Father Francis, the priest at the Catholic church back home in Chetham, Rhode Island. *"How very thoughtless you are. And that is one thing a professional singer cannot be. If you want to make it in the world of singing, Grace Picoletti, you must mind what you are doing."*

And she would. With firm steps, she descended the staircase, forcing herself to live in the moment. To feel the chill of the unheated stairwells, a difference from the warm dorm-room from which she'd just emerged. To sense the goosebumps rising on her arms. To listen to the groans behind the dorm-room doors she passed as other Gladstone Conservatory girls awoke. To concentrate on whether Judy Everich's scales – heard from the community practice room on the lower floor – were exactly in the center of the pitch or not. (They were not.) To call out a cheery "Hello!" to Maude and Charity when she passed the giggling twosome on the stairs, their heads parting only for a split second to respond.

Concentrating worked, alright. Grace could pay attention to the moment. Live her life precisely in the focused sphere of Gladstone Conservatory. As she'd been trying to do for the past school year.

Until she reached the dorm lobby, that is. There, beneath the Victorian-style architecture, Violet Simmons leaned against the solid dark-wood table, a stack of mail several inches thick in her hands, the individual mailbox cubbyholes rising before her. The second-year student scrutinized each envelope, even sniffing it in some cases, before depositing it into its appropriate cubbyhole. *She is so nosey!* Grace winced inwardly but kept a pleasant expression on her face. She was too late. Too late to face the mail delivery herself, bravely receiving the whole stack from the postman's hand. Now she had to let Violet mosey through the pile, commenting on each person's mail, while Grace waited for…

For what? You know he'll never write. Not now. She clenched her teeth in an effort to push down the looming disappointment and stepped down to the lobby floor. *He hasn't written since September 4th, 1936.* Strange how a date could engrave itself in her mind so deeply.

Stranger still how her heart could still hope.

Violet's eyes darted up at the clatter of Grace's low-heeled shoes on the waxed wooden floor. The girl smiled as though she'd not just been caught trying to figure out exactly what cologne saturated Phyllis Gain's correspondence. "Looking for your mail?" Violet asked, her light-pink fingernails scuttling through the stack. Her cinnamon hair still coiled in its overnight spirals on her scalp, crisscrossed with bobby pins.

Best to pretend nonchalance. Despite having spent nearly a full year with her fellow students, living with them day-in and day-out, Grace had never become intimate friends with any of them. Something always stopped her. Maybe it was the feeling that no one was from the kind of background from which she came. Perhaps it was the sense that so many of these girls – privileged, talented young women from the best families on the East Coast – had no clue what real life outside their carefully-sheltered bubble was like. And maybe just a little of it was the fear that, if they knew the real Grace beneath her expensive cardigans and stylish saddle shoes, none of them would want to be friends with her *just for her sake*. So she'd kept mostly to herself, studying hard and interacting when she had to. It was kind of soul-deep lonely, but at least it was safe.

However, there was no time to think of that right now. Violet's pointed finger finally stopped halfway through the pile. "Here's one!" She pulled out the square and handed it to Grace.

Grace didn't even need to tamp down her hopes. She'd known that one letter would certainly arrive with her name on it. She barely glanced at the old-fashioned cursive. Sure enough, it was from Mama. She tucked it into her dress pocket. "Thanks, Violet," she murmured, turning back to the staircase. She'd read the letter later, thankful beyond measure for the way her relationship with her mama had grown over the past few years. Had sprouted from a hard, infertile seed sleeping in the dark, dead ground to a young, tender plant that already had begun to bear fruit. *I have much to be joyful about.* Maybe a lecture about her blessings was just what she needed.

"Wait, Grace. Here's one more." Feeling her heartbeat pick up at Violet's words, Grace barely kept herself from losing all self-restraint as she whirled back toward her schoolmate. *Stop it, Grace. It's probably from Doctor Giorgi. That is, from Dad.* No matter how often she tried, she couldn't change her impulse of calling her stepfather by his professional title rather than by his well-earned role in her life.

She received the second thick, square missive from Violet, unable to stop her eyes from falling too eagerly on the handwriting and the return address. And unable to hold her heart in its rightful position. Slowly, it sank from its place in her ribcage down to her feet for the hundredth time in nearly three-hundred days. *Stop it, Grace. It's kind of Doctor – er, Dad – to write.* Papa never would have. *"Writing letters is for women,"* he'd have said. Doctor Giorgi probably didn't even realize just how much his letters did mean to Grace: how she saved them and read them over and over. More than Mama's, even. *When you don't grow up with a father's love, you appreciate it even more when it comes to you.*

But a letter from her stepfather wasn't all that Grace's heart desired. *If Paulie would write to me even once…*

But he wouldn't. Hadn't for many months. Unless she counted the times her mama added that, "Paulie says to tell you he's praying for you."

But she didn't want just his prayers. She wanted his letters. *And his love. Oh, Paulie, why did you fall out of love with me?* Her heart choked up at the question.

With a thank-you to Violet, Grace shoved all thoughts of Chetham, Rhode Island aside. She began to climb the steps again, more quickly this time. The big hand on the lobby cuckoo-clock neared the nine, and she couldn't be late to music theory. That class was difficult enough as it was.

"Oh! One more for you, Grace!"

Her mouth dried. *Surely, it's not…*

Grace turned to find Violet smirking up at her. "And it's from a young man," the girl teased, waving the envelope like a broken wing. "Oooh, I didn't know that you had a fella."

Keeping the same smile on her face, Grace shook her head. "I don't," she said, willing her voice to remain steady as she descended the stairs again with the slowest of steps. When had her joints turned into overcooked macaroni?

She reached out for the envelope, but Violet withheld it, running it beneath her nostrils. "Does it smell like cologne, I wonder?" she teased.

Grace heard the clatter of high-heels and saddle-shoes on the staircase above the lobby. Her neck prickled. "Violet, please give me the letter."

Violet's eyes widened. "Oh, so it *is* from a boyfriend?"

"No." Grace forced herself to remain calm.

"Then why are you so nervous?" Violet raised her eyebrows. Her cheeks glowed pink with merriment. Obviously, she was enjoying this.

Grace was not. *Lord, help me to behave with kindness. And make her give me the letter!* "I'm not nervous. I – I have to get to class." Which she did.

Violet's mouth dropped open, and all signs of merriment fell from her face. "Class!" She smacked down the stack of mail onto the heavy lobby table. "I have class at nine o'clock, too, and I still have to take out these pin-curls!" Her hand to her head, Violet brushed past Grace and thundered up the staircase.

Before the lobby filled with the other descending young women, Grace grabbed the stack of mail, nearly crushing the edges in haste. The top one bore her name. But the return address…

She swallowed down the aching lump that rose in her throat. Clamping her jaw again, Grace faced the mail cubbies and, with shaking hands, shoved the remaining envelopes into the general spot for someone else to sort. She took her own third letter and pushed it into her pocket with the other two. *I'll read them later. Not now.*

Noisy high-heeled shoes tapped down the steps behind her. "Hey, Grace, Violet said that you got a letter from your young man," Christine Emerson jabbered in her loud parrot voice as she paraded toward Grace, her black eyebrows cocking in anticipation, her painted lips curling up.

Grace smiled with the woodenness of a Christmas nutcracker and felt the hollowness of her expression straight down to her toes. "I did," she replied. "My little brother Cliff wrote to me."

CHAPTER TWO

"Heyya, Benji." The half-friendly thud of Aldo's fist hit Ben's shoulder. *He knows I hate it when he calls me that.* Irritation crawled through his veins. *One of these days I'm gonna smack ya one right in the kisser, Moldy Aldy, my friend.* Not bothering even to answer Aldo's greeting by raising his eyes, Ben kept his seat in the tack room. In fact, he didn't even break the swish-swish rhythm as he sponged the leather bridle lying across his legs. Two more and then he'd stop for breakfast.

When Ben didn't respond, Aldo's nasal whine began again, "Benji-boy–"

With a swiftness that belied his outer calm, Ben rose to his feet in one smooth motion. He grabbed Aldo by the jaw with iron fingers and smiled. "Aldo, next time you call me that, I'm gonna break your teeth."

Aldo's throat bobbed twice at Ben's words, causing Ben's former irritation to swirl away in a tide of satisfaction. With effort, Ben resisted the urge to back up his threat with a shove. Adrenaline pulsed through Ben's arms, but he maintained his coolness. Mr. Clay, the barn manager, didn't look well on fighting, and Aldo had gotten the point; that was clear from his angry scowl.

How he'd like to give Aldo a good punch, though! The guy had never done nothing but make trouble for him since he'd come. *Jealous. That's what he is.*

Ben took a deep, silent breath as he reached for the bridle again. *He knows I'm sitting pretty here.* Plenty of times, Mr. Clay had told Aldo and Pretty Joe to watch Ben's work if they wanted to see the way things oughta be done in a racing stable.

He'd thought that surely, given the way he'd treated Aldo, the coward would've scrammed. But, ten seconds later, Ben looked up and the short kid still stood there. *Why's he almost… smiling?*

"Now, whatdaya want?" After that card game last week, Aldo sure hadn't sought out Ben's company more than was necessary. "To what do I owe the honor of this visit?"

Aldo raised his chin and folded his hairy, ham-hock arms across his dirty, half-buttoned shirt. "*I* don't want nothin'. The boss does, though. Says it's important." A strange satisfaction hovered just beyond reach on the man's face, as if he was trying to hide something that tickled him pink, blue, and every color in between.

Shoving back the wave of nervousness that lapped at his bones, Ben frowned. "The boss? Mr. Clay?"

A mean delight curled at Aldo's lips. "Oh, yeah, Mr. Clay. And Bousquet himself."

Ben found himself on his feet, heart pumping faster than a stallion fed only on oats. Something was off about this. He opened his mouth to ask Aldo but then thought better of it. No use throwin' his pearls to swine, as Grace had said in one of her long-ago letters.

And Aldo sure is swine.

~ ~ ~

Ben shook his head. "I don't understand it, sir." He ran his hand down the filly's left front leg. She flinched and made a faint sound deep down in her throat. And no wonder: her skin felt hot as a bonfire in July. The leg had swollen to twice its normal size. *Almost as if she got an infected cut. Or as if somethin' hit her. Hard.* He stood slowly to avoid startling the horse and faced his employer and the barn manager.

Their twisted scowls turned Ben's body stiff with fear. Why did they seem angry at *him,* not just with the situation of a lame horse? Lame horses happened, especially at a racing stable. Cracking his knuckles nervously, Ben licked his lips before asking, "Didja call the vet?"

Mr. Clay exchanged a stony glance with Mr. Bousquet. "Anderson's on his way," he replied, "but I think there's little he can do to get her back into racing condition. Not this season."

Ben frowned. "Whatdaya mean, sir? I mean, lotsa horses go lame for a bit. Could just be a touch of–"

"I think it's time you stopped pretending that you don't know what's going on, boy," interrupted Bousquet. He crossed his arms over his chest as if to emphasize his sternness.

As if Ben needed that affirmed. Bousquet in a normal mood could be a frightening, unreasonable man. Bousquet angry... Well, he didn't want to consider that. Especially if the anger was directed at him. "W-What?" Ben stammered, feeling his cheeks turn hot with surprise and fear. "I dunno what ya mean, sir. I didn't got nothin' to do with this horse goin' lame. Applesauce! Ya know I take good care of the horses for ya. And this filly's my favorite. Mr. Clay, tell him," he heard his own voice begging. What a hateful sound! Whining, begging, pleading. Why should he have to prove his innocence here just because a rich man's prize filly had a lame leg? *I didn't got nothin' to do with it!*

Mr. Clay raised his eyebrows and pulled something from behind his back. He held it out to Ben. "We found this in the filly's straw bedding."

Half-afraid to know what the mystery object was, Ben forced his eyes to examine it. "My hammer," he murmured aloud. His voice sounded as if it came from somewhere outside himself. As if someone other than he spoke.

"So you admit that it's yours?" Mr. Bousquet spat, his fury fully taking over. Purple rage spread over his face. In his neck, the stressed tendons pressed against the florid, smooth skin.

How Ben wished that he could deny ownership of the hammer! But he couldn't. There, on the well-made handle, he'd carved his initials, *B.P.*, just to make sure that none of the other employees stole the necessary tool. And he had been in the filly's stall just yesterday, making repairs on the door, like Mr. Clay had asked. *But I'm sure that I took my hammer back to my quarters.*

He swallowed hard and sucked in an oxygen-less breath. This situation was giving him the screaming meemies. "Yeah. It's mine. But why does it matter? I mean, an old hammer lying on the straw wouldn't up and hit the horse, make her lame. I—"

"What made you do it? Were you stewed, boy?" Mr. Clay growled, advancing on Ben with slow, steady steps. "The horse has obviously been injured – hit in the leg – and now she's lame."

"I ain't been drinkin'! I swear it on my father's grave!" The words rattled out of Ben's shaking lips.

The taller man shoved him in the chest. Ben fought the urge to retaliate with a push of his own. If he did, it would undo him. He'd be out on his backside in less than thirty seconds. Forcing his face into passivity, Ben permitted his hands to curl into fists at his sides.

His oiled black hair falling across his right temple, the barn manager continued, "What, then? Make you mad, did she? So you lost your temper?"

"N-No, sir!" His eyeballs drying out from not blinking, Ben backed up against the wall, horror gripping his innards when he realized that Mr. Clay really believed the garbage he was spouting. *And Bousquet's buyin' it, too.*

"Doc Anderson's here, Mr. Clay, sir," Aldo's voice interrupted the storm inside the filly's stall. His self-satisfied, innocent voice.

Mr. Clay turned his attention away from Ben and toward Aldo's submissive, concerned face peering over the half-door. "Bring him right away, boy," he snarled. "I don't have all day. This horse is bad-off."

"Yes, sir!" Aldo's voice now wore a mask of distress, but Ben wasn't fooled. *He's happy that I'm in trouble.* Aldo had no worry for the horse. That one only cared about the contents of his pocket. *And about getting even with me.*

How his hammer had gotten back in the stall, Ben didn't know. But he did know one thing: He had to convince the barn manager that he had nothing – nothing whatsoever – to do with the prize racehorse's injury. "Mr. Clay, sir–" he began.

But Mr. Clay cut him off again. "Get out of my sight. You're restricted to your quarters until further notice. Got it? And don't even think about leaving the premises, or I'll be calling the police."

The lump in Ben's throat nearly choked him. "Yes, sir," he mumbled.

~ ~ ~

He didn't have to wait long for news. Within an hour, Mr. Clay appeared at the open door of the stall in which Ben made his bed. "Leg's not busted."

A sigh of relief whooshed from Ben's too-tense lungs. "Thank God."

Mr. Clay raised his eyebrows. "I wouldn't be so quick with giving thanks to the Almighty if I were you."

Ben's mouth dried. "Wh-Whadaya mean, sir?" His fingers gripped the edge of his cot until his knuckles turned white. "I know that it seems like I hurt the horse, but really, I don't know…"

He trailed off when he saw that anger still soured the barn manager's face. "Yes, you really don't know, do you, Ben? Perhaps you haven't accounted for the fact that that filly won't be able to race for the rest of this season, possibly losing Mr. Bousquet thousands upon thousands of dollars? Perhaps you haven't recognized that there's plenty of evidence – including your own admission that the weapon belongs to you, as well as the attestations of your fellow grooms regarding your infamous bad temper – to show in a court of law that you intended to injure that animal, a man's valuable property? Perhaps you don't realize that your hefty offenses could – No, let me speak plainly, since we're friends – *will* land you in prison?"

The torrent numbed Ben's mind and emotions as surely as plunging his body into a winter river would desensitize his flesh. He couldn't speak. How had he gone from the respected head groom for a powerful politician to a falsely-accused criminal in less than two hours?

"Of course," Mr. Clay went on, "there's a way out of this mess, Ben. Mr. Bousquet has decided to be gracious to you. If you can come up with some money to reimburse him for the loss of the filly's racing season, then he will be content with your dismissal. We're not talking about much, you understand. Seven, eight thousand would satisfy Mr. Bousquet."

Disbelief joined the numbness. Ben shook his head. "You know I ain't no rich guy, Mr. Clay. Where would I ever come up with money like that?" he gasped out.

The barn manager raised a shaggy eyebrow. "True, you don't have that kind of money at your disposal, but…"

"But what?"

"Your old man does, doesn't he?"

The very mention of Papa caused his skin to crawl. "I don't got no father," he replied gruffly. "I told you before. He's dead."

Mr. Clay's gaze stayed steady. "Oh, I think you know whom I mean. I've heard the rumors spread around here: about how your gold-digger of a mother married again to a rich something-or-other."

Doctor Giorgi. Ben's jaw hardened. He gave a stiff nod.

Mr. Clay leaned in a bit. "My advice, kid? Get the jack from him, and save your hide from jail."

"Can't. Ain't on speakin' terms with the guy." He hadn't been since 1935. The last he'd seen of the Doc, the man'd been covered with vomit. *My vomit.* The idea of facing him again turned Ben cold with repulsion.

16

Mr. Clay sucked in his leathery lips. "Well," he finally said, turning back to the barn aisle. "It's your choice, then. If you're sure you don't want to ask the old man, I'll call the police. Get it over with, you know. Better for all of us."

His heart jumped into his larynx. "Wait!" Ben stumbled forward, grabbing at Mr. Clay's shoulder. Anything to stop the man from calling the police. "Please. Wait. I-I'll write to my mother. I'll get the dough from her."

Mr. Clay smiled. "Good. I didn't think we needed to get the law involved. That's not how friends operate, you know. You have paper and a pencil?"

"Huh?"

"To write your mother."

"Oh." Ben swallowed. "Yeah." Somewhere in his locked personal box, he was sure he could scrape up a sheet.

"Good," repeated the barn manager. "Whenever you've got the letter ready, call for me. Mr. Bousquet will pay for the stamp." Without another word, he stepped into the barn aisle and pulled the stall door shut behind him.

The sound of chains and a padlock turning hit Ben's ears. "What're ya doing?" he yelped, despising the way his voice cracked with fear. Cages, prison, bars…

"I want to make sure you stay nice and cozy in there, kid." The chains clanked one last time as Mr. Clay secured them. Then the man's footsteps retreated back toward the lame filly's stall on the other side of the stable.

Ben let his head fall into his hands. How had this happened? Hammers didn't rise up by themselves and strike a horse, even if he had left the tool where he shouldn't have. And hit the horse himself? *As if I'd do such a thing!*

Chuckling interrupted his gloom. Ben looked up to see Aldo's olive-toned face sidling along the barred opening of the stall. How that guy reminded him of a snake. "You really got it coming to you this time, Benji, dontcha!"

Ben gritted his teeth, but his spirit had sunken so low that he wasn't able to think of an appropriate retort. He glared up at Aldo with silent vengeance. Why waste his breath on that kind of a creature?

Aldo smirked. "Maybe this'll teach you not to cheat at cards, huh?"

Outrage clogged Ben's throat as the full import of Aldo's words soaked into his mind. "You…" He felt his knee joints lock against the edge of his cot. He fixed his eyes on that backstabber who stood on the wrong side of the bars. If he could've bumped him off with a gaze, he would've. Ten times over. "You did this to me, didn't you? You scum," he breathed.

Aldo answered with a snorting laugh before dissolving into the increasing darkness of the stable.

CHAPTER THREE

Chetham, Rhode Island

The morning light splashed across her desk as Sarah reached into the drawer for a fresh sheet of stationary. How thankful she was for these mid-morning hours of solitude – after the hustle of getting Cliff off to high school and Sam out the door to his office, yet before her own afternoon activities.

Taking the fountain pen from its holder atop her neatly-arranged desk, she breathed deeply, silently asked her Heavenly Father for the words to write, and began her letter:

Dear Grace,

I have not heard back from you yet, but this snippet of a hymn came to my mind this morning during my quiet time with the Lord Jesus. I thought that you would find it helpful, especially during these last weeks of the – what do you call it in college? – the semester? You'll have to forgive your old unlearned mama her mistake, if she's made one! Here it is:

Blind unbelief is sure to err
And scan His work in vain;
God is His own interpreter,

And He will make it plain.

You said to me in your last letter that you still have no idea of what to do after you've graduated. That's a long way off yet, I know, but time goes faster than we expect it to, doesn't it? This hymn – well, I felt comforted that "God will make it plain." We don't have to try to figure it all out for ourselves, Grace – We can rest in Jesus, knowing that He will lead us as we obey Him. He will lead you, Grace, even if it's not in the way you thought your life might go. I've seen that in my own life.

I hope that you know that your stepfather and me, that we are both so happy with the good work you've done at the Conservatory. I know that He will direct your path, Grace. We are praying for you every day.

Your loving,
Mama

Sarah set down her pen and stretched out her back, enjoying the feeling of her muscles loosening. Outside her window beside the desk, she could see that a pair of robins had begun to build their nest. The male partner of the cheerily-vested team must have found mud near the small fountain behind the house, for Sarah could see a large glob of sticky brown held between the two halves of his beak. Patiently, the robin waited for his mate to finish her interior design work before he dashed into the nest to deposit his own findings.

A smile stayed on her lips as Sarah turned back to her letter, folding it and tucking it into an envelope. She addressed it and then moistened a stamp to affix to the upper right corner, shaking her head as she did so. Three cents to post a letter. What were things coming to?

She'd just risen from her chair when a strong knock – just short of a rap – sounded on the bedroom door. "Yes?"

Mrs. McCusker pushed the door open. The housekeeper's steel-colored dress and matching eyes had not changed in the two years since Sarah had married Sam Giorgi and moved into his large house on River Avenue. *Though her attitude toward me has certainly become more respectful.*

"Pardon me for disturbing you, madam, but the postman has delivered the mail," the woman interrupted Sarah's thoughts.

Sarah tilted her head, surprised. Usually, Mrs. McCusker just left the mail on the entryway table for the Giorgis to look through at their leisure. "Thanks for letting me know," Sarah replied after a moment's hesitation. "I'm going for lunch with my daughter Lou and will look at it when I return."

Mrs. McCusker hesitated, then gave a half-nod. "Very well, madam." A faint frown stained her pale lips as she turned back toward the hallway.

A familiar feeling wrapped tendrils around Sarah's heart. *Fear.* But why? That was silly. There was nothing in the housekeeper's actions or words to give Sarah a reason to become afraid! Still, she'd better check the mail before she left the house.

Gathering her powder-blue coat and handbag, she descended the curved staircase slowly, her low-heeled pumps click-clicking on the polished wood. Above her, the crystal chandelier threw off rainbow-colored beams of light and reminded her of her favorite childhood novel, *Pollyanna*, whose heroine had seen the glory of heaven in the most unlikely places. As she came closer to the hallway table, Sarah's gaze focused on a piece of mail resting there. *The letter.*

Her heart pounding, she picked up the envelope, not recognizing the long-and-thin cursive scrawl. Perhaps the sender had written his or her return address on the flap. She turned the envelope over, holding it away from her farsighted eyes. Sure enough, there it was...

She stopped breathing. *It's from Ben. Oh, dear God, thank You!* It had been so long since he'd written that she'd forgotten what his handwriting looked like. The tears rose to her eyes as she forgot her dismissive words to Mrs. McCusker earlier and slid a shaking finger beneath the sealed flap. In her hurry, she tore the envelope and let it fall to the polished floor like a cast-off autumn leaf.

Dear Ma,

Sorry I ain't wrote to you in so long. I've been busy. Thanks for your letters. I got them all. Ha – You guessed right that I'd get back in at the same stable. Not much can keep a Picoletti down, huh?

Sarah frowned, and a little of the hope trickled out of her swollen heart. *He sounds the same. Just the same.* And if he was just the same, why did Ben write now? When he'd not answered a single one of her bi-weekly letters for two years? Praying for the grace to face whatever else lay in the letter, she continued to read:

I'm in a little trouble. I ain't done nothing wrong, though…

~ ~ ~

Three days later

Sam Giorgi drew a deep breath into his lungs. His eyes rested on the fields, newly greening and studded with grazing horses and foals. Their coats shimmered bay, black, gray, and chestnut in the bright spring sunlight: a vision of splendid peace.

A peace that could not find a resting place in Sam's own heart.

Sam's old driver, Taylor, steered the car around the final curve of the dusty driveway. "Park here, sir?" Taylor quirked a fuzzy eyebrow in the rearview mirror as he slowed the car.

"Uh, yes. Yes, this will be fine." Sam paused. "I'm not sure how long I'll be, Taylor." A twinge of unaccustomed nervousness spread through his body. Usually, he was the person in control – in surgery, in the exam room, and even in his family. But here, Sam knew, only one person would determine the course of action. And that person wouldn't be he.

The car shuddered to a stop, and Taylor began to open his own door so that he could assist his employer, but Sam arrested his action. "Don't trouble yourself, Taylor. Just wait for me here, please. They're not really expecting me, so I'm not certain how this will go. I'll return

22

shortly. I hope." He opened his door and propelled himself to his feet with one motion. The brick house – larger even than his own comfortable home back in Chetham – towered among swaying willow trees. He straightened his tie and jacket and then strode up the walkway, pushing through the nervousness tingling in his chest. *Oh, Lord! I don't know how this all will go. But You do. I will trust in You.*

He raised his chin and rapped the golden lion knocker with an authority he didn't feel. *So this is how a politician lives.* Sam hadn't called to make an appointment. Hopefully, the man would be at home. If not… Sam tightened his jaw as the time lengthened on. *If not, I'll be staying in a hotel tonight and returning here tomorrow.*

Just when Sam had begun to relinquish hope of setting foot inside the man's home that day, the thick, carved door opened four inches. A young woman – a maid, Sam assumed – peered through the opening with large plum-colored eyes fringed by satiny lashes. A starched black-and-white uniform dressed a body that was as round and plump as a spring cabbage.

"Good afternoon," Sam began, smiling in a way that he hoped would secure his welcome. "I wonder if Mr. Bousquet is at home. I wish to speak with him."

The door eased open a few more inches, and Sam saw the maid's gaze dart past him to his late-model Ford and then, quick as a wink, back to him. His conveyance must have met with her expectations for someone who wished to speak with her master; she stepped back so that he could enter. "Please come in, sir."

His shoes clacked as he stepped onto the multicolored marble entryway floor. The stone blended seamlessly in a mosaic pattern, though Sam couldn't tell what picture it mimicked from the cursory glance he afforded it.

"May I have your name and business with Mr. Bousquet, sir?" the maid interrupted Sam's visual tour.

Sam removed his hat and placed it on the entryway table, his eyes still roving the glimmering and polished surfaces of his surroundings. "Certainly. Tell Mr. Bousquet that Doctor Samuel Giorgi has come about a personal matter."

"Very good, sir," she replied and moved toward an open door that veined off the entry. "If you'll wait in here, Mr. Bousquet will be with you shortly."

With a nod, Sam stepped into the room she'd indicated. It was a formal sitting room, the kind furnished with couches uncomfortable enough to make unwanted guests leave quickly and decorated with the sort of manmade elegance that caused Sam to look out the paned windows for relief.

Oh, Lord, help me to be wise with this man. Give me Your discernment.

He barely had time to finish the one-sentence prayer when a voice cracked the room's silence with the subtlety of a jockey's whip. "Welcome! Welcome, sir!"

His curiosity piqued, Sam turned to face the owner of the words. He'd never met or seen Gerald Bousquet – though he'd certainly read in the newspaper of the man's successes, in the racing business at least. From what Sam understood, Bousquet had operated a breeding-only stable in the early Thirties. Then, once Suffolk Downs had opened outside Boston a couple of years ago, the man had leapt into racing too. As Sam rose from his place on the awkward couch, he eyed his host. Like the maid who had met Sam at the door, Bousquet was a stout, squat fellow; the top of the man's balding, oiled head came only to Sam's chin. For not the first time, Sam wondered exactly what – besides the horse business – Bousquet did to maintain his lavish lifestyle. Everyone knew that he was a politician, but no one seemed to know what that entailed for the man.

"And whom do I have the pleasure of addressing?" Bousquet extended his hand, interrupting Sam's thought.

As Sam stepped toward him, the faint scent of black licorice touched his senses. *He drinks anisette in his coffee, I'd wager. If I was a wagering man.* "I am Doctor Samuel Giorgi. I've come about a personal matter. I hope it is not an inconvenient time?"

Mr. Bousquet wriggled his fleshy lips, as if in an effort to itch his nose without using a finger. "If you're the Samuel Giorgi I think you are, then you've not come about a personal matter. Any matter that involves money is strictly a *business* matter, you know." His shaggy eyebrows reached halfway up his round forehead in emphasis.

Sam remained silent but kept his chin up.

Bousquet's jaws worked into a puffed smile. "Please, sit," he invited Sam as he himself sank into the one comfortable-looking chair.

Perching on the edge of a hard couch, Sam began again. "As I'm sure you know, I'm Benjamin Picoletti's father," he said slowly, "and–"

"*Stepfather*, I believe, is the correct relationship," interrupted the politician, easing himself deeper into the cushioned leather chair. "Not to offend you in any way, Mr. – that is, Doctor Giorgi, but the young man was *very* clear on that point. However, I don't wish to distress you by delving into the – ah, awkwardness of your relationship. So, please, go on."

Sam took a breath. This man rubbed him like sandpaper on a sunburn. *And he delights in doing so.* "I understand that the boy has gotten himself into some trouble here." He paused to see what Bousquet would say. Perhaps Ben had exaggerated. Maybe the situation wasn't as dire as he'd said.

Bousquet merely cocked an eyebrow with the flexibility required of an Olympic gymnast on the parallel bars. "Yes, I'd say that."

"Ben wrote to his mother and explained the situation," Sam continued. "I believe that you think he is responsible for an injury done to one of your racing fillies and that you wish to be compensated."

"I don't believe it, Doctor Giorgi. I know it. And if you're not prepared to reimburse me, then I will have that *boy*, as you call him – I call anyone over twenty-one a man – locked up long enough to teach him a good lesson. A very good lesson." Bousquet slid his sausage fingers into the silver box on the coffee table between them. "Care for one?" he asked amicably, drawing out a plump cigar.

"Uh, no, thank you," Sam managed. How could this man offer him a premium cigar in one breath while informing him in another that he planned to lock up Ben and throw away the key? He cleared his throat. "Have you considered whether you have adequate evidence to convict Ben? In a court of law, I mean?"

Bousquet's fingers froze in the midst of lighting his match. He leaned forward, eyes boring into Sam's. "You listen well, Doctor. I own the courts in this county. The judges, too. They'll do what I tell them to. Your *boy* committed a crime. Ruined a prize racing filly. And he's going to pay for it – or you will. One way or the other, I'm getting my money's worth. All eight thousand dollars of it."

A retort flew up Sam's throat, but he restrained himself. He'd heard rumors that Bousquet was involved in underhanded activity; this conversation certainly added credibility to that gossip. *You don't mess with the mob, unless you wanna end up with a hole in your heart,* Sam remembered his barber advising him one Saturday afternoon not too long ago. "May I see Ben, please? Is he working out in the stables?"

Amusement flickered in Bousquet's eyes. *Why?* "Yes, he's in the barn. He's not working, though. I'll tell you that much. I can't take that risk after what happened." The man rose to his feet. "I'll take you to him."

CHAPTER FOUR

There were exactly fifteen whorls in the wood ceiling over stall seventeen. Ben had counted them. Fifty-three times as he lay on his back on his cot for the past five days.

His breath pulsed out with an angry whoosh, and he lurched upright. How much longer would it take for Mama's money to reach him? Or, at the very least, a letter telling him that she couldn't send it? That he'd have to pay in jail-time for that scum Aldo's set-up? His feet crunched the straw as he paced toward the barred stall window. Was this legal? Keeping him under lock-and-key while he waited for Mama's reply?

Ben gritted his teeth, his hands wrapped around the iron bars. Legal or not, Bousquet could do it. And had done it. *Come on, Ma. You gotta come through for me.* Funny, when he was younger, Ben might have felt guilt at using Mama and the Doc like this, but now… now he felt nothing. Nothing but a bitterness that numbed and brought anger surging through his bones from time-to-time.

He heard footsteps approaching. Craning his neck, he could make out the boss' plump, eel-like form far down the stable aisle, silhouetted against the late afternoon sunlight. But the man with him… Ben squinted, but the outside light contrasted too strongly with the interior of the stable for him to distinguish the man's face.

Who cares, anyway? He turned away from the bars and hunkered down on the straw. He'd wait for the two men to pass by. Watching them from behind the bars made him feel too much like a caged animal in the zoo.

"He's in here," Bousquet's bass voice slid down the aisle.

Me? Ben tensed. Had they gotten impatient and sent for the police?

"You've imprisoned him in a horse stall?" An answering tenor rose, tinged with fury. Something about the man's voice struck Ben's ears as familiar, but he couldn't immediately place it. "What is he, an animal? How many days has he been in there?"

Whoever it was didn't like Ben's imprisonment. Confusion brought Ben's eyebrows together. *Who in the world?*

The footsteps stopped in front of the stall.

"What does it matter? Better locked up in here than in prison. Which is where he'll go if…" Bousquet trailed off.

"Let me inside. I need to speak with my son."

My son? Ben ceased breathing. The Doc had come here? The word "son" hung in the air, alien, repelling. Ben's heart couldn't have allowed it to penetrate even if he had wanted it to. Which he *did not.* He made a conscious effort to suck in air, feeling his nostrils flare like a hyped-up stallion. *I ain't your son.* And he never would be.

Why's he here? Why didn't they just send the money? Anger ripped through Ben's chest, throwing his thoughts into a personal version of Hooverville. The realization flooded his mind. *They ain't gonna give me the money. He's here to tell me to get lost for good.*

The clank of a key in the old lock prompted Ben to lurch to his feet. No way would the old man find him pathetic and groveling on a cot in the straw. The heavy door slid back just as Ben swiveled to face it, chin raised, fists balled at his sides, letting his hatred for both the Doc and Bousquet flash clear and loud from the storm clouds of his navy eyes.

Ma's new husband – well, of almost two years now – stood just over the threshold, Bousquet at his side. Accusation and avarice filled every line of the politician's face. To think — Ben had once been his favorite employee! *If I ever get my hands on Aldo, I'll rip his throat out.*

His breath came heavy, pumping out of his chest, bare beneath the thin button-down shirt and suspenders. Eyes narrowed, he stared at the two men, both his opponents. *If they'd just let me at 'em in a fair fight, I'd get 'em down. But they're too chicken-livered.* Bitterness pooled in his mouth. Look at them, silent in their tidy, finely-made clothes, acting calm and authoritative! Who were they to condemn him? To slam him for a crime he didn't even commit?

The Doc stepped over the threshold. "Hello, Ben." He held out his clean right hand.

Ben stared at it. What did the old man mean by wanting to shake his hand? His eyes skipped back up to the Doc's face. He couldn't read whatever was written there. His own fist stayed balled-up at his side; he didn't know if he could have met the Doc's proffered handshake if he'd wanted to. He still wanted to punch him one. *The old one-two.* To make up for taking Ben's place as the rightful head of the Picoletti family. To make up for... everything.

"May I have a moment alone with my son?" Mama's husband made the request in a quiet voice.

Bousquet looked as if he wanted to protest, but the Doc's tone had carried such a note of authority in it that the other man's resistance wilted. The boss gave a single nod at his guest. "Don't let him out." The flimsy warning flapped in the air like stockings pinned to an April clothesline.

The Doc met Bousquet's warning with a level stare. Shooting a last menacing glance in Ben's direction, the boss turned on his heel and swaggered down the aisle. Ben waited, muscles tensing. What would the Doc say to him? Would he try to shred him with words? A smile twitched at the corner of Ben's mouth. Bad luck for the Doc if he did. For Ben, the old saying held true: *Sticks and stones may break my bones, but words'll never hurt me.* It'd taken years, but from the day he stepped out of Papa's house for the last time — not counting that overnight stay in '35 — Ben had set his heart to crusting over, hardening, numbing until he knew that he was nearly as impenetrable as a tightly-closed mussel, washed up on the shores of Oakland Beach.

The Doc had been following Bousquet's departure with his gaze, but now he turned back to Ben. "Shall we sit down, son?"

"I ain't your son," Ben growled, unable to stop the words from crawling out of his throat like lice. His fists tightened until he could feel his fingernails, stubby as they were, bite into his palms. *Cool it, Ben. This guy's your last chance before they throw ya in the locker.* He dragged in a breath. *Wish I had a cigarette.* "You sit," he mumbled.

The Doc found a straw bale and perched on it. He balanced his gray hat on his knees. "Your mother and I received your letter." His eyes held a foreign tenderness as he looked at Ben – a softness that turned Ben's stomach and filled his mouth with ashes. On a woman's face, that sort of kindheartedness would be understandable, but on a man's? Well, on a man's, it flat-out gave him the heebie-jeebies. *Can't be real. Don't trust it.*

"The letter wasn't written to ya, but okay," Ben contented himself with remarking. His arms came up, crossing his chest, blocking any flow of feeling from that wolf-in-sheep's-clothing who'd married Ma. *Just to redeem his own conscience.*

"We'd like to help you," the Doc went on, his hands loosely clasped in his lap, so smooth and well-groomed. Had the man ever worked – really worked – a day in his life?

But wait – Was Ben hearing things? The Doc was going to help him? "You mean, you're gonna pay my way out?"

The Doc nodded.

Should he feel gratitude? Maybe, but he didn't, and he wouldn't pretend that he did. Leaning back against the corner, Ben smirked. "And then what? It's the last time you hold the end of the rope for me? Is that it? You want me to scram for good, huh? That's whatcha mean, right?"

The Doc just held his gaze levelly. Something inside Ben turned inside out – the kind of feeling he got when he swallowed a lump of tobacco, instead of spitting it out.

"It's eight-thousand bucks, ya know. That's a lot of jack." Ben raised his chin, daring the old geezer sitting on the hay bale to retract his word. No point in reiterating the fact that Ben hadn't done the malicious act, hadn't actually harmed the filly. Bousquet would have his money, regardless of who had really injured the animal. *Should never have mentioned the Doc's money to him when I came back here.*

"I know that. You explained it in your letter." The Doc rose to his feet. "I'll speak with Bousquet."

"Well…" What more could he say? "Guess I have to say thanks." *Why do I have to be indebted to him, of all people?* Unable to hide the disgust on his countenance, Ben turned his back, waiting for Ma's husband to leave as quickly as he'd come. *He'll probably be as glad as I am to see the last of this place. And I'll never have to lay my eyes on him again.*

"There is something I need in return." The Doc's voice cut into his thoughts.

Ben swiveled. What did the old bird mean? His eyes narrowed. Oh, yeah. "Don't worry. You won't never hear from me again," he snarled. "I'll disappear."

The Doc stood silently, hat in his hands. Ben grew uncomfortable. Sweat beaded at the back of his neck, right where his ratty collar met the uncombed dark auburn mess of his hair.

"Come back with me."

Ben started. "What?" Surely he hadn't heard right.

The Doc kept his eyes fixed on Ben. "That's what I want in return."

A laugh gurgled from Ben's throat. "You're outta your mind, old man." He couldn't be serious. "I ain't never comin' back to Chetham. And I sure ain't comin' back with you, of all people."

"Come back with me," repeated the Doc, his tone deepening into a near plea. "Work off the money I'm paying Bousquet for your release."

A smirk found its way to Ben's lips. "So that's it? You want free labor on some project of yours, huh, Doc?"

"Eight thousand dollars is hardly free labor," the Doc mildly replied.

Ben opened his mouth, then shut it. Much as he hated to admit it to himself, the guy was right. *Why do I hafta be obligated to this fool?* For not the first time, the noose in which his situation had placed him tightened around his neck. Swallowing hard, he let the anger in his heart make his decision. "Nope." He turned his head away. "If that's the price you want, I ain't payin' it, so you can just beat it, old man." Return to Chetham? Where he'd made a laughingstock of himself the last time, getting drunker than a New Year's punch? Where he'd have to live with the shadows of the past for twenty-four hours a day? Hadn't he nearly promised Grace that he'd not come back there, that he was going for good? Just thinking about the town made the memories he'd tried to put six feet under crawl up his spine and back into his head.

And work for *him?* Probably sleep under the Doc's roof, eat at his table, see Mama and Cliff cared for because of *him?* The bitterness burst into flames, consuming all other emotion. *I'd rather go to prison.*

The Doc stayed silent for a long moment. Ben peered out of the corner of his eye and saw him placing his hat on his head, face fallen into somber lines. "Are you sure?" the Doc asked, his hand on the door, ready to pull it back for his exit.

Ben tensed his jaw and nodded once.

"Alright." Sadness had crept into the Doc's voice. He sounded like a homeless dog alone on an abandoned porch. Pulling back the door, he left, the recession of his footsteps echoing.

Moments later, Ben heard Bousquet approach and chain the stall shut once more.

And the loneliness in which Ben found himself weighed on his shoulders until he could stand on his feet no longer. He sank onto his cot with a weariness belonging to an older age than his twenty-two years.

~ ~ ~

"Lord my God, open his heart. Change his mind." The mumbled prayer escaped Sam's mouth every few moments as Taylor drove away from Bousquet's grand house. The plea constantly renewed itself in his soul, pressing there.

"Did you say something, sir?" the driver asked, looking at Sam in his rearview mirror.

"No." Sam turned his gaze toward the grazing horses in the glinting fields beside the car. *I've done everything I could.* There was nothing left but for him to return to Chetham. Without Ben. The idea brought tears to his eyes.

Stay. The thought pulsed potently through his brain. *Stay.*

For a moment, Sam fought against the seeming impulse. He had patients to see back in Chetham – a full schedule tomorrow. And Sarah expected him to arrive in time for dinner tonight. *I can't stay.*

Stay.

"Yes, Lord," he said aloud. The tension eased within him.

"What was that, sir?" Taylor asked, turning onto the main road.

"I've changed my plans, Taylor. We need to find a hotel near here to stay for the night."

The driver didn't blink. "Very good, sir."

~ ~ ~

He didn't rise from his knees that night. Kneeling beside the soft bed in his lamplit hotel room, Sam poured out his soul as he hadn't done since that day two years before when Sarah had abandoned him. He begged for the boy to be placed in his hand. For mercy to be shown. For grace to be given.

And a little after three in the morning, he sensed in his soul a question from the Eternal One.

Was he holding anything back? Was he unwilling to place all he had in the Father's hand – to trust Him completely in this redemption for which he asked? Was Sam willing to give *anything* that the Father asked for?

For a long moment, Sam struggled, not knowing what, precisely, might be exacted from him. But in the end, the breath whooshed out of him, and, prostrate on the floor, he yielded all the matter to Him who had given Himself for him. *My hands are open to You, Lord. Take from me what You will. I trust that You will give me one-hundred-fold back whatever You ask of me to give, in this life and in the one to come.*

At last, weary in soul, worn-out in body, Sam's head hit the hotel pillow, and he clicked off the lamp.

CHAPTER FIVE

The deep clearing of a man's throat pulled Ben's gaze straight toward the barred stall door. The corners of his already-dour lips headed straight south. He let his groan sound out loud and clear. *Not him again!*

Ben lurched to his feet. "What are you doin' here? Thought I told you to beat it," he growled, eyes narrowed. Head aching and restless from the week's inactivity, Ben's mood had turned marsh-water-foul. *And I got no problem with letting you get the brunt of that, old man.*

"I'm leaving today," the Doc stated.

"Good. That's like you, ain't it, Doc? To leave others in a lurch." Hopefully, that'd sting.

The Doc was quiet for just a moment, looking down at the floor. Then he lifted his eyes and murmured, "I came to ask you to come with me."

A scoffing laugh burst from Ben's lips, mingling with anger at having been disproven in his judgment. "You're joking. Told ya already I ain't comin' back to Chetham. And I ain't workin' for *you*."

But the Doc's firm jaw showed just how serious he was. "Are you afraid?"

The question poured kerosene on Ben's wrath. "Who do you think you are, old man? I ain't afraid of nothin'!"

The Doc's gaze stayed steady. "Then prove it. Come back to Chetham. Let me pay off Bousquet, and you come back and work off your debt."

"I ain't gonna be obligated to nobody! I didn't ask you to pay my way – I asked my ma." Though, even as he said it, he realized how asking Mama also meant he'd asked the Doc.

"If you work it off, you will have no obligation to me, Ben."

He had a point there. And, this morning, something vice-like twisted Ben's guts at the notion of heading off to prison. *Wastin' my life behind bars for years... or going to Chetham for a few months?*

"And you would have a clean record."

Much as he hated to admit it, the Doc made a good point. *I would be free. Free to do what I wanna do.* Ben stared at the middle-aged man before him. Could he really stand to be around this judgmental, religious, hypocritical bluenose for...

"How long did ya say I'd have to work?"

A slight smile pressed up the side of the Doc's mouth. "Well," the Doc considered, "it *is* eight thousand dollars. That's a lot of money."

Ben tried to tamp down his irritation. He breathed in deep, feeling the air whoosh into his lungs.

"Tell you what," the Doc said, "I know that you're a hard worker, Ben. I've told you: I have a project that I want completed. By the end of the summer. When that project is finished... Well, then, we'll consider your debt to be paid in full. You will be free to go."

"What kind of work?"

"Carpentry. Your mother tells me you're very handy with a hammer."

One summer. Well, the tail-end of spring, too. Ben took another deep breath. *I can do one summer.* One summer with the ghosts of the past haunting his every step. One summer with this creep lurking around every door. He'd have to drink a lot. He shut his eyes. "Alright." He bit the word out as if it was as disgusting as horehound candy. "But you get me outta here this morning, old man."

~ ~ ~

Even if the day of the week hadn't stared at her from the wall calendar across from her bed, Grace would've known from the emotional excitement surging through the dormitory. At the Conservatory, Friday night was date night, and many of the girls – especially those with steadies – would spend much of the day getting ready for that evening's escapades at the picture show, the local diners, and the soda shops.

I, on the other hand… Grace pulled the covers back over her head, willing the next twenty-four hours to pass without her further knowledge. The Conservatory held few classes on Fridays, so what was the purpose of the day, anyway? *If only we could go straight from Thursday to Saturday.*

This is the day the Lord has made; let us be glad and rejoice in it…

With a sigh of acquiescence, Grace threw back the covers and heaved herself off the too-soft mattress. She winced at the hour on her round alarm clock, squatting on the bedside table. Nine-thirty. She knew she shouldn't sleep in so late, even though she didn't have a class to attend. *I probably could use these hours more wisely.* But how tempting it was to try to doze through the romantic buzz humming through every room in Saville Hall on Friday mornings!

Despite the rain pattering on the window, Grace's roommate had already hurried off somewhere. Probably to get her hair styled, though with the weather, Elaine would have to tie on a scarf to retain even a hint of her fresh hairdo. Stepping across the small, narrow room, Grace drew back the lace curtain to see a drizzly street below. *A perfect day for heading off to the library.* In the reflection, she saw a smile rise unbidden to her lips as she began to plan her Friday – a day which, for Grace Picoletti, held no "date night."

She brushed her hair thoroughly, thinking back to last year, her final year of high school, before she'd left Chetham for the Conservatory – how Mama had often taken ten minutes at night to visit Grace's bedroom and brush out her hair for her, sometimes pinning it in little circles for the next day's style. An ache took hold of Grace's heart as she remembered all those she'd left behind: Mama, Doctor Giorgi, Cliff, her school friends… *And Paulie.* For not the first time, she asked her Heavenly Father why He'd bidden her to leave them all – all she loved – for a dream she'd long forsaken: a professional singing career.

She opened her bureau drawer, pulled out a pair of stockings, and shut the drawer harder than necessary. If only she could closet away her memories of a certain young man so easily, one whose dark hair curled around the nape of his neck, whose chocolate eyes shone with a sunniness that Grace knew came directly from his loving heart. *But I can't forget him, Lord.* As naturally as breathing, her thoughts turned into a prayer. *I remember Paulie's kindness, his joyful face, his gentleness when he held my hand that day at Crescent Park…*

The tenderness in his expression when she'd brought him ice for his split lip. *After Ben slugged him in the jaw…*

How expectant his eyes had been that first Christmas she'd known him, when he'd given her the pearl earrings that now sat on her bedside table, resting inside their velvet box, beside her alarm clock…

How he'd come out to the old Picoletti house nearly two years ago to tell her that he would not hold her tightly – he was freeing her to make whatever decisions about her future that she thought God had laid on her heart – but he loved her nonetheless. And always would. *So he said.*

And then the slow, nearly-hidden expression of shock that had come over his face when she'd told him that she planned to attend the Conservatory. That God had opened a door she'd not even known was there – was giving her back an old desire of her heart – that she had to see what He would breathe into it.

The sound of a door slamming below jolted Grace from her maze of memories. She pulled on a thick cabled sweater the color of hot cinnamon oatmeal, necessary to combat the draftiness of the old stone library. Plucking her Bible and journal from the nightstand, she headed for the door. But one question nagged at her heart as she made her way down the flight of steps to the door: *If I had stayed in Chetham, would Paulie still love me?*

~ ~ ~

And the Word became flesh and dwelt among us…

The whispers and soft giggles floated over the wide tables arcing across the cozy library's ground floor, reaching Grace's ears with ease. Her eyes wandered from the Book of John toward the source of the noise. Near the mahogany card catalogue, complete with its gold plaque memorializing the generous patron who had bestowed it, two young people sat, their heads bent over their textbooks, pencils in their hands.

Grace's heart clenched. The sight of them – he dark-haired, she, light; sharing laughter and sweet schooldays – reminded her so much of…

Stop. Stop it. You mustn't, Grace. It only brings you pain.

She forced her gaze back down to her Bible, but the rest of the verse dissolved in her now-watery vision. Seemingly without her permission, her fingers flipped back to the inside cover and drew out the two creased pages tucked there. Bearing her name. And his.

September 4, 1936
Dear Grace,

I don't dare call you "mine." Well, not yet, anyhow. We both know that will be for God to decide. In His acceptable time. But I can pray and hope. And write! Dad said that would be "perfectly appropriate," so we have his permission, as long as I don't get too mushy on you.

Yes, Grace, I certainly plan to write to you over the next four years, becoming quite a "pest-pal" (haha!) as you sing your heart out and I turn myself to my own studies – though I don't know at this point where they'll lead. If Dad has his heart's desire, I'll follow him into the medical field. Personally, I'm not certain yet where God is leading me – I've been thinking about medicine for sure, but I don't know. Something in my spirit sometimes seems to hesitate, if you know what I mean, when I think of that. I wonder if it's the Lord's way of telling me He has a different path for me. Wouldn't that be something? I'll keep praying about it, and I'd appreciate it if you would, too, Grace.

Speaking of the house, though you've been gone only a week, the very walls seem to ache for your presence. I know that I do.

Better cut that kind of talk off before I get too carried away. But you should be aware of how I feel, Grace. How my feelings for you go unchanged by the seasons. In fact, my love for you grows more and more – whether or not you can or do return it. You've never said, and I'm half-glad for that. If I knew – If you'd assured me of your own love for me, I'd go completely crazy waiting for you. Regardless, I know that you've made me a better man for God to use, and I will always be thankful for you. I will always love you, Grace.

Well, I must sign off now before I turn too romantic and Dad starts censoring my letters! You won't tell on me for what I've said, will you? Just kidding.

Everyone sends their love, but I guess you already know that! Don't worry; I'm keeping an eye on Cliff for you, though he's turning into such a fine young man, he hardly needs watching anymore.

Keep out of mischief.

Sincerely,

Paulie

"Grace!" The vibrant voice exploded her reverie. Jerking her head up, she saw Violet Simmons quick-stepping across the library toward her. Her friend pulled off a rain cap that dripped water as she walked. "What are you doing here?"

Grace pulled a smile onto her face but kept her voice low in an effort to placate the frowning elderly librarian at the check-out desk. "Hello, Violet." She pushed Paulie's letter back into her Bible and closed it.

But she didn't do it in time to avoid Violet's curious eyes. "What's that?"

Grace shook her head. "Nothing. Just a letter." She'd told no one about Paulie; it wasn't a Picoletti trait to spread all one's business on one's lawn. Maintaining eye contact with her friend, she ignored the warmth in her cheeks. *Oh, don't notice it, Violet!*

But Violet's lacquered lips spread in a wide smile. "Just a letter? A love-letter, you mean? So this is why you so rarely accept dates!"

"Uh…" Grace struggled to respond. After all, Paulie had written a kind-of-love-letter. *But it's none of Violet's business!*

"Is he from back home?" inquired Violet. Apparently, she wasn't bound by any notions of privacy.

"Yes." Grace swallowed. How many more questions would Violet ask? Her nervousness found an outlet through her fingertips, and she began to shuffle the edge of her Bible.

"Are you engaged?"

Grace's eyes shot up. "No! Not at all." Wasn't her bare ring finger indicative of that?

Violet looked taken aback, and Grace immediately felt remorse for her abruptness. "I'm sorry. I didn't mean to answer so… strongly. It's just…"

Violet slid into the chair beside Grace. Looking into her dark eyes, Grace saw understanding there. "Hey, I left a boyfriend back home, too. Proposed to me and everything." Violet sighed. "But, in this business, you gotta do what you gotta do. Music performance is my life. At least, I want it to be. And being tied to a guy from the backwoods of Alabama…" She shook her head, her curls brushing against her smooth cheeks. "That would *not* have worked. For me or him. Did… Did you break up with him, or did he do it? You don't have to tell me if you don't want to," she added. "Sometimes, it does you good to talk to somebody about it, though."

Grace shrugged, feeling her nervousness drain away in the face of Violet's concern. Really, what was there to hide, after all? *Nothing.* "Neither, actually."

"Neither?" Violet tilted her head. "What do you mean? Someone had to do the –"

"He's just never written to me again," Grace interrupted, feeling the sharp sadness squeeze her heart. "He wrote once, at the beginning of the school year." She held up the letter. "But that was it. That was the last one."

"And you're sure that you wrote him back?" Violet pursed her lips.

"Of course."

"More than once? Because maybe the letter got lost or something…"

"I wrote him twice." And much as Paulie's silence confused and hurt her, Grace wouldn't lower her dignity by writing a third letter. She refused to beg for his affection if he was unwilling to give it freely.

"And still no reply?" Violet let out a gusty breath, disgust coating her expression. "What a jerk."

"He's not a jerk!" Grace surprised herself with how quickly she came to Paulie's defense. "He's a wonderful young man." Though never writing back didn't ring strongly in his favor; she could see as much echoed in Violet's face. "I don't know what happened."

"Did you ever ask him? I mean, when you went home for Christmas or something?"

Grace swallowed. Confrontation had never been a strong suit of hers. And, from the moment she'd arrived home to River Avenue, Paulie had seemed so… unromantic toward her. Acting more brotherly than he ever had. Well, she'd just felt too awkward to be the one to bring up their relationship-that-never-was. "No."

She looked away. "Anyway, what is there to ask? He just – It just…" Her throat clogged, she couldn't continue. The rain poured down the window to her right. "He acted like nothing had ever occurred between us. Like we were just friends again."

After a moment of silence, Violet took an audible breath. "Well, anyway, I'm glad that I saw you today here. You like children, right?"

Surprised at the turn in conversation, Grace hesitated a second.

"I've seen you teaching the primary children's Sunday School class, right?" Violet pressed. Like many of the Conservatory students, she attended the same church as Grace did, right in downtown

Crocksville.

"I help; I don't teach," Grace corrected. As if Mrs. Cleary would ever give up the children's Sunday School instruction to her! But she did really enjoy it – actually, she'd been surprised by how much joy telling the little ones Bible stories brought her.

Violet shook her head as if that was of little consequence. "Same thing," she stated. "Anyway, I don't know if you know it, but my uncle is the headmaster at the charity school here in Crocksville. You know, the Helen Higgins School. That's part of the reason my mother let me come all the way here from Alabama: We have family in this area."

"I know of the Helen Higgins School, of course." The fifty-year-old tuition-free school accepted impoverished city children from all over New York and New Jersey, giving them an exemplary education in an effort to raise them from their difficult circumstances. "But I had no idea that your uncle is the headmaster there."

"Well, he is," Violet continued, "and they are in desperate need of good volunteers to lead the extracurricular classes after school. I told him that I thought that I knew of a few good candidates. Including you." She smiled triumphantly, as if she expected Grace to shout with joy at the news.

"But… I've never actually taught children in my life," Grace sputtered, forgetting to whisper and earning a hissed *shush* from the librarian. "And I'm so busy with classes at the Conservatory."

Glancing at the frowning woman behind the desk, Violet leaned over to talk more closely with Grace. "Oh, teaching can't be too difficult, Grace. Uncle Timothy isn't expecting you to be Eleanor Roosevelt, for goodness' sake. And it's not every day, either. Just a couple of days a week. Teaching them music. Voice or… piano. It doesn't matter so much as long as there's music. You know how to play piano, right?"

"A little," Grace answered honestly. Visions of her already-back-breaking class and church schedules floated before her eyes. She opened her mouth to tell Violet that, no, there was absolutely no possible way she could shoulder any more.

But Violet had already taken off running with the notion. "Well, that's fine. My uncle wanted me to take it on, but you know I can't do it. I'm already swamped with schoolwork, and I'm helping him out on the administrative end of the school. And my new boyfriend Andrew is forever complaining about how few nights we get to spend out on the town together. I just can't take on one more thing, Grace."

Determined not to let Violet plow over her, Grace began to shake her head, but Violet placed her manicured hand on Grace's shoulder. "Just come talk to Uncle Timothy, Grace. At least then he'll know that I did really try to get someone for him. Please?" She drew out the last word with a smile.

Sighing, Grace nodded. And in her heart, she even began to entertain the idea of doing a bit of teaching at the charity school. *Maybe what I need is to keep busy.* Maybe God could use her dateless hours. And perhaps then she could forget about the curly-haired young man who had captured her heart over Mrs. Kinner's kitchen table back in 1934.

CHAPTER SIX

Bousquet had thrown Ben out with nothing more than his sack of personal belongings and the clothes on his back. "And don't even think about asking for the wages due you, boy," his former boss had grumbled, eye-level with him in the driveway. "You know what I could've had done to you. You're lucky I'm letting you off like this."

Like this… Considering that the guy had just pocketed eight-thousand bucks he had no right to!

The Doc had stood there, silent beside his fancy car, all shining in the May sunlight. *As if he was a Grand Duke or somethin'. Whatever a Grand Duke is.* The sight of the man raised the hair on Ben's back, nearly made his spine crackle with anger. Who was he to stand there, self-righteous prig, as if Ben *needed* his help?

But the thing that really rankled? That dug its unsheathed claws into the skin of Ben's spirit? *That I do need his help.* He'd be crouching in the corner of a prison cell right now if the Doc hadn't performed this knight-in-shining-armor rescue. *Now I'm in his debt. Always gotta pay….*

Ben turned from Bousquet with a huff, slinging his sack over his shoulder. Every step toward the Doc and his car pressed the hot iron of slavery deeper into Ben's heart. At the last few steps, he couldn't even meet the old man's eyes; he knew that if he did, the loathing in his own expression would liquefy into words. And he needed – much as he hated it! – he *needed* the Doc to stand by him.

Gotta get myself outta here. And that's all. I don't need him after this! Ever again!

A spry driver with velvety gray hair capping his head opened the back door of the car. *Must be nice to live with so many people at your beck-and-call!* Ben stopped short and finally raised his eyes to meet the Doc's. "Sure you don't want me to ride in the front? I'm your hired help now, ain't I?" He made sure to inject extra sarcasm into the question.

The Doc met his gaze without fear and – frustratingly enough – without answering anger. "You're welcome to sit where you wish, Ben. But I'd like it if you'd sit in the back with me."

Ben cocked an eyebrow. "Oh? Why's that?"

"Because I'd like to get to know my wife's eldest son better."

Ha. He let the bitterness curl his lips into an open sneer. "And here I thought I was *your* 'son,' old man. That's what you're always saying, ain't it?"

The taller man paused for just a moment. "That's what I consider you, Ben," he said, and his voice… For just a moment, Ben froze to hear a tone so foreign to him in it. Could it be tenderness? He'd bet two dollars it couldn't be – just couldn't be for *him*. Could it?

Throwing off the spine-shivering thought, he jutted his chin out. "Well, you're wrong there, old man. I'm Charlie Picoletti's son, for better or for worse. Ya know, the first guy married to your *wife*. Didn't I show that to ya last time I visited you and your happy family?" He hesitated. Well, why not say it straight out? "And I guess I gotta show you again before the summer's over."

The Doc met his gaze. "We need to get going." He gestured toward the backseat.

As if he would give the old man that satisfaction! "I'll sit in the front," Ben growled.

"Suit yourself." The Doc ducked into the car. The driver seemed at a loss for a split second before turning toward the front door, moving to open it for Ben.

"I'll get it," Ben asserted, glad to give the little man a shove out of his path. In a way, it felt like he was shoving the Doc. And Bousquet. And Papa. Plopping down in the plush interior of the vehicle, he made sure to spread out his legs as rudely as possible before rustling for a cigarette in his shirt pocket. He struck the match on the bottom of his loose-soled shoe and lit the cig just as the driver took his own seat.

A few yards out on the main road, Ben cricked his head around to peer at the Doc. The older man had taken some papers out of a leather briefcase and seemed engrossed in their contents. Ben faced the front again. "Ya know," Ben said loudly, "I didn't do nothin' to that horse."

Silence.

Did the Doc think he was guilty? *Why does it matter one iota to ya if he does?* Still, Ben would feel a whole lot more comfortable if he knew that the Doc believed that he was guiltless...

"I said, I'm innocent. I was framed by some goon."

Silence.

Ben turned his whole body around. "Didn't ya hear me?"

"Yes."

Man, this guy was a peach! "And you believe me? That I'm innocent?"

The Doc put his sheaf of papers down on his lap. "To be frank, Ben, it matters very little to me whether or not you hurt the horse."

Nope, his first conclusion had been wrong. This guy was just plain batty. "Huh?"

"What matters to me is that you are coming home."

Oh-kay. This guy really *was* batty. As though Chetham could ever in a million and one years be home to him. Dread curdling his stomach juice, Ben turned and faced the front all the way back to Chetham. Hopefully, he could stay out of the old man's path as much as possible for the rest of the spring and summer and then hightail it as far away as was humanly possible. Away from everything that had happened to make him the man he was.

~ ~ ~

"I hope that I didn't come at a bad time."

Sarah smoothed her sweating palms down the front of her pink-printed dress and forced her lips to curve up into a smile at her kind-hearted pastor's wife. Bertha Cloud and her daughter had walked all the way from the center of Chetham on this warmer-than-usual spring day. *The least you can do is make them feel welcome.* "No, no, not at all, Bertha," she replied, trying to keep her gaze from travelling past the Clouds' just-grown daughter Betty to the driveway. If Taylor didn't hit any traffic, Sam would arrive home very soon. *With my son.* Her heart leaped as a deer over field fences at the thought.

Opening the front door a little wider, she invited Bertha and Betty into the sun-splashed entryway. Hopefully, they wouldn't see the tension in her smile.

"You see," Bertha went on, "I've been having such trouble with this knitting pattern. I didn't know if you would help me figure it out, Sarah."

Sarah tore her gaze away from the driveway again and met Bertha's eyes. *Stop being so distracted!* She forced herself to take a calming breath. *Take every thought captive….* "Sure. I'd be glad to help."

Bertha tilted her head. "Are you expecting someone? If you are, I can come back at a better time."

"No. That is…" She paused. She'd shared some things about Ben with this woman who'd quickly become a friend to her over the past couple of years, since Sarah had met the Lord Jesus in a personal way. How would Bertha take the news that Sarah's sometimes-wild but tenderhearted eldest son was returning – not because he wanted to, but because the only other path led to imprisonment for a crime he may or may have not committed? She swallowed. There was no way around it. "You see, Ben is coming home."

Bertha drew in an audible breath, and the next thing Sarah knew, her friend's solid arms had enveloped her in a hearty embrace. Instinctively, Sarah stiffened as her body had been accustomed to react to close contact for so many years. Folks like the Clouds just didn't understand that, when they threw their arms around some people, it made a wall go up. *She means well.*

Pulling back, Bertha held Sarah at arm's length. "Sarah! That's wonderful! You must be so pleased."

Sarah nodded slowly. Yes, she was pleased, as Bertha put it. But wariness also hovered around her spirit. The last time Ben had visited, he had gotten drunk – very drunk – and violent, to the point of hurting both Paulie and Grace. *Though, of course, he hadn't meant to. Not really. Surely not Grace, at least.* And two years away – Well, could that have done any good? If so, certainly Sarah would have heard from him before now. No, the time apart could have only hardened him… made him more the son of his now-dead father, Charlie.

"I just hope we're doing the right thing," she let the words slip out, held up by fretting. "Last time, well…" She hesitated as her eyes fell on the Cloud girl, her sweet round face void of understanding hardship or heartache. Had the girl ever even met one such as her eldest son? "It was difficult," she finished, knowing that Bertha would comprehend what Sarah had omitted saying for the sake of Betty's unworldliness.

Bertha's expression became serious. She looked Sarah straight in the eyes. "George and I will keep praying for your family, Sarah. It's not an accident to the Almighty that Ben is returning home."

"No, you're right, but still—" The words dissolved on Sarah's tongue as the sound of crunching gravel met her ears. They were here. Sam had brought her son back to her.

She felt a touch on her sleeve. "We'll come back another time," Bertha spoke.

Sarah nodded.

Bertha and her daughter turned back toward the still-open front door and stepped outside ahead of her. Sarah's legs moved. She found herself on the wide brick steps, just within the cool shadow of the overhang, straining for a first glimpse of the boy who had opened her womb twenty-two years ago.

But the person who entered her field of vision wasn't a boy, any more than he had been the last time he'd visited. Instead, a wiry-limbed but well-muscled man slouched up the path, his dark auburn hair too long and his face wearing the grizzle of several days without seeing a razor's edge. His expression... hard as frozen tar, bitter as bad wine. *Just like last time.* The thought pressed hard in Sarah's stomach, making her lose what little appetite she'd had for Tabitha's lasagna, waiting to be pulled out of the warming oven for supper.

Ben caught sight of her. He stopped several feet short of the steps, his eyes catching hers. Sarah's whole throat closed off. Her son – whom she'd thought she'd never hear from again, never see again – stood before her, in flesh-and-blood. *Oh, Lord, You know...*

He spoke first. "Hey, Ma." It was a quiet phrase, awkward, as if he didn't know what to say. His eyes went toward the Clouds, narrowed; then tripped over to Sarah before darting over his own shoulder. He gestured toward the driveway, half-hidden by the flowering trees. "The Doc's talkin' to the old guy who does his drivin'. Taylor or somethin'." Though he hid it well, Sarah could read the signs of discomfort traced on his face. *He doesn't want to be here. Sam had to force him.*

Sarah nodded. Why wasn't it the magical reunion she'd imagined? With tears streaming down his face and hers, him so glad to have a home to rest in, a real father at last to teach him how to be a man? With repentance in his heart and a desire for the salvation of the Lord to overtake him? *That was a dream, Sarah. This is reality.* Sam had warned her that it would not be all tulips and dandelions. *Help me, Lord. Help me to accept whatever You bring. Help me to be compassionate toward him.*

A deep breath rattled into her lungs, and she stepped down off the dais-like front stoop until she was a hairsbreadth from her son. With a trembling hand, she reached up to touch his shoulder, hard and firm from hours of stable work. He stiffened – as she had moments before in response to Bertha – and she realized that this was perhaps the first time she'd touched him intentionally since he was a little boy on her lap. The years with Charlie had not been good ones for developing outward tenderness in Sarah, even toward her own children. *It felt safer to not be vulnerable, even with them.* There was much reparation to do; she'd thought that she'd done some of that in her letters – letter after letter, written with no response.

But how different to see him face-to-face! To see what perhaps no one else could see in Ben: the deep hurt lacquered over with bitterness; the boy who never had a chance to become a true man but was rushed into early adulthood by knowledge of his father's adulterous habits; the inability to rise above the mud in which he'd been born.

Only You, Lord. Only You can change the heart of stone into a heart of flesh…

"How ya doin', dollface?" Ben called out, his gaze trained on the Cloud women beyond Sarah. His eyes crinkled at the corners in fun as Charlie's had, his mouth curling up in a flirtatious smirk.

Sarah cringed. Her hand dropped from her son's shoulder, and dread pooled in her chest. Could she bear to see the most-likely horrified expression on Bertha and Betty's faces?

"I apologize. I should have introduced us." Bertha's mellow voice broke into Sarah's train-wrecked thoughts. "I know who you are through your mother, but you've never met us."

Sarah turned to see Bertha approaching, Betty trailing behind her, eyes darting to-and-fro. Bertha stuck out her gloved hand. "I'm Bertha Cloud, and this is my daughter Betty. We just stopped by to see if your mother could help me out with a knitting pattern. I'm all thumbs when it comes to handicraft, but your mother could knit in her sleep, I think." She smiled.

Ben said nothing, but his face told Sarah that he was surprised at the friendly reception from this conservatively-dressed woman – especially since he'd just hit on her daughter. Slowly, his work-crusted hand rose to meet her gloved one. "I'm Ben. Haven't met ya before, but I seen you around town years ago when I used to live here."

Sarah's insides relaxed ever so slightly as she thanked God one more time for a pastor's wife who was down-to-earth, who actually loved the souls of people and not just the appearance of goodness. She glanced over at Betty, and saw the look of reserve icing the daughter's face. Well, no wonder. She could hardly think that Betty had ever been called *dollface* before!

Bertha smiled. "Well, we'll look forward to seeing you at… uh…" She stumbled over her phrasing, and Sarah knew that she'd meant to say, "at church," but realized too late that Ben very well might decide not to go to First Baptist. "We'll be seeing you," Bertha repeated, ending simply this time. She glanced at Betty as if to see whether or not her daughter might make an attempt at civility, but Betty merely maintained a frozen, tight-lipped smile.

"See ya," Ben replied.

Bertha strode away, knitting bag in hand. Her more petite daughter hurried to keep up with her, walking in the shadow of her mother. Betty glanced behind her twice, her eyes wide as if she couldn't quite take in the uncouthness of this man. The second time she did it, Sarah caught Ben giving her a bold wink. Betty turned as pink as fresh bubblegum and nearly tripped on Bertha's heels as she sped away.

Ben turned back to face Sarah, a grin splitting his mouth, showing lemonade-colored teeth. Weariness draping over her, Sarah half-wished she could send him right back where he'd come from. *And he's only been at the house for five minutes.*

But he was here now. There was no turning back.

CHAPTER SEVEN

"I had Mrs. McCusker make a room ready for you. I think you'll like it. It's blue. That was always your favorite color." Sarah knew that she was rambling, but Ben's silence unnerved her. He tromped along behind her, his loose-soled boots making a *thump-thump* on the polished staircase. Sam was still outside, ostensibly talking to Taylor about the automobile's maintenance. *Really, he's trying to give me and Ben time alone.* She glanced back at her silent son. *To talk?*

A few more quick steps brought them to the room right across from Paulie's and several doors down from Cliff's. Sarah pushed the partially-closed door open wider. "Here you go." She smiled with a brightness she didn't feel.

With hardly a glance her way, Ben shuffled into the bedroom. She watched his eyes move from the cushioned window seat that looked out on the yard back to the perfectly-made double bed, its bleached-white pillows floating above the blue coverlet and finally to the small private bathroom. He blew out a breath. "Swell digs, Mama. Didn't get to look around proper last time I was here. But I can see now – Ya did good, huh? Marryin' the Doc, I mean. Second time's a charm, I s'ppose."

Sarcasm soaked his words, but Sarah chose to ignore that. "Sam is a good, godly man," she stated, her voice quiet as she clung to the peace in her heart. "I'm glad that the Lord brought him to me. His money wasn't the reason I married him." *Though it was in a way, wasn't it? You had to get out of the debts Charlie left you.* "Not the most important reason, anyway," she amended, disliking the way a lie pressed on her heart.

Ben raised his eyebrows, just in the way Charlie used to when she'd said something dumb. Sarah struggled against the feeling of intimidation that traveled through her body. "The Lord brought him, huh? Awfully friendly with the Old Man Upstairs, ain't ya?"

The indignation that rose in Sarah's breast surprised her. She didn't like hearing the Man who had rescued her from her own sin being referred to in such a flippant way. *Even by Ben.* But, when she looked at him, so cold and angry in the sunlight that trickled through the striped curtains, pity doused her own ire. *He doesn't know any better. And much of that is my fault. Forgive me, Lord.* Aloud, she said, "Yes. He's a Friend who sticks closer than anyone else." And she held her son's gaze so that he'd know that she meant it. "And anyone can come to know Him so."

After a moment, Ben looked away, toward the window. "Well, I wouldn't know anything about that, Ma. God and I aren't exactly on speakin' terms these days."

"You can be." The words flew from her throat, gentle as a gray mourning dove landing on the driveway's gravel edge. "He wants to be on – what did you call it? Speaking terms with you. More than that, He—"

"All that doesn't sound very Catholic, Ma," Ben interrupted. "Least, not the way I understand Catholic-ness. Ain'tcha gonna get yourself anathematized or whatever for that? Saying you can talk directly to God? Like you got some kind of special favor with Him? Who do ya think ya are? The Pope?"

He was sneering at her now. When had he ever done that, in all their hard days with Charlie cheating and Ben angry, in the time when he'd come to visit after Sarah'd married Sam and he'd been enraged because he'd thought Sam and Paulie were just like Charlie – using the Picoletti women for their own gain? *Never. He's always respected me. He's always loved his mama.* What had happened to the heart of her little boy?

But he wasn't a little boy anymore. She decided to answer his accusation first. Maybe that'd clear the way for the Gospel to shine clearly. "It has nothing to do with being Catholic or Protestant. Nothing at all," she replied, praying for the words to speak to this gaping wound of a man. "It's just this, Ben: By myself, I'm nothing. Nothing but a sinner. Saved by His grace. Jesus alone makes me able to speak to the Father and know that I'll be heard – because I'm loved by Him. And so are you, Ben," she finished, wishing she possessed the courage to walk over to her son and grasp him in a hug reminiscent of Calvary. But her arms and hands felt stiff as cake left uncovered overnight.

He blew out a breath. "Yeah, I'm real loved, Ma." She could scarcely hear his muttered words as he turned his back to her, staring out the window at what she knew was a view of the lawn leading down to the pond out back.

Her mouth ran on, her heart rushing ahead of her mind, desperate for her son to know peace. "And I know – I *know* – that God will work all the bad things that happened to us – your papa, you running off, everything – out for good." The paraphrased verse, though Sarah believed it with all of her being, tumbled from her lips without power.

He turned to her again and she saw the utter unbelief that spread across his face. He made no attempt to disguise it. "You say that 'cause you live here in the lap of luxury now, Ma. And you only got here because Doctor Sam Giorgi felt guilty that he left you in the dust way back when."

He smiled, and Sarah felt the chill of his expression deep in her bone marrow. "So now you're here, and to make yourself feel better about the course through which your life's run, you use the excuse that God meant for it all to happen… that He's gonna work it all out for good. Is that right? Well, I wanna know, Ma. What about the rest of us? It's alright for Grace and Cliff. Even Evelyn, I guess. They've feathered their nests well, and I'm glad for them. But what about me and Lou and Nancy? We got all messed up. Our lives are wrecked. We just gotta make the best of it now. Pull ourselves up by our broken bootstraps, huh?"

The guilt from the mothering years she'd wasted, trying to do it alone, the old shame of Charlie's betrayals pulsed through Sarah's consciousness, silencing her. Wordless, she stared down at the carpet. *I failed them. Why didn't I do differently in life? Why did I take so long to come to You?*

"So don't talk to me about your God of love and mercy. I don't wanna hear it. Don't come telling me again that I've gotta repent of my sins or I'll be damned. Be damned for what? For doing what I had to do to survive? To keep myself from going crazy? For raking a little bit of enjoyment of this hopeless life I got no choice but to live?"

Sarah stood stunned at the words pouring out of Ben's mouth. She'd never told him that he must repent – though, of course, he did. Repentance was the only way Home. She'd only spoken of the Father of love and His mercy to her, both now and in her letters to Ben. What should she say to this? What *could* she say?

"I'll stay for the summer. The rest of the spring and summer. I told the Doc that I would. To pay off the money he gave Bousquet so's I didn't get locked up for something I didn't do." He emphasized the last three words. His eyes ground into Sarah's. "But then – you listen, Ma. You wanna live this kind of life? Slave to a God who doesn't care about none of us and never did? Fine, you do that. But I'm outta here. Outta this town. And I'm never comin' back. You hear me?"

She swallowed, willing herself not to show him how his voice and stance reminded her so much of Charlie. *You have not given me a spirit of fear, but of love and of power and of a sound mind.* How glad she was now that she'd spent many spare minutes these past few years committing

Scripture to memory. "Yes," she said, thankful for the way her voice stayed steady despite her crumbling nerves. "Whether you stay or leave will be your decision, Ben. We're all so happy to have you home."

He snorted.

Cringing inside, Sarah moved toward the door. The freedom of the corridor pulled at her, but she turned one last time. "Supper is in twenty minutes."

~ ~ ~

"Where's everybody?" From his place at the head of the table, Sam felt his body tense as his stepson entered the dining room, letting the door bang behind him. *He should've been a hammer-thrower in the Olympics.* A quick glance told Sam that Ben had not used the half-hour or so of time before dinner to work on his appearance: He'd appeared unshaven, unwashed, with the same surly smile muddying his expression.

"Cliff's gone on an overnight trip with the youth group. Camping," volunteered Sarah. Sam noticed she appeared nervous but still at peace – a drastic change from her unwound behavior the last time her son had paid them a visit.

Ben lifted his chin in acknowledgment. "Well, that was convenient. Wouldn't want me to poison my own brother, huh?"

Sarah went on. "And Paulie's working."

A sneer replaced the smile. "The rich kid's gotta *work*? What's he do? Hairdressin'?"

Despite his desire to love Ben as his own, Sam felt anger stir inside his heart at the abuse heaped on Paulie. Paulie – who had *chosen* to work, saying that it would be a good way to learn how "real people" lived. Sam picked up his glass and took a long gulp of water to avoid having to answer Ben. *Help me to love him, Lord. Give me the love you have for him. A love that doesn't compromise, but sacrifices.*

"Paulie works at Dickie's, dishwashing, a couple of nights a week," came Sarah's reply after a moment's hesitation.

Her pause seemed to have incited just a touch of embarrassment in Ben. Without another word, he pulled out a chair and landed in it. His hand was halfway to a biscuit when Sam gained control of his emotions enough to intercept with gentleness. "May I ask God's blessing?" He wondered why his heart pounded. Surely not in fear!

Ben's head jerked toward him. "Don't matter none to me, Doc. Your house – your rules." He grabbed the biscuit he'd aimed for, threw it down on his plate, and pretzeled his sinewy arms across his chest.

With that, Sam and Sarah bowed their heads. Sam thanked his Heavenly Father for their food and for Ben's return, but his heart also held deeper pleas that he couldn't express aloud.

When Sam opened his eyes, he found Ben's gaze fixed on him. The coldness of that storm-blue stare made him feel as though he'd been plunged into the Providence River in January. *He hates me.*

"So whatcha gonna have me workin' on, Doc?" Ben took half the biscuit into his mouth in one bite. "Specifically, I mean?"

Sam took a breath. Funny, he could be in complete control of an operating room, but when it came to his family, he always felt incompetent. It was probably a good thing though; the consistent humbling kept Sam dependent on God. "I'd like it if you would call me Sam. When you call me Doc, I feel like I'm still at my office." He smiled, hoping his friendliness might massage out the knots in this conversation.

Ben merely gaped at him for a long moment, all good humor absent. Then he gave a mixture of a shrug and a half-hearted nod before poking another half-a-biscuit between his lips.

Sam figured he'd have to take what he could get with this one. At least they were conversing with some level of civility, which was an improvement on their time in the automobile on the way back to Chetham. "As I told you at the stable, I understand from your mother that you have a good set of carpentry skills in those hands of yours," he began, glancing at Sarah. Her expression serious, she continued eating small bites of lasagna, the stringy mozzarella looping from her fork to the plate.

Ben let the front legs of the chair drop heavily, and Sam tried not to think about the nicks in the waxed floor. "Yeah, I can handle a hammer," his stepson replied around his mouthful of biscuit.

Sam nodded. He dipped his fork into his own lasagna but didn't bring it up to his mouth. His nerves wouldn't permit him to eat. "Good." He braced himself. Who knew how Ben would take this? If he were in his stepson's shoes, well… he wouldn't be a happy camper, to put it lightly. Filling his lungs with a deep breath, Sam plunged forward. "My plan is to have you work on repairing the old brick house and cleaning up the property."

Ben's eyes narrowed. He swallowed, the lump of food shooting down his throat. "What… brick house?"

"Your mother's. We've let it sit for a long time – the market was bad – and it seems like a good time to get it going now. But it's a mess; I'll warn you of that. A couple of summer storms – hurricanes, really – over the past couple of years haven't helped, either." He was rambling; he knew that. *But it's for his good, even if he doesn't see it that way. This is for Ben's good. I know it.* Sometimes, a man had to go back through the old paths he'd trod before he could rise to a new and brighter calling. Sometimes, there was no way forward except by going back.

Without meeting his eyes, Ben plucked another biscuit from the basket. He didn't bother buttering it but instead began tearing it into little pieces and dropping them into his plate. His jaw pulsed.

Sam swallowed. If Ben refused now… He watched his stepson, so full of easily-wounded pride.

And, surely, *that* was how he could persuade him to agree. "I know it's a big project. Maybe you –"

Ben's chin rose. His eyelids lowered. "Ya think I don't got it in me? Think I can't do it?"

"I know you can do it," Sam replied, trying with everything inside him not to get ruffled.

Apparently satisfied, Ben dug the serving spoon into the lasagna steaming before them and heaped a miniature mountain onto his plate.

Sam drew in a breath. *This is right. I know this is right, even if he hates me even more for pushing him to do it.* "But you'll still have help."

Ben paused in the act of raising a bite of meat and pasta to his mouth. "Help?" He frowned. "Whatdaya mean, *help*? I told ya, I can do it myse—"

"Paulie will help you."

Ben's fork clattered to the plate, flinging the uneaten clot of lasagna toward his left. With a plop, the mass of sauce-laden cheese-and-pasta landed in Sam's water glass.

If not for the murderous expression on his stepson's face, Sam would've laughed. As it was, however, he merely called for the maid and asked her to replace his water.

~ ~ ~

Deep in the night, Sarah woke to the sound of springtime crickets serenading one another with love-songs. The darkness covered the house with a soothing mantle; a breeze tiptoed through the half-open window, fluttering the white curtains until they rose and fell against the upper panes like waves on the beach.

Eyes heavy, she turned over and reached for Sam. But his space in their bed was empty; her skin felt the coldness of the sheets, telling her sleepy mind that he'd been absent for many minutes. Shoving the hand of sleep away, Sarah pushed herself up against the headboard, peering into the darkness. "Sam?" she whispered.

But he didn't answer. Maybe he'd gone to use the bathroom. Their supper with Ben had been enough to make even a grown man's belly sick. *Poor Sam. I'm sure he didn't expect to take this kind of a situation on when he married me. Give him strength, Lord God. Give me strength. You know how much we need it.*

When Sam didn't return for a few more minutes, Sarah's inherent loneliness roused. Pushing back the light coverlet and woven blanket, her feet found her slippers, burrowing into their fur-lined coziness. "Sam?" she whispered again. But still he didn't answer.

She peered more deeply into the shrouded room. At last, her eyes widened. There, at the foot of the bed, a rounded lump slouched. Wordlessly, she shuffled over. "Sam?" She touched him on his shoulder.

But he had fallen fast asleep on his knees, his Bible open before him on the rug. In the patch of moonlight, Sarah raised the Book up to see what he'd been reading.

And this is the record, that God hath given to us eternal life, and this life is in His Son. He that hath the Son hath life; and he that hath not the Son of God hath not life. These things have I written unto you that believe on the name of the Son of God; that ye may know that ye have eternal life, and that ye may believe on the name of the Son of God. And this is the confidence that we have in Him, that, if we ask any thing according to His will, He heareth us: And if we know that He hears us, whatsoever we ask, we know that we have the petitions that we desired of Him.

Beside the passage, in Sam's careful looped cursive, she read one word, a name: *Ben.*

He was praying for my son. Suddenly, she felt ashamed. She, the woman who had given birth to the man snoozing away in oblivion several doors down, the woman who had professed in weeping and worried words how much she cared for Ben, had been slumbering while this man, whose only interactions with her son included rancid insult and even violence, lost sleep begging God to grant mercy to him.

She would wake him. Get him under the coverlet, where he could get his much-needed rest more pleasantly. But not yet. First, Sarah knelt on her own knees and took up the torch of prayer from her weary husband, bringing her lost sheep before the Father of lights during the first night he spent under the Giorgi roof.

CHAPTER EIGHT

en stared up at the decrepit house. What a wreck. Always ill-cared for by Papa as he tended to his own affairs, it had looked ready to expire and collapse two summers ago, when Ben had last entered the Picoletti home. By that time, Mama had married again, leaving the house to the ghosts of the past. It appeared that they had taken full advantage of the Picoletti family's abandonment.

We might as well tear it down as fix it up. He let out a lungful of pent-up frustration. *It ain't worth anyone's time. Ain't worth my time.*

But it was worth the time he would've spent behind bars. He knew that much was the truth, no matter what kind of fool the dear ol' Doc was – and Ben could think of plenty of variations. Yet why the old man wanted Ben to fix up this house for the princely sum of $8000, he couldn't guess. The Doc'd be lucky if he could get half that when he finally sold it. Though there *were* acres of land around the house. In a booming town, some new-fangled developer would love to get his hands on it. He'd chop Papa's fields and woods into little plots, eager to get the most money for his investment.

But Chetham was too small a town and too far away from any decent-sized city for anyone to want to do that just yet, so Ben figured the old brick Picoletti house was safe from developers mowing it down. *Safe? What do I care what happens to this heap of junk? It's just a house.* His jaw pulsed, though, and he shoved down the strange melancholy that stole over his whole person – the emotions that he had thought he'd adequately burned in the oven of anger so that they could never again make him vulnerable.

I wish the Doc'd torn it down. I wish a fire would start in the night and…

He tightened his fists against the flood of thoughts pouring through his brain. Tightened them so much that his gnawed-off fingernails bit into his palms. Why could he almost see his papa standing there on the broken back stoop, bare-chested as a sailor, always ready to make a back-alley deal? Always ready to get Mama pregnant again; always ready to hang around with any floozy who caught his eye? And yet also always ready to stand in the church loft, raising his hypocritical voice in song as sweet as any seraph's…

He swallowed down the odd burning in his throat. Pushed back the rage that throbbed softly, always ready to break out. *I can't spend a lot of time thinkin' while I'm here. Just gotta do my work, get it done, and move on with my life. There's no point in wishing…*

Tearing his eyes away from the house of memories, Ben forced himself to survey the rest of the property. Among the overgrown trees and tangle of bushes, he caught sight of the dilapidated barn at the end of the lane. The outbuilding's roof hunched, as if in apology for its shabby condition.

It was unfixable; he could tell that at a glance. He'd have to knock it to the ground before the summer was through. A snort found its way out of his nose. Figured. The only place he'd thought of as his refuge in his youth would have to be demolished. *But that's life for you, old boy, huh?*

He straightened his shoulders. The sun had fully risen. If he was ever to leave Chetham behind him, he should get to work. *Might as well look in the barn to see if any of Papa's old tools are still there.* The Doc had told him to buy anything he needed at the hardware store on Main Street – "Put it on my bill there," he'd said – but Ben figured that he might as well delay a trip into town as long as possible – avoid the prying eyeballs as long as he could.

He turned from the brick house and strode down the dirt path made by so many pairs of feet over the years. No matter that no one had lived here for nearly two years – Nothing on God's green earth could make the grass grow again in that hard-packed path.

The door had relinquished its always-tenuous clutch on the barn. Without pausing to think, Ben ducked into the semi-darkness. He sucked the nearly-palpable air-borne dust into his lungs and experienced a circus-elephant of a sneeze. Stumbling from the ferocity of it, he heard a rustle to his left. Any country kid knew without looking that it must be a rat or a mouse, scrounging around the ancient, dirty straw strewn on the floor.

In the seconds that it took for his eyes to adjust, the scenes of the past rose before him. There, in that loose-limbed stall, had stood the old cow, Bessie. How he'd hated coming out here to milk her on frozen winter mornings when he was thirteen or fourteen! He'd pushed off the job on his sister Lou as soon as he could do it without incurring Papa's wrath – and she'd promptly shoveled it onto younger Grace's much more frail shoulders, without so much as a "Please, wouldja…?"

A half-smile crept onto Ben's face unwished-for. Ol' Lou. What was that scoundrel of a kid sister up to nowadays? If he remembered correctly, one of Mama's letters had mentioned that both the twins were married – had a kid apiece even. And had both stayed in Chetham or thereabouts.

He shivered. How could they do that? This place – this whole town – gave him the creeps. It stank in the nostrils of his soul. Didn't they feel as he did? Didn't the anger roll through their veins on sleepless nights, 'til they nearly wanted to dig up Papa's body and tear it limb-from-limb?

Oh, never mind. Lou and Nancy had most likely – no, certainly – stayed in Chetham for some free handouts from the dear ol' Doc. That would be just like the twins he remembered. Always lookin' out for theirselves. Compulsively, Ben's teeth ground. What right did that

64

goody-two-shoes have to take care of Lou and Nancy, of Mama and Cliff...?

Of Grace? The memory of his favorite sister – pale and golden and worried, eating chocolate babies on a hay bale a few years ago – made his protective instincts toward her kindle with a warmth he hadn't known that he still possessed. It must be this place – with its visions of the past – that stirred his mind. He would say his soul, too, but he wasn't sure he still had one. A smile cracked his lips. Maybe Papa had drowned Ben's soul at birth like he used to drown misbegotten puppies. Ben could remember how his eight-year-old self had begged on his knees for Papa to spare even one of the old dog's litter. *"Please, Papa! Please! Don't kill them all!"*

It had never mattered what he'd said. Or how hard he'd begged. By nightfall, some six or eight puppies would hit the bottom of the lake, loaded into a weighed-down flour sack. He could still hear their squeals of fright...

The tightness of his jaw startled him. Shaking his head, Ben began to scour the sides of the two stalls, looking for Papa's old toolbox. Anything to take his mind off Papa himself. He'd nearly given up trying to find it, assuming some hooligan had stopped and snitched it one day (he would have done it himself) when his toe banged against something hard, covered in straw, dust, and old rope, frosted with cobwebs.

Wincing at the pain drumming through his toe, Ben bent down and retrieved the buried homemade toolbox, pieced together from odd boards and old nails. How strange to stand there with his papa's toolbox in hand, feeling the worn groove in the handle where both Papa and his papa before him had wrapped their thick Italian fingers! And now Ben wrapped his own there, too. *Just like them.*

A shudder went through him. "Get to work," he admonished himself aloud.

Forcing himself to forgo one more glance at the abandoned interior of the barn, he strode outside into the early morning sunlight and back up the path to the house, refusing to let himself feel anything this time. He set the toolbox down on the back stoop and tried to turn the knob.

Locked.

With a grunt, he applied his shoulder to the barrier. On the fourth try, the door burst open, taking one of the hinges with it. The action gave Ben the feeling of mastery, of power, that he needed to fortify himself against the interior of this hated house – a house that was the bone and gristle of so much of his past, of so many of his memories. *Of so much of what I've become.* The realization smote him for not the first time. He knew that's why he'd wanted to leave Chetham behind him for good. Leaving it felt like leaving himself – the wretched inward parts of himself that he didn't like to think about.

He stepped inside Mama's kitchen. Here again, cobwebs hung suspended from the ceiling. The floorboards creaked underfoot. One had rotted out, leaving a hole through which Ben could peer into the abyss of the cellar. He looked overhead and found the reason behind the rot: the whole ceiling above wore a dark waterstain. He sighed. Maybe the work this house required *was* worth all that dough.

In the silence, the clearing of another man's throat shot Ben's heart with adrenaline. An intruder. Hand tightening on the hammer, he whirled around, ready to face whoever had dared to trespass.

The person who met Ben's eyes made his heart drop back to its regular thumping. Loathing replaced the nervous excitement rushing through his veins. A disgustingly clean-cut young man stood there – a bit broader and maybe a smidgeon taller than when Ben'd last seen him – but still wearing that innocent, sympathetic church-boy expression. It was enough to make Ben upchuck. *Paulie.*

"Whatda *you* want?" he growled, fists tightening into balls at his sides, nearly dropping the hammer as the rage swirled through his body with the power of a tidal wave.

Hesitation flitted across the clear face, but it disappeared as soon as Ben had seen it, replaced by the same easy-going smile Ben had hated the last time he'd seen him. "Didn't know if you'd recognize me. It has been a couple years."

Mockery lightened Ben's mood. "How could I forget you? Last time I saw you, you had a nasty run-in with a door-jam, if I remember." He let the viciousness of his comment color his own expression.

A faint flush rose to Paulie's face. Not anger, but close. Satisfaction spread through Ben's heart.

"So what're ya doin' here?" Ben turned away to examine the still-decent cupboards. The Giorgi boy wasn't worth his while, and he'd show him that good. Real good.

"Uh, Dad said he wanted me to work with you. On the house. I was planning on walking here with you this morning, but when I came down to breakfast, you'd already left."

"Didn't want breakfast." Ben turned his attention to Mama's old stove. It still wore the grease stains of the last time she'd cooked on it. Yikes. How would they move this thing? It had to weigh a ton, literally. Finished inspecting the stove, he leveled his gaze directly on Paulie, fastening him with those eyes that he could make as frosty as a pitcher of ice-cold lemonade. "And I don't need your help on this house. Your dad's paying me to do this job. I'll get it done." Well, it was more like Ben was paying the Doc back for forking over those bucks for Bousquet. But Paulie Giorgi didn't need to hear that from Ben. *I'm sure the Doc'll tell him, though.*

Much to Ben's surprise and annoyance, however, Paulie didn't wilt at the harsh tone. He'd thought he would cower like a dandelion plucked from a summer meadow, deprived of water. Instead, the poor little rich kid stood tall and straight – not proud but with something Ben couldn't identify right away. Something that made a part of Ben's own spirit blush. *Dignity*. The *gagootz* of a kid had dignity.

"My Dad wants me here, Ben," he said, his voice full of determination, "and there's nothing you can do or say that'll make me leave. The sooner you realize that, the better for both of us."

Ben opened his mouth, trying to think of an angry retort, but the words died on their way from his brain to his tongue. He raised his

67

chin. "Well, if ya wanna work," he finally said, "let's see if your lady's hands can swing a hammer, kid."

CHAPTER NINE

Grace felt the warmth of Rosie's breath on her ear as her friend released a sigh before delivering her whispered thoughts – for the fourth time this church service. Trying to be as discreet as possible, Grace edged slightly farther down the pew to get away from the moist exhalation. Her eyes stayed fixed on Reverend Haverland, whose toad-like face filled with fervor as his preaching continued.

But, despite Grace's movement, Rosie would not be dissuaded from speaking her mind. "Have you ever seen someone so dreamy? He looks like a prince from Greece or something."

Grace cringed. Rosie had whispered loudly enough for the people on either side of them, as well as those behind them and directly in front of them, to hear her. *I shouldn't have moved. Rosie wouldn't have spoken so loudly.* Filled with a feeling that fate would not be denied, Grace edged back toward Rosie to prevent any further communications from floating into others' ears.

"Look at those beautiful waves. And that profile." Grace felt Rosie sag against the nearly-straight-backed pew. She'd not known that sagging there was possible, but Rosie accomplished it.

Grace gave Rosie a nervous smile. "Hush, Rosie. I'm trying to listen," she murmured back, barely moving her lips. The pastor had been preaching about taking up the shield of faith for the past few weeks; this would be the last sermon in the series, and Grace craved hearing every word. Her faith could surely use bolstering lately. She felt more than a bit adrift – not sure where God was leading her with the degree she'd gain in a few more years; sensing that Paulie had withdrawn his affection from her without any intention of restoring it.

But just as Grace's attention latched onto Reverend Haverland's words once more, Rosie's pink silk dress brushed her arm. She felt her friend's body lean into hers. *Honestly, even if she doesn't want to hear the sermon, doesn't she care what other people think of her?*

"Who do you think he is?"

Finally, Grace had had enough. "Who?" she hissed.

Rosie appeared pleased to have Grace's full attention. With the brilliance of morning glories, her blue eyes opened widely as she gestured with her chin toward the front left of the congregation. "Over there. In first row."

Grace's eyes roved, but she didn't immediately find the object of Rosie's fascination. "Show him to me later if you must," she muttered, softening her words with a smile.

Rosie sighed. And since her friend appeared willing to give up on provoking Grace's interest in the young man, Grace forgot all about the incident as she paid attention to the last ten minutes of the sermon.

Before the closing hymn, the minister reminded the congregation about the soup-and-sandwich luncheon that would take place after the service in the fellowship hall. Grace winced. She'd forgotten to bring anything for the communal meal. Knowing that she would still be welcome, she made her way down the flight of cement steps into the church's drafty basement. The air was filled with the mingled smells of soup: chicken noodle, split-pea and ham, Manhattan chowder. The deaconesses hovered about, especially in the church kitchen, still fetching napkins, bowls, and more to feed the congregation, fairly starving after the sermon.

Having left Rosie talking to a gaggle of other young women, Grace headed over to the kitchen, where she found the reverend's wife in charge.

"Do you need some help, Mrs. Haverland?" Grace asked. She'd forgotten to bring soup to share; the least she could do was to assist in serving.

Ladling stew into a bowl from a giant pot on the stove, Mrs. Haverland smiled at Grace. "Well, isn't that nice of you to offer? Let's see here. Why don't you take this bowl of stew out?" She hesitated for just a second before asking, "Think you can handle it?"

Grace smiled back, finding it funny that, for not the first time, a person questioned her strength based on her rather frail physical appearance. If only they knew how she used to carry heavy pails of milk up to the house or scrub the floor on her hands and knees! Aloud, she simply replied, "I can handle it, ma'am."

She picked up the brimming serving bowl, the steam from the hot, rich stew wafting upward. She had just turned toward the open door leading into the fellowship hall when...

Bang!

Before Grace knew what had happened, she felt the burning hot broth splash into her face and soak through her blouse. Clutching the bowl against her chest, she stared up to see who had gotten in her way.

She locked gazes with the most beautiful eyes she'd ever seen: the deep color of blueberries allowed to ripen fully in the June sun. Grace realized that this must be the dreamboat of whom Rosie had spoken as the man's startled expression clouded with horror at what he'd done.

"Oh, oh, my goodness! I am – I cannot tell you how extremely sorry I am, miss!" he babbled. "What a clumsy oaf I am! Here, let me take that." The man reached out for the now nearly-empty serving bowl.

And, dripping with brown broth from both her body and her clothing, Grace couldn't help herself. She began to laugh, just a little at first, then fully giving herself over to the humor of the situation.

He appeared stunned by her reaction. But, as he watched her and figured that she was not really crazy, the sides of his own mouth tilted up. A short puff of a laugh came first, but before long, he'd joined in her rolling laughter.

Wiping the mixture of laughing tears and broth from her cheeks, Grace finally turned toward the countertop to place down the serving bowl. Mrs. Haverland stood there frozen in place, ladle poised, mouth open, eyes darting from Grace to the young man.

"I'm sorry, Mrs. Haverland. I…" Grace trailed off. The relief from the tension she'd felt over school and Paulie spread through her heart, and she couldn't wipe the smile off her face. Perhaps the first genuine smile for many weeks.

The minister's wife shook her head. "It wasn't *your* fault, Grace." She shook her ladle in the direction of the young man. "It was *his*. But never mind. If you'd still like to stay for the potluck, Grace, you could probably find something to wear in the giveaway room."

"Thank you, Mrs. Haverland." Grace turned toward the door, heading for the small room in which the church collected used clothing for the poor.

As she ducked out, she heard Mrs. Haverland addressing the man. "As for you, sir, I'll need you to bring out another bowl of stew for all those hungry people! Now scoot!"

~ ~ ~

Grace found a worn but clean dress in the clothes room. At least the stew hadn't gotten on her stockings. She rinsed out her soiled clothing in the washroom and used soap to get the splashes of brown juice from her arms and face.

Washing up took quite a few minutes. Grace felt sure that she would get only the scraps of the potluck luncheon. But no matter. It was the fellowship that she really enjoyed, reminiscent of her last year at First Baptist, surrounded by friends and her family. That had been a wonderful, golden time, with friendships she'd cherished.

You have friends here. She pushed her way through the washroom door and spied Rosie chattering away with Violet, both of them bent over their bowls of soup. Heading toward them, she knew that she should be thankful to have the goodhearted, if sometimes silly, girls as friends here in New York.

But it's not the same as the friendship I had with Paulie.

She shook her head. No one – girl or boy – could ever fill the spot in which Paulie'd stood in Grace's affections. He'd seemed to know where the doors of her mind and heart led. Along with Emmeline Kinner, Paulie'd been the one to lead Grace to the Cross, where she'd found the Friend who would never leave her, neither here in New York or back home in Rhode Island.

But Paulie wasn't here now. The knowledge that no letter from him had arrived since that first one – and that he'd never made any excuse for it when Grace had visited home for Christmas vacation – made her wonder if she'd been mistaken about him all along. Or at least mistaken about where his heart really lay. She knew that he'd held affection for her, but maybe, as he matured, he'd realized that they simply were not suited. People did come to those kinds of conclusions.

She just had never thought that she and Paulie would be among them.

Now, walking across the crowded room, filled with families and college students, elderly folk and children, Grace aimed for the empty seat next to Violet. She'd put her purse and Bible down and then get her serving of soup. And maybe one of the crusty rolls she'd seen one of the deaconesses piling into baskets…

"Excuse me." A familiar, rich voice rumbled. She turned toward the table at her right, from where the voice issued. There, the spiller-of-her-soup sat at a table with several others – the McGrath family of six, as well as old Mrs. Arable and her middle-aged daughter Miss Janie Sue.

When he saw that he'd gained her attention, the man rose from his place at the table. "Seeing as I kept you from getting your soup when the pots were full, I took the liberty of getting you a bowl while you cleaned up the mess I made."

Grace looked from him to the place he'd set for her – right beside him, complete with two large bowls of soup and both a buttered and unbuttered biscuit. "You overestimate my appetite, mister," she replied, giving a little embarrassed laugh.

Smiling, the young man shook his head. "No, I just didn't know which kind of soup you'd like, so I got two different kinds. Mrs. Haverland said that you'd surely enjoy one of these two. Look, chicken noodle and clam chowder. I, uh, thought that we should stay away from the beef stew." Merriment danced in his eyes.

Her heart lifted strangely, and laughter bubbled up again. Moving toward the chair, she allowed him to help her into her seat.

She greeted the McGraths, Mrs. Arable, and Janie Sue before bowing her head to say a silent prayer. To her astonishment, she realized that not one twinge of nervousness touched her as she sat beside this young man. Well, that was a change from how she usually felt around men she didn't know well!

Opening her eyes, she ate a spoonful of the red clam chowder. Not as delicious as the clear chowder she liked back home, but quite adequate. Setting down her spoon, she picked up the buttered biscuit and tore off a small bite. *Who is he, and why do I feel fascinated by him?* The thought whirled through her heart and mind. *Take your time, Grace. No need for him to think you're overly interested in him.* "Am I allowed to know the name of the person who got me my part in this fine luncheon?"

Strange, the bold words just glided off her tongue and sent a zip of excitement through her – a sensation she hadn't felt since…

The man smiled, making his eyes crinkle a bit at the corners. He was older than she'd thought. At least in his late twenties. Maybe in his thirties. Funny how wiping the beef broth from your eyes changed your perspective. *He's even more handsome than I thought at first.* In the moments before he replied, she noted the sandy blond waves that he'd combed straight back from his forehead and the kind yet determined set of his jaw. She remembered the gentle way he'd helped her into her chair. Everything about him spoke of strength of character and purpose.

"I'm Kirk Haverland, Miss Picoletti."

Her mouth fell open. In her chest, her heart quickened its beat. "How do you know my name?"

"I know the right people," he answered with a wink. At her frown, he went on, "I'm Reverend Haverland's nephew, and I'm very pleased to meet you."

CHAPTER TEN

The sun shone hot as cracked red pepper – much too hot for the first Monday of May in Rhode Island. Using her unoccupied hand, Betty swatted at the fly that kept flitting into her eyes and picked up her pace until she nearly trotted along the dirt backroad that cut through the south side of Chetham. The lunch bucket hung heavily on her arm, banging against her hip with every step. *The sooner I get there, the sooner I can leave.*

Not that she minded being around Paulie Giorgi, of course. What girl *wouldn't* want to be around *him*? Of course there were more handsome young men to be had in Chetham, but few who could boast the genuine Christian faith and walk of Paulie. If only Grace Picoletti didn't have first dibs on him… *And she does, even though she's been gone for nearly a year with hardly even a visit for Christmas.*

Because of Grace's lack of visits home, up until this past month, Betty had held out a hope that she would, one day, somehow, capture Paulie's attention. She'd kept her hope a secret, as she knew that Daddy wouldn't approve of her "setting her mind on things below, not on things above," as he liked to say – especially when the boy in question obviously had no interest in her. But two weeks ago, Betty had found her hope all in vain, anyway, when that forward Mary Cracker actually asked her older brother Stephen to question Paulie on why he was dating so little. Not at all, actually. And Paulie'd replied that he loved someone already and was just waiting for God to bring her back to him.

Well, any featherhead could figure out exactly whom Paulie meant from that clue, and so, with a few whispered words, Mary had dashed Betty's secret hopes. *At least for now. Who knows if he'll ever get Grace back, now that she's gone out into the world like that.* Betty wiped at the perspiration gathering on her upper lip. *She* certainly hadn't wandered away. Betty had stayed right here in Chetham. She'd waited, nearly in a fever to become an excellent wife and good homemaker for… well, God only knew for whom. But Betty certainly had an idea of whom; that was for sure!

Now, if only Paulie Giorgi would cooperate a little – would just get over his fascination with Grace – nice girl though she was – and realize what he had right in front of him – displayed every Sunday at the First Baptist piano, for goodness' sakes!

A sigh escaped the bubble of frustration in her heart. At any rate, Betty would see Paulie today. While Mother visited with Mrs. Giorgi, Betty had been sent to the old Picoletti house, bearing the young men's forgotten lunch pail. Yes, she'd see Paulie… but would Paulie ever see her? Really see her?

The let-down when he didn't take particular notice of her – as he was sure not to – almost wasn't worth the treat of seeing him. *And I have to see that horrible stepbrother of his.* Though she'd barely met the loathsome creature, Betty certainly had no desire to ever interact with Benjamin Picoletti again. Not after he'd called her a… She fairly blushed at the thought. *Dollface! He called me dollface, just as if I was a girl from a burlesque show or something.* She pursed her lips. Well, poor man. He hadn't been in church yesterday, had he? He obviously needed the Lord.

But, really, what could Betty Cloud do about that?

~ ~ ~

The rotten shingles fell away from beneath Ben's knees as he crawled from one section of the roof to the next. "Whoa!" He cursed aloud, enjoying the knowledge that Paulie must be wincing at the torrid stream coming from his mouth. *He can't stop me, though. His papa ain't here to stop me, neither.* A smile curled at Ben's lips and he began pulling away the next swath of worthless roofing with gusto. Soon – two months, tops – he'd be finished with this job and never would Chetham – or Doctor Giorgi – see his face again.

In the meantime, he'd decided that this little preacher-boy needed to be taken down a peg. *Or several.*

And Benjamin Picoletti was just the person to do that. After what his mama had endured at the hands of men like Sam Giorgi – who had abandoned her to the whims of Ben's own papa – why shouldn't Sam's son learn a lesson or two? Learn to eat humble pie? Learn that maybe he wasn't the goody-two-shoes that he believed himself to be? Every amateurish pounding of Paulie's hammer reinforced Ben's conclusions.

"Hey, looks like Mother sent lunch to us!" Paulie's voice held newly-infused enthusiasm. He squinted intently across the yard from his place a few feet away from Ben.

"Ain't *your* ma, kid. Your ma's dead," Ben stated, turning his own eyes toward the yard to see what in the world this stooge was going on about.

A petite brunette, her hair carefully curled, her dress as neat as if it'd come off a dress-shop mannequin, picked her way across the piles of discarded shingles and rotted wood in the yard. Two things were clear: She looked familiar, and she was dang pretty.

"Hiya, Betty!" Paulie stood up, obviously without thinking, and nearly pitched headlong off the roof.

Ben didn't bother to lend him a steadying hand. If the kid was gonna be a goner, he might as well go now as later. "Watch it," he merely commented. "You wanna end up dog meat?"

There. He'd done his part in keeping the Doc's son safe.

Paulie nodded and began to clamber over to the edge of the roof, toward the ladder leaning up against the side of the house. "We're coming down."

Ben raised his eyebrows. *We are?* What was this guy made of? In the real world, you didn't get lunch served to you on a golden platter. Sometimes, there was no lunch at all.

The girl shaded her eyes against the sun. Ben saw the look of admiration she held for Paulie there, though she tried to hide it beneath that demure little smile. Slowing his hammering, Ben watched Paulie out of the corner of his eyes. Did the loser – who'd once pretty much professed undying love to Grace – return the pretty girl's admiration? Ben figured he'd better watch and see what kind of gig was going on here.

The two exchanged a few words, though Ben couldn't hear them. Paulie took the pail from the girl; he appeared to joke about the heftiness of the lunch. Then, without a wave in Ben's direction, she left the way she'd come.

He couldn't resist. Before she'd gone out of hearing distance, Ben set down his hammer and let out a piercing catcall. "Thanks for lunch, cutie!" he hollered.

Paulie's head jerked up, and Ben felt intense pleasure when he saw the look of anger that passed over the younger man's face. He picked up his hammer and went back to roofing with vigor.

"Why'd you do that?" Paulie had climbed back up the ladder, apparently determined to confront Ben.

Ben didn't give Paulie the satisfaction of looking his way. "'Cause I wanted to. And 'cause she's a stuck-up prude who thinks she's too good for everybody else. Just like you are, kid." There. That should spark some anger in the Doc's beloved son.

"Betty Cloud is a good girl who—"

Ben met Paulie's eyes. "Oh, defending her honor, are ya? Why? Is she your trollop, too? Kinda like my sister was?"

The next thing Ben knew, his fingers clutched for a grip on the roofing shingles. The metallic taste of blood lay on his tongue. Paulie crouched beside him on his haunches, face drained of color. "I'm sorry!" The words choked out. "I-I don't know what I... Please forgive me, Ben. I shouldn't have reacted like that."

Disgust flooded Ben at the sound of the apologies running off the boy's tongue. How low could you stoop, to beg the pardon of someone you'd just slugged? He sent a look toward Paulie that should wither his miserable, cowardly self to less than nothing, wiped his bleeding lip with the back of his sleeve, and retrieved his hammer. "Don't worry about it. Didn't think ya had it in ya, preacher-boy. But that's good – ya do got blood in them veins, not just milk."

Paulie was silent for moment, keeping his eyes on the roof. He licked his lips carefully before beginning. "But I want you to know – to know for certain – that I never... that is... your sister..."

Ben found himself smirking as Paulie struggled to express what he had to say without sounding coarse. "What? What're ya tryin' to say? My sister what?"

Paulie looked away. "Your sister and I – Our relationship was pure. In the way you're thinking."

Ben whistled. "Oh, so now you know what I'm thinking?"

Paulie stayed silent.

But one word held Ben's attention. "Lemme ask you a question, lover-boy. You said, *was*. So you're no longer... *with* my sister?"

Paulie picked up his own hammer, turning it over in his hands for several long moments before he replied, eyes down, "I don't know."

"Well, lemme tell you something I do know." Ben let the words fly out. "I may not be religious. I may not be a *good* man, but at least I ain't no hypocrite. I don't tell a girl I'll never leave her and then chase after some other skirt."

Paulie's eyes flashed up. "I'm not—"

"But that seems like it runs in your family, huh, kid?" Ben interrupted, feeling relief as his pent-up anger toward the Doc poured out. "But you listen to me: You ain't gonna do to my sister what your dear ol' dad did to my mama."

And then the Doc's son began hammering in such a way that Ben knew he'd get no more from Paulie that day, try as he might. Wiping his still-bleeding mouth on his sleeve, Ben took up his own hammer again. The sooner he finished here, the better. Then he would be free to leave.

~ ~ ~

Grace tamped down the nervous tingling in her chest, refusing to let it travel down her arms. Taking a deep breath, she closed her eyes for just a moment and shut out the sight of her first teaching assignment. *Lord, make me a good teacher. Help me to reach these children and to not only give them a love for music, but also a love for You. I don't know how to do this, but I know that's no reason I shouldn't try. I know there's a need here, and if You want me to be here, make me of use please.* Maybe – just maybe – she'd find her calling here. Maybe *this* was why she'd come to the Conservatory.

Opening her eyes again, she took in the sight of the enormous charity school. The Helen Higgins School's main building stretched three stories high, rough gray stone extending several dozen feet in all directions. Her eyes caught on the morning glory vine traveling around the solid metal door, the only source of color against the drab building.

"Well, what are you doing here, Miss Picoletti?" The familiar male voice caused her head to swivel to the right.

Kirk Haverland stood there, a kind – and seemingly delighted – smile curving along his well-formed lips. *Why is he here?* For some reason, Grace couldn't stop her heart from skittering. *And why am I blushing? What reason do I have to blush, for goodness' sake?*

Well, she would just have to pretend that her face wasn't flooding with color. Straightening her shoulders, she clung a little more tightly to her music textbooks and returned Kirk's smile with one of her own. "I teach here. Well," she amended, "I *will* be teaching here."

Now there was no doubt that he was positively, absolutely delighted. The smile broke into a grin. "Really? What subject?"

She opened her mouth to answer but, before she could, he

slapped his forehead and shook his head. "How silly of me. You're a vocalist. Of course you'd be teaching music. That's wonderful. Just great."

She nodded, and a moment of silence ensued. The awkwardness descending, Grace almost began to hurry up the few steps to enter the school building when an unusual boldness came over her. "And you," she said, looking far up to his face. *He must be at least six feet tall, if not more.* "Why are you at the school today?"

"I'm your new boss, I suppose," Kirk replied, and she noticed that he had a dimple – just one perfect dimple punctuating his smoothly-shaven, tanned cheek.

Why am I thinking about his dimples? Really, Grace. Stop it. It wasn't like her to get caught up in how men looked! "My boss? I thought Mr. Whitely…" Wasn't Violet's uncle the headmaster? When she'd spoken to him about volunteering a few days ago, Mr. Whitely had said nothing to her about a replacement. Especially not *this* replacement!

"Yes, Mr. Whitely will serve until the end of the school year in June. Then he'll be retiring. Most deservedly, from what I hear. He has been an excellent headmaster. I moved to Crocksville to train under him for the final month so that I'm ready to go for next year. Of course, I'll be conducting the summer school after Mr. Whitely departs as well." He smiled again, very warmly, and Grace felt the heat in her face rise another several degrees. *I must be the color of a July tomato!*

"Well," she said, grasping for her bearings in what had suddenly become an emotionally-clouded atmosphere, "I must go inside, Mr. Haverland. My class starts in fifteen minutes, and I want to have time to set up. I've never done this sort of thing before and…"

"And you're just a bit nervous? Am I right?" He tilted his head, his face so open and encouraging that Grace felt some of the tension drain from her.

"Yes, a little," she admitted. "But I'm trying to trust in the Lord to help me through it."

"Ah, for when you are weak in yourself, then you are strong in Him." Mr. Haverland nodded his approval. With a confidential expression, he bent toward her as if they were conspirators. "To be honest with you, Miss Picoletti, I've never done this sort of thing before either. Headmastering, you know. So God will have to help the both of us."

Grace found herself smiling back at him freely. His manner was so easy yet without pretense, and he quickly admitted to his human frailty and dependence on God. He seemed exactly the sort of man that she would love to have as a friend here at the school.

With the gallantry of an Austenian hero, Kirk offered her his arm. "Let's go inside together, shall we?"

Feeling happy with the anticipation of what awaited her at Helen Higgins, Grace placed her arm on his forearm. "Alright, Mr. Haverland."

He gave her a sideways smile. "Please, call me Kirk."

"Alright… Kirk." The name slid from her lips as though they'd been made to say it.

He took the steps with steadiness and grace, leaving her in no doubt that he had been born to lead. And it was only long after her class had finished for the day that Grace realized that she had thought much more of Kirk than of any other young man all afternoon.

CHAPTER ELEVEN

Despite the way his protectiveness could grate on a guy's nerves, Sam Giorgi couldn't be faulted with providing an inadequate Sunday breakfast. *Or any day's breakfast.* Ben sliced through his cinnamon French toast, studded with plump raisins. He speared four bites on his fork at once and popped them into his mouth. He'd only been in Chetham for a week-and-a-half, but he already had settled into a solid, doable routine: wake early, grab some grub from the kitchen lady, work on Papa's old place for ten hours or so – with or without Paulie's silent help, depending on the kid's school schedule, arrive home after supper'd finished and gobble up the leftovers. Bypass the sitting room where everyone else gathered. Fall into bed. Repeat.

Except for this morning. When he'd arrived home last night, a bottle of his old pal Frenchie's bootleg alcohol – "coffin varnish," Frenchie called it – smuggled in his jacket pocket, the Doc had informed him that no one in the Giorgi household worked on "the Lord's Day." The old killjoy's tone held so much iron in it that Ben knew that he couldn't outright defy him. He'd just wait until all the family had left for church. Then he'd hightail it out to the brick house and get a few hours of work in, same as he'd done last Sunday. Though thinking on it now, the Doc must've found out about that somehow, or he wouldn't have come down so heavy last night.

The sooner the house gets done, the sooner I can leave. He kept repeating that to himself; that – and the booze – helped him get through the days working on Papa's place.

But while he waited for them to leave, he might as well eat up. He reached across the table to spear another few sausages from the heaped platter and caught the Doc's son staring at him. As soon as his eyes connected with Paulie's, the kid dropped his gaze. But not before Ben saw the resentment slow-roasting there. *Yeah, kid. I know how it feels to wish someone would up and get lost for good.* Hadn't Ben longed for dear ol' Papa to do just that for years? *Beat it, Papa. Just get out and leave us be.* How many times had his heart cried for that at eight – ten – twelve – sixteen years old? That old jalopy steamrolling Papa had been a gift from God – if Ben still believed in God, which he wasn't all that sure about.

Flinging the sausages onto his plate to release a little extra steam, he turned his attention to Cliff. How that boy had shot up! When Ben had last visited, Cliff had been – what? – fourteen? Now he was sixteen, sprouting patches of chin hair and stinkin' to high heaven when he'd run home from school, sweating through the nice duds he had, courtesy of the Doc, of course.

Cliff must've felt Ben's eyes on him because he looked up from his plate and grinned straight at him. *Poor Cliff – having to come and live with Doctor Giorgi. Sure don't got the freedom I had at his age.* Actually, Ben had already left school at Cliff's age – had his first job, too, pulling in a few good dollars a week. Never mind that the law said you couldn't leave school 'til you were sixteen; lots of kids did it. *It made a man of me, too.*

Nostalgia for the brotherly bond he'd missed having with Cliff swept over Ben as he chomped through the sausage links. *I can miss one day of workin' on that old house. It's Sunday, after all, like the Doc said.* "Hey, Cliff," he offered, "wanna come fishing with me this morning?" Surely the kid wouldn't choose church over a fishing trip. "Thought we could head down to Jeffer's Pond. He still lets people fish there, right?"

Silence came over the entire table. The Doc exchanged a glance with Mama, but Ben couldn't read what was in it.

Cliff's face held the expression of a confused Golden Retriever puppy – not sure if he should wag his tail or not. He swallowed the big bite of French toast he'd been mushing around in his mouth. "Uh, we go to church this morning, Ben. It's Sunday."

Ben shrugged. "Yeah, I know. I figured you could skip a week. Just one week. Or'll God throw ya into hell for that?" He winked, sure that Cliff would find that funny.

But from his brother's face, Ben could tell that Cliff didn't find it funny, just a little bewildering. "Whatdaya mean, Ben? Not repenting of your sin is what'll throw you into hell."

Cliff stated it so sincerely that Ben had difficulty resisting the urge to roll his eyes. What sin? What was he doing that was so bad? *I'm just doing what I gotta do to get by in this crazy world.* What was anybody doing, for that matter, that was so bad that God would send them to hell for it? *Except for murderers, maybe. And Papa.* Yes, Ben would love to see that man burn in the deepest pit hell could offer. But Ben figured that God – if He existed – didn't care all that much about what ordinary folks did to get by in the world. "Yeah, well," he said at last, "I don't believe in that stuff, Cliff."

Cliff glanced at Paulie, as if to see what old preacher-boy would say about that. But Paulie wore a mask of disinterest as he sliced his own sausage into small pieces.

"So you'll come?" Ben pressed.

Cliff glanced at the Doc and then shook his head. "No, thanks."

Ben felt his hatred transfer with ease from the memory of Papa to that man sitting at the head of the table, eating scrambled eggs like he was innocent of jailing this whole family to his self-serving ends. *If it wasn't for him, Cliff would've come and we could've had a nice, brotherly time together. Cliff's afraid of going against him, just like Mama was afraid of going against Papa.* Ben dug his fork into his own eggs with such vengeance that the tines scraped against the china. *I ain't afraid, though. In fact, I'd like to face God Himself and tell Him what a lousy job He's done with the world.*

"You should come with us, Ben. You're more than welcome." That was the Doc, butting in. He was good at that.

Ben didn't bother to hide his smirk. "No, thanks."

Across the table, Paulie stayed silent, pulling his fork through the remains of his eggs. Wouldn't that kid love to have to sit next to him in church? *Don't worry, Paulie, ol' boy. I ain't darkening the door of your church any more than I'm going to Confession anytime soon. You can have every last inch of the pew.*

But when he next glanced up, he found Mama's eyes on him. They were filled with tears. Ben swallowed hard and stared down at his plate. *Oh, come on, Mama! Don't cry on me. You know I can't hold up against that!*

Without bothering to ask to be excused, he threw down his fork and shoved his chair back from the table.

~ ~ ~

Knotting his tie before the mirror in the entryway, Paulie wondered whether Dad wanted to take the car to church this morning or if they'd walk. The sun shone, and the day promised temperatures in the upper 60s. *We'll probably walk unless Mother's knees are bothering her.*

He hoped they'd walk. It would provide him with a chance to exercise off some of his irritation with Benjamin Picoletti. A chance to get into a frame of mind more conducive to worship and less to boxing.

Thinking of boxing… He couldn't *believe* that he'd actually punched Ben right in the face the other day. How unlike Christ could he be? All the man had done was insult Grace, the sweetest, most desirable girl alive. Oh, and whistle at Betty Cloud, like she was a woman of the street.

Ben Picoletti had deserved that punch. Paulie had nothing to repent of, did he? *Even though you've repented of it half a dozen times this week already, Paulie. Guess you weren't sincere, huh?* With a hardening of his jaw, Paulie adjusted his tie to his satisfaction and turned to call up the staircase for Cliff to hurry.

Instead, he came face-to-face with Ben. Well, really, chin-to-nose, seeing that Ben was a couple of inches shorter than he was.

That couple of inches gave Paulie immense satisfaction.

"When's the gate open, preacher-boy?"

It took Paulie a moment to realize that Ben's analogy to a race starting gate meant that he wanted to know when the Giorgis were leaving for church. *Wonder why? Wonder what he'll be up to while we're gone.* Aloud, he said, "If we're walking, we should leave in a couple of minutes. As soon as Mother and Dad are ready."

"Great." Ben flopped down on the second-to-last step and crossed his arms over his chest. "Well, I'm ready."

Paulie rarely found himself speechless, but, just for a second, Ben's comment rendered him thus. "Wha – What do you mean? You mean, you're coming with us?"

Ben raised his eyebrows, the side of his mouth curling a bit. "Your daddy asked me to. Didn't ya hear him?"

Paulie swallowed past the tongue that had turned to sandpaper. "Yes. Yes." He faced the mirror again, desperate to hide the anger surely spreading over his countenance. How could Ben do this? He'd spoil a perfectly good Sunday morning. And probably afternoon, too, since the Clouds had invited them to have an early dinner at their home. *Knowing Ben, he'll come, too. Even though nobody wants him!* That might be unfair, yes. But was it untrue? Much as Paulie didn't like to admit it, yes, considering the other three members of the Giorgi household. But it sure felt good at the moment to vent his feelings, festering with all the discomfort of an infected toenail!

"What, my duds not good enough for ya?" Ben taunted.

Pretending to fiddle with his tie, Paulie eyed Ben's reflection. The young man wore the same clothes as yesterday. And the day before. And the day before. *This, despite Dad having given him two entire sets of new work clothes and a suitable outfit for church, too!* Ben's daily attire consisted of nearly-threadbare corduroy pants, a dirt-stained button-down shirt (*without* an undershirt; Paulie was certain of it), stretched-out suspenders, and sloppy boots-sans-socks.

Paulie closed his eyes. *Help me, Lord.* He had no idea how God would accomplish that, but perhaps He would deem it in Paulie's best interests to remove Ben…

A hard slug hit his shoulder, jolting Paulie's eyes open. Ben stood behind him, smirking. "'Come as ya are.' Ain't I got that right?"

"Yeah," Paulie muttered. "You sure do."

~ ~ ~

Betty had just begun playing the introductory hymn when she saw him out of the corner of her eye. At the tail-end of his family's line, that horrid Picoletti individual shuffled. No. This time he didn't shuffle, exactly. He *strutted*, as if to say that he had every bit as much of a right to be at First Baptist as Betty Cloud did.

Resisting the urge to look at him again, Betty stared unseeing at the hymnbook spread before her. Usually, she enjoyed what Daddy called "feeling" the hymn: letting the lyrics shape the way she played, adding emphasis to certain parts and softening others. But Ben's entrance had shattered her concentration. With difficulty, Betty staggered through the music and waited for Deacon Melbourne to take his place behind the podium so that he could read the week's announcements. *Get ahold of yourself, Betty.* She dropped her hands from the keys and forced them to stay in her lap calmly.

Eighty-six-year-old Deacon Melbourne climbed the two platform steps with more spritz in his steps than Daddy did. He had always reminded Betty of a cricket, his large, round eyes peering out from behind his wire-rimmed spectacles, his shoulders bobbing to emphasize certain important announcements. Instead of listening to the man's sing-song voice tap-dance down the list of First Baptist's small happenings, Betty let her gaze slide across the congregation so that it wouldn't be obvious when she at last looked at Ben. *It'll seem like I was just looking at everyone and he happened to be in my line of sight.*

Betty's eyes traveled from Mrs. Sowams and her brood of five in the second row to Geoffrey and Emmeline Kinner with their son in the third pew. She let her eyes stay on sweet David, who cuddled up to his mama, for a moment before moving ever-so-casually toward the Giorgi family again. Though why she wanted a second look at Ben, who could know? He certainly wasn't the most attractive creature to have ever entered First Baptist's sanctuary. Nor the most gentlemanly. The cat-call still echoed in her mind. And, of course, there was very little reason to suspect that he was a Christian, for that matter.

No, Betty Cloud, the reverend's daughter, had no business at all seeking another look at his rough-hewn but sensitive features… nor his intelligent but so very stormy eyes… nor…

And then he met her gaze, and… he winked! With a sharp but silent intake of her breath, Betty darted her gaze back to Deacon Melbourne, who had just finished speaking. *Do not look in that direction again. Ever again!*

But the fact remained: Ben Picoletti had winked. At her!

She knew that it shouldn't matter to her. It should disgust her, in fact. *Imagine, winking at a girl. In church! What does he think he is, an owl?*

Yet, try as she might, Betty could not deny that the wink very much disturbed her. In fact, it was the reason she couldn't concentrate on Daddy's sermon at all that morning.

CHAPTER TWELVE

B en decided that he'd rather not go to the Clouds' house that afternoon. The man's sermon was boring with a capital B. How could his at-home personality be any different? Bertha Cloud was alright as far as middle-aged women went, he supposed, but was a roast-beef dinner worth the agitation that sitting at the table with the Doc and the Reverend might bring?

Though of course, there was the daughter to consider: pretty Betty Cloud, whose tailbone must be sore from never getting off her high-horse. How much enjoyment could be derived from irritating her in every little way he could think of! She played it confident, alright, but he could tell he'd rattled her with his behavior over the past few days. He remembered the way her innocent dark eyes had opened round as Christmas oranges when Ben had winked at her during church.

A smile pulled at Ben's lips, drawing them upward like a hooked bass. He strolled toward River Avenue alone. Betty Cloud, for all her hoity-toity ways, *had* noticed him – maybe not romantically, but he knew when a girl was intrigued at least by his wildness, his bad reputation. And he'd certainly caught her staring his way today when she should've been concentrating like a proper church girl on the old deacon's announcements. *For being such a virtuous girl, she sure don't mind ogling at a fella, does she?*

He reached the turn-off from Main Street onto River Avenue, but instead of striding right down that dead-end road to grab one of the Doc's fishing rods, Ben stopped short. Something tugged at him. He wanted to go to the old house. Why, he couldn't say, but not another minute had passed before he found himself heading back the way he'd come.

He took the old short-cut through the woods to get to Papa's house. *Why am I bothering?* He asked the question of himself several times as he pushed through overgrown brambles and newly-budding branches, as his corduroys caught and ripped on a thicket of thorns. He saw the Picoletti place every day – would be seeing it every day for the next several weeks at least, whenever he came to work on it. But his feet moved on down the path, as if they had a mind of their own.

This path – the memories it alone held! Ben could recall forging his way to elementary school on the dirt, slick with January ice, his lunch pail in his hand. The pail held lunch not only for him, but also for the twins and Grace, all three trailing behind him, eager to reach the school before their thinly-mittened hands turned numb. Cliff hadn't been old enough to tag along yet. Before they'd left home, he'd made sure that everybody had their homework – ready to hand into the schoolteachers, from no-nonsense first-grade teacher Mrs. Katz to lenient third-grade teacher Mr. Alfredo. But his own homework wasn't ready…

The bitter tang leaped into Ben's mouth as he remembered Mr. Johnson's sharp reprimand and insistence that Ben stay after school to clean the blackboards. He'd sent a note home, too, one that Ben was afraid to hand to Papa – and afraid not to hand to Papa. Mr. Johnson was right – Ben hadn't completed his homework; Ben had received a failing grade on his spelling test for the fifth consecutive week; Ben had trouble concentrating in school…

But how could I help it? He'd been sitting out in the barn for so long, waiting for the yelling to subside, waiting for the final sharp crack of Papa's fist to Mama's cheek, telling Ben that their argument was over, that now he could go inside and concentrate on his studies. And how could he focus even then, when Mama's eyes dripped silent tears into the soup pot she stirred? He'd rather escape and play ball on the streets until the streetlights turned on and Matthew Henderson's father called for his son to come wash up.

Matthew Henderson's father... Even now, the memory of the man's round face, shiny, pale, and solemn, gentle as a contented walrus, caused a longing to rise in Ben's own heart. He ground his teeth and shoved aside a low-hanging pine bough. How many times had he seen stout Mr. Henderson, hands tough and dirty from his ploughing and planting, stride up? How often had he wished with all his heart that Matthew's papa called for *him*, invited *him* to sit around the supper table and eat up his looks of approval and love?

Inevitably, each evening, as he'd watched Matthew scuttle away, his papa's protective arm wrapped around his shoulders, his own papa's whistle had rung out. Fear had entered Ben's heart upon hearing that sound; it meant that if Ben didn't sprint home, he'd be late and liable to get a heavy hand across his own face. If he came on time, he'd get a grunt. No more, no less.

He never cared nothing for me.

Even now, the pain of it all still stung his heart so badly that he longed for the day when he could not be touched by it – when the hardness that he already felt emotionally in other areas of his life could seep into and fill all of his memories of childhood as well. *Would to God that I didn't have to remember!*

At least Papa was dead. That should give Ben a small portion of satisfaction.

But it didn't. *Because every single day I think about him and how he hurt me and hurt Mama and all us kids.*

Though Papa's body lay cold as ice on Lincoln's birthday, though the worms were having a feast on his carcass, laid out in his best suit six feet under, Papa's spirit continued to haunt Ben's footsteps.

Up at the track, he'd managed not think about it during the days at least. But at night, the memories would come flooding back. Some nights, he'd up and gone into the town, looking for fun and girls and what passed for friendship – anything to distract himself and fill those long hours – to keep something coming into the doors of his heart at all times so that he could tell the memories of his childhood that there was no room at the inn.

He pushed past the final bramble, and the old house towered above him. His soul hated every last faded brick – hated with the kind of loathing that is powerless to do anything but gape. How to expel the demons? Who knew – certainly not Ben.

Powerless. That awful feeling clung to his mind and bones and crawled up his nerves. At the mercy of memories that were part of his very self: the reason why he was a gambler, a cheat, a liar, a womanizer, even. *I've become what I hated in him.* The thought that had popped into his mind on more than one occasion burst again onto centerstage.

I will never escape. He plunged forward across the grassy expanse, determined to face the memories of Papa and to laugh in their face. To dare them to prevent him from walking as a free man, haunted no longer, untouched by his past.

Striding up the path to the door, he passed the makeshift scaffolding he and Paulie had devised and entered the house. He'd rather not start with the kitchen – He could still remember seeing Mama, pregnant with her last child, hovering over the stove, the same night Ben had found out that Papa had a steady mistress for the umpteenth time – though God only knew what the Doc had made her do with the baby, for surely Mama had borne it. If Mama had lost the baby, Grace would have told him straight out when Ben had asked her two years ago.

Mama should've told me. Anger toward the Doc – for certainly that was who prevented Mama from confiding in Ben – blossomed afresh in his heart. *She should've told me whether the Doc made her get rid of it or give it up or what.* The old man had probably wanted Mama all to himself – hadn't wanted a baby to interfere with his plans for "his" family.

Passing through the kitchen, Ben drew his hand through a mess of cobwebs stretching across the doorway that led into the sitting room. The space stood naked except for the crippled piano crouching in the corner. The curtains shrouded the light, and Ben felt brave enough to cross the room in a few strides and pull them back. But as he did, the rod came loose and the entire caboodle crashed to the floor in a flood of dirt, dust, and frightened spiders.

Startled, Ben stared at the tumble of metal and faded fabric for just a moment before he shrugged. He and Paulie would eventually remove everything in the house anyway. At least there was sunlight now.

Sunlight...

Why did that memory flood back to him now? The one of Mama, her hair long and wavy down her back like a mermaid in one of those old fairy-tale books, sitting at the piano over there? He had been just a small child, leaning his body up against her warm, plump thigh.

And he'd been happy.

Happy? He'd not thought that one memory of his childhood reverberated with that feeling. As the agony of it all had replayed over the years, he'd forgotten that any part of those early days of his life contained... happiness. *Was I really? Was I truly happy?*

Almost without his permission, Ben's legs moved woodenly across the room until he stood just above the instrument. He lifted the rollaway fall that covered the ivory. His eyes trickled over the broken keys of the piano. What had Mama been playing that afternoon? Not a show-tune; he was nearly certain of that. There'd been peace, not just merry-making in what she'd played...

He sat down on the stool gingerly, testing his weight on its aged material. It creaked and wobbled but seemed as if it would hold him. His fingers touched the stained cream keys. Some were missing now, but it had once been a beautiful instrument. A smile rose unbidden to his lips. Mama had taught him to play a little, before she had become overburdened by her wandering husband and the children he'd sired but refused to father.

Perhaps if he could etch out on the keys the piece Mama had

95

played back then, that happy time would return to the house of his memory. And maybe – just maybe – the peace he'd felt that one day would come back to his heart again. How he longed for it!

He pressed his fingers into the keys. The notes sounded broken, out-of-tune. He ground his teeth. Why did tears rise to his eyes? He was no kid in knickers, no youth that underwent the lash of Papa's tongue. His lungs clenched as he forced the moisture back – *back* – and pushed on. His fingers found seemingly random keys and drew a ramshackle harmony out of them, playing until the tide of his memories receded. Feeling the satisfaction of conquest, he played on, controlling the blur of broken music, not caring if it was beautiful or ugly – just that he could make it start or stop at the command of his will…

"Oh! Hello."

He whirled around, jolted back into time, his neck twinging from the sharp turn. A dark-haired woman stood in the doorway that connected the kitchen and sitting room. She held a little blond toddler by one hand; the child's other hand grasped a lollipop which he kept popping into and out of his pink mouth.

Anger pulsed through his veins. Embarrassment, too, that he'd been caught at a vulnerable moment. "What are ya doin' in here? Dontcha know this is private property?"

Surprise flashed across the woman's face, but it ended with a small smile. Odd; this woman's smile appeared to hold no guile. She seemed as if she genuinely meant to be friendly. "I'm Emmeline Kinner," she said after a smidgeon of hesitation.

Stepping toward him, she held out a long-fingered hand toward him. Her fingernails were neatly trimmed and her skin looked soft. *A woman with a cushy life*. He didn't trust her. He ignored her hand.

"You're Ben. Am I right?"

Ben nodded warily. He'd keep his guard up with this one.

The smile widened. "I thought so. I'm a friend of your mother and your sister Grace. I know that the house belongs to your parents. I didn't mean to intrude," she continued, "but your mother told me how you and Paulie have been working here, fixing the old place up. David and I were out for our Sunday afternoon walk, and – I don't know – I figured I'd take a look at your progress. Then I heard the piano…"

Ben felt his skin crawl. "Didn't mean for nobody to listen. I ain't no piano-player." And what emotions had she witnessed shadowing his face? How long had she been standing there in the doorway?

The woman raised her eyebrows. "If you're not, you've got me fooled. You have a good ear for music, Ben. That's obvious."

The attention discomfited him. Anxious to get the woman to focus on something else, he gestured toward the little kid she held by the hand. "Who's that?"

What had he said to make the woman pause the way she did? Then her full, rich smile spread across her mouth again. "This is my son, David. David, say hello to Mr. Picoletti."

"Shucks, he can just call me Ben. Wouldn't know who he was talkin' to if he called me Mr. Picoletti," Ben put in before the boy could respond.

The kid turned his large gray-blue eyes up to his mama, as if to question whether she would agree.

"How about Mr. Ben?" the lady suggested, pushing a chunk of her son's hair back from his face.

David let go of her hand so that he could retain his sucker while extending one small narrow-boned hand to Ben. "Hello, Mr. Ben," he said.

The kid's shy charm and bird-like fingers reminded Ben of his sister's manner. *Back when I actually spoke to Grace.*

And thinking of Grace made him realize…

"Hey, I know who you are!" He rose from the stool, knocking it to the ground with a crash. He set it on its feet again and faced Emmeline, looking from her to David. "You're that lady Grace used to write me about. The one who gave her that flower or something. K-Kenter? The Kenters? Is that who you said you were?"

"Kinner. I'm Emmeline Kinner. And yes, I do know Grace very

well. Well, at least until she headed up to the Conservatory. Nowadays, I get most of my word about Grace from your mama. From what I hear, she's doing very well." Emmeline looked as if she expected him to know more than she did. Well, maybe he should. Grace was, after all, his sister. But he couldn't recall more than tidbits of what she'd written to him lately.

Not sure whether to affirm or deny Emmeline's assumption, Ben gave a noncommittal grunt. He then turned his attention back toward David. "How old are ya, kid?"

"Two." David held up his outstretched fingers to emphasize.

"Wowsers. You are a big boy." Ben couldn't help but feel as though he'd met this cute kid somewhere before. Had he seen him in church this morning? That must be it. Naw, it wasn't that. David *reminded* him of… of his own siblings, so strongly that it made him shake his head in disbelief. *Crazy.* "Hey, ya wanna sit up on the bench with me? Plunk out a tune?" Where had that idea come from? Hadn't he just told this lady that he weren't no piano-man? And why'd he want some sticky-fingered kid on his knees?

But before Ben could take back his words, he saw that David's eyes shone at the prospect. Once again, the kid looked up at his mama to see if she'd agree. At her smile and nod, Ben took his seat again at the piano, and David scrambled up onto his lap.

"Now, listen, kid. I'm gonna put my fingers down on the keys, and you put yours right over 'em, like icing on a cake. Got that?"

David nodded, squirming, so that Ben had to grab him under the arms to keep him from taking a tumble to the dust-covered floor. "Watch it, kiddo. You wanna kill yourself?"

David shook his head.

"Keep still, David, or you'll have to come off the bench," Emmeline admonished.

The kid kept still, but Ben could feel the anticipation bubbling through David's skin. He set his hands down on the old, chipped ivory. "Okay, kid. Pop your hands over mine."

Ben hadn't been prepared for the wave of nostalgia – of yearning

– that poured over his entire being at the feeling of the soft child-fingers covering his own. In one moment, he became wholly aware, to the exclusion of all else his senses received, that the sweet innocence of childhood was what he longed for – what he felt had been robbed from him, taken so unjustly by Papa's folly. Here, on Ben's lap, sat a kid who trusted him with the whole-hearted belief of those who have never known betrayal. *I never was that kid.* The realization brought such pain! Ben swallowed, trying to keep the bucking emotion from surfacing. He couldn't do this; he was too exposed...

David sat, waiting for Ben's hands to move beneath his. But Ben felt his own fingers curl up and drop from the keys. The kid turned, questioning Ben with his eyes.

Ben set him down on the floor. "Sorry, kid," he managed. "Maybe another time. I gotta get back." He ruffled David's hair and, without another glance at Emmeline, strode from the house before the storm broke over his spirit.

CHAPTER THIRTEEN

The days were getting longer. Knowing that she had a good hour before the gong rang and all the boarding students gathered in the dinner hall, Grace took a detour on Monday afternoon after teaching her class. Crocksville, New York bordered on Lake Champlain, and Grace had often found her way to the shore over the past year. Though different from the salty Atlantic beaches of home, the slow rhythm of the waves not only calmed her sometimes-troubled heart but also seemed to help clarify her thoughts and prayers.

She paced down the boardwalk, noticing that few cars had parked along the road leading to the beach. Tourism hadn't yet reared its ugly head this season, and the sky promised rain. Likely, Grace would have the shore to herself, except for a few other solitary souls like herself – those who needed to withdraw from the teeming mass of humanity to think things through.

Her steps slowed as she approached the end of the wooden walk. *And I have a lot to think through.* Lowering herself carefully to the edge, she removed her fashionable heels. She looked first one way and then the other to make sure that absolutely no one was within sight, and then she carefully slid her knee-high stockings down until she'd rolled them off her legs. Sighing with relief, she pushed her toes deep into the cold sand and rose to her feet. She tucked the shoes beneath the boardwalk, stockings hidden within their toes, to retrieve later.

Grace strode forward toward the lake's edge, into the wind, feeling its forceful coolness filter straight through her pale gray dress and loosen her hair from its pinned-up style. She clutched her hat with one hand and realized that she should've left it with her concealed shoes. The sand shifted under her feet, dry and chilly. She began to run toward the incoming waves, stopping when she reached the moist sand before the wide gray-blue of Lake Champlain began.

Facing the water, she closed her eyes and breathed deeply, knowing the presence and power of her Almighty Father. The One who had called her out of darkness and into His marvelous light. The One who had set His love upon her. The One who lived in her and through her. The One for Whom she was willing to give her life, for had He not given His for her?

Lord, thank You. Thank You for the job You've given me teaching at this charity school. It reminds me of my old desire to teach — back before You gave me the scholarship to the Conservatory. Do You have something for me to do, after all, with teaching? I need Your wisdom to know what to do after I graduate. The pressure to sing professionally is always there, yet I've never felt drawn to do that — not for You, only when I wanted the attention before I was born again. But if You want to use me in that way, well, then I'm Yours, Lord. You show me; You direct me, and I'll do what You want. Give me the grace to do what You will.

A seagull cawed nearby, and Grace opened her eyes. There, on a piece of driftwood, he sat, staring at her with shining eyes that reminded her of the black buttons on an old pair of boots Mama had when Grace was a little girl. She smiled at him, seeing the beauty of his feathers against the tan sand, and closed her eyes again.

But, Lord, I want to go back to Chetham. I want to go home. I will… wander for the rest of my life if that's what You want, but I would rather go home. You know my heart. You know that sometimes I ache for Mama and Cliff and…

She swallowed. The lump clogging her throat hurt. *And Paulie. I need him. I still want to be his.*

Enough. She opened her eyes and stretched out her hands, open-palmed to the heavens. "But I am first and foremost Yours, Lord. Do with me and my life as You will," she whispered. "For some reason, You saw fit to bring me here. And I've loved it. I'm so very thankful that You gave me this. But I don't quite understand why Paulie... I thought he loved me. And I thought that You had planned for us to be together. I think that maybe I was wrong."

Tears rose to her eyes, blurring her vision, causing the water and the sky to fade together. *Though He slay me...*

She blinked, and the tears fell. "I will trust You."

A peace came over her heart, slow and lush as the dusk on a spring evening. The pain was not erased, but she knew that Jesus walked with her – and that He would continue to keep her in the hollow of His hand. Burying her feet deeper in the dark, wet sand, Grace wrapped her arms around her torso and let the wind fully blow in her face as she sang the old hymn softly:

"This is my Father's world,
And to my listening ear,
All nature sings
And round me rings the music of the spheres."

The sun had begun to slip down into its dark horizon-bed when she turned from the smears of orange and pink to head back to her dormitory house. Surely, she'd missed the dinner gong. Well, no matter. She had some saltines and peanut butter and an apple in her dorm room – a good enough supper. She turned for one last glimpse of the sunset, walking backwards for a few steps to fully take in its beauty.

Grace had almost reached the boardwalk when she saw that a man sat there. She stiffened and nearly stopped walking, suddenly very aware that the beach lay empty behind her. She strained her eyes, trying to see what he looked like, but she had stayed too long, relishing the sunset. Murky dusk concealed the man's identity. He stood then, towering against the sky, much taller and broader than she.

Heart pounding, Grace couldn't swallow, much less speak for a long moment. Her bare feet and legs made her feel even more vulnerable, as did her hair, undone by the wind. *Oh, Lord God, protect me!* Perhaps it would be best if she spoke first; after all, the man sat right above where she'd tucked away her shoes and stockings. She couldn't leave the beach without those.

Fear twisting through her body, she came to a full halt, ready to run if she needed to. "Good evening, sir." She forced out the words, keeping her voice as steady and formal as she could. The last thing she wanted was to encourage this man to think –

"Good evening, Miss Picoletti." The man bowed from the waist and removed his hat.

Her mouth fell open. "Mr. Haverland, is that you?" The fright she'd felt died away, but annoyance crept to life toward him. How dare he sit there watching her? Had he heard her singing?

He came toward her, his shod feet mushing through the sand. "The very one, though I wish that you would call me Kirk." He shuffled his hat in his hands. "You left the school before I could catch you today. Mr. Whitely asked me to let you know how pleased he is with your teaching. He tells me that the students are ecstatic about learning with you. Well done. It appears that you have a gift."

The final drop of displeasure at his having silently watched her drained away in the face of his compliment. If another man – barely an acquaintance – had said such a thing to her, Grace would have put up her guard. But Mr. Haverland – er, that is, Kirk – appeared extremely sincere. As he always did.

"Thank you," she said quietly, meeting his eyes – or what she could see of them in the failing light. "God has been gracious to me."

Her heart, wounded by Paulie's year-long silence and weary from longing for human affection, felt soothed by Kirk's kindness. At least he appreciated her.

Smiling, he stepped toward her, narrowing the space between

them. Her breath caught in her lungs when she saw the admiration clearly in his gaze. She tensed. Wasn't it too soon in their friendship – if that was what this was – for him to display such a regard? He hardly knew her. He didn't know about Paulie…

Why should he have to know about Paulie? He's not asking you to date him or any such thing, Grace. He just wants your friendship.

Grace forced herself to relax and even gave him a small smile in return.

At her response, a new boldness appeared on Kirk's face. "Miss Picoletti, I know that I'm your supervisor, but I want to ask you a question as, well, just as a man to a woman. Nothing to do with work."

Grace stopped breathing. She'd been wrong about his goals. They had been more inclined toward romance than she'd thought. Part of her leaped at the interest she saw in Kirk's expression; another part of her recoiled, stepping backward, looking for shelter from…

She met his eyes. The unaffectedness she saw there told her how foolish she was to fear him: this godly man whose intentions appeared entirely honorable. "What is it?" She pushed the words out of her mouth like a mama-bird urging her overgrown hatchlings to leave the nest.

"May I take you to dinner this evening? I would like to get to know you better." His smile quavered just a bit, revealing his nervousness. "Much better."

In the second of silence before Grace answered Kirk, the memory of Paulie tiptoed through her heart. If only he stood on this beach – as he had once stood on Crescent Park beach with her – courting her! *I can't. I can't do that to Paulie.* "I have work to do for my Conservatory classes tomorrow," she said at last, looking away. She didn't want to see the disappointment on such a good man's face. "Excuse me. I have to get my shoes." She ducked around him and reached beneath the boardwalk for her heels.

"Well, what about just coffee then? There's a wonderful little café that Uncle Howard told me about, on the corner of Hope Street."

After making his proposal, Kirk turned away to give her privacy while she put on her shoes.

My, but he was persistent. Tucking her loose hair behind her ear, Grace sat down on the boardwalk, feeling the grit of sand beneath her on the wood. Her stockings were rolled down into the toes of her shoes. They'd just have to stay there, as there was no way in this world that she would pull her dress up to her knees, even with Kirk's back turned like it was. Hopefully, the heels would fit with those stuffed in there! She unbuckled one shoe and pushed her foot into it, dusting off the sole with her hand first. Tight, but they still fit. "No, not tonight." Then, lest she sound rude, she softened it with, "But thank you."

His back still to her, Kirk asked, "Wednesday evening, then? After the prayer meeting, of course."

A smile pushed its way to Grace's lips, despite herself. The memory of Paulie had all but faded in the face of Kirk's relentless pursuit. *Why am I even worrying about "doing that to Paulie"? From all appearances, Paulie has abandoned me.* Still, a hesitation tugged at her heart. "I'll have too much practicing to do on a night like that." She buckled her other shoe and stood. "I have a difficult theory class on Thursday mornings."

"All set?"

"Yes. You can turn around."

He did. "How about Thursday evening, then? Or Friday? Saturday? This week? Next week? The one after that?" His eyes held the glimmer of the stars as he gazed into her face.

She opened her mouth, but, really, what could she say? Should she lose out on a possible romance that God might desire to give her because she couldn't forget one He'd withheld? Should she let the memory of what could have been with Paulie ruin her opportunity for a future with anyone else? Was that right? It couldn't be.

Yet something in her spirit still wavered and hesitated to walk forward with Kirk's suggestion.

Grace turned toward the road and walked away from the lake,

leaving him there in the melting sunset and rising moon. A few steps from the pavement, she stopped and faced Kirk again, seeing him silhouetted against the fast-fading horizon. He stood strong-legged and firm, his golden hair whipping in the wind like beach-grass, waiting for her to answer him.

And the answer came to her own mind: She could love a man like him, couldn't she? From what she knew of Kirk, he had many of the traits she'd adored in Paulie – kindness, gentleness, the ability to lead, love for the less fortunate, seriousness in his walk with God. What was stopping her from accepting this date, other than a misplaced belief that Paulie had been the one for her?

Maybe, just maybe, my relationship with Paulie was like that sunset… beautiful while it lasted. And I should appreciate it, but not build all of my hopes around it. Not think that just because God gave it to me for a season, then it should last forever.

Wait. The impression came with the softness of a long-ago dream. *Wait? Wait for what?* Had the Lord impressed that word on her heart? But why? Why should she wait? Tears pressed up to her eyes without warning as she realized how tired she was of checking the mail-cubbyhole for letters that never came. *I don't want to wait. I want to be loved now. And even if I waited, it's obvious that Paulie's not for me. He doesn't care enough even to write.*

Wait. The impression was stronger now, taking more effort to push away. *Wait.*

The last ray of the sunset dripped into the lake, and the crickets began their lovely age-old melody on strings. The light wind caught strands of Grace's hair and swept them across her face, veiling her vision for a moment. She pushed them behind her ear. It was silly to be guided by an impression. "Saturday," she stated before she could change her mind, hearing her own voice as if it belonged to another. "I'm free on Saturday."

Kirk's mouth split into a joy-filled grin. "Wonderful! Dinner and—"

"Just coffee would be fine," Grace interrupted. Her arms tingled with anticipation even as she told herself that this meant nothing. She crossed them tightly against her chest. She was just having coffee with a young man. *Paulie has probably taken many girls on dates since I left.*

Kirk sobered at her limitation, but she could tell that excitement still fizzed inside him. "Just coffee, Miss Picoletti." He paused. "*This* time."

She couldn't prevent the smile from turning her lips up. How good it felt for a man of character to pursue her – to *want* to be around her again. And it didn't hurt that he was more handsome than Cary Grant.

"Now please, let me walk you home."

She opened her mouth to protest.

"I insist. You never know when something might be waiting for you in the dark." He winked.

She thought of Kirk sitting on the boardwalk, waiting for her. *No, you never do.*

CHAPTER FOURTEEN

"Watch yourself!"

Paulie heard Ben's admonition just in time to catch himself from falling straight off the roof. "Thanks," he bit out, hating the ugly feeling he could discern in his own tone. Why couldn't he keep his feelings from seeping into the open?

Ben didn't respond. Whether that was because he held a handful of nails between his lips or because he refused to give Paulie more of his attention than absolutely necessary, Paulie didn't know.

And he sure as anything didn't care one red cent, much as he shouldn't want to admit that. *In fact, I wouldn't mind if Ben fell and broke his thick head. Maybe that'd knock some sense into him.* Though it probably wouldn't. Paulie shoved aside the guilt that laid soft fingers on his heart. It was true: Ben Picoletti was an ignorant, no-good bum who had no right to lay claim to Dad's time or money. Dad could've gotten this job done faster and cheaper than the $8000 he'd shelled out for Ben's release.

And he probably did hurt that horse, too. Paulie gritted his teeth and swung his hammer hard enough to macerate his thumb if it was foolish enough to get in his way. *I hate him. I really do.* The thought pulsed through his heart, traveled along his veins, and settled into his mind, begetting other thoughts. *I'm angry with him. Angry enough to want him gone. For good.*

He doesn't deserve Grace's love. Not like I do.

Now where had that come from? Startled, Paulie tried to turn his focus toward the job at hand. He wasn't the best at multitasking; that was why he had thought such a strange thing…

No, it really wasn't. *I thought it because it's true.* He eyed Ben, sweat dripping down his face and neck, tanned as an exotic kiwi fruit. He crouched on the shingles with an ease Paulie envied but couldn't mimic. *I should ask him…*

His better judgment told Paulie to get the day's work in and then hurry up home, where a hot supper would await them, as well as a refreshing bath to wash away all his troubles. Better by far to do that than to delve into a Pandora's box…

"So do you hear often from my sister?"

Paulie nearly dropped the hammer. How had Ben guessed what was on his mind? *He didn't. It must've been on his mind, too.* His thoughts felt more jumbled than scrambled eggs. "Uh," he wobbled, "you mean Grace?"

That was dumb. Paulie winced.

Ben didn't even look at him. "Yeah, I mean the one you gave them firecracker earrings to. Ya know. The one up at that singing school in New York. Yeah, that one. You talk to her a lot?"

He could've cut the silence with a butter knife. "No," Paulie answered. "Not much." *Not at all.* "You?"

Why was his heart pounding? Why was he asking – silently pleading – for his eyes to have deceived him when he'd stepped into Ben's bedroom yesterday to deliver an armful of clean laundry. There, he'd found a stack – a stack! – of letters from Grace. Half of them not even opened. What a lousy brother. *If I was him, I'd have those letters memorized.*

"Yeah, I get a letter from her every two weeks. Have for the past two years. Always writes the same things. 'I love you, Ben. I care about what happens to you. Turn to God, Ben.'" Ben stopped hammering, sat back on his haunches, and hoisted the waistband of his pants a little higher. He smirked. "Guess she threw ya over, huh, preacher-boy?"

Paulie met Ben's eyes with a burning stare of his own, but he had nothing with which to reply. He knew, in his heart, that what Ben stated was true. Had she responded to any one of the more than three dozen letters he'd posted this year? *No.* Not one. Grace had forsaken him. And it was that knowledge that crushed his spirit.

Ben resumed hammering. "Well, ya know what I say to that? Good for her."

~ ~ ~

As she brushed the curls so that they would hang around her face with the fluffiness of Ginger Rodgers' hair in *Swing Time*, Grace's eyes went to the clock. Six-thirty. Drawing a deep breath, she turned toward her jewelry case. Something simple would be best; she didn't want to look like she was trying too hard for Kirk's admiration.

She'd not brought much with her to Crocksville; she hadn't had ample jewelry to begin with. And she couldn't very well wear anything too cheap-looking with this mauve dress. The pair of earrings that would best complement it? *The pearls, of course.* The ones she'd received three Christmases ago, in a little velvet box just outside Chetham's First Baptist Church. *Paulie's pearls.* That was how she always had thought of them.

And it had been how she'd always thought of herself as well: as Paulie's Grace. She closed her eyes. *I can't do that anymore, Lord.* She'd never been Paulie's to begin with, had she? And hadn't she already gone through all of this before she'd left Chetham? Even before her last year of high school, she'd known that she was utterly, completely her Savior's. Not a man's.

Yes, but a part of her had always thought that she'd surely – yes surely – return and marry Paulie. *And I thought that he believed the same.*

But it simply wasn't true.

When she opened her eyes, they fell on the small blue velvet box. Calmly, she picked up the box. Resisting the wave of desire to open it and stare at the round baubles, she opened the top drawer of her dresser and tucked the case deep behind her folded silk stockings. She had no intention of throwing them away, but she no longer wanted them on display, distracting her from the future God might be giving her – tempting her to place her hope in a charming boy from the past – a boy who had never written past the first week of college. *I was just a high-school sweetheart for him.* The thought punctured her heart still, despite having come to a slow realization of it for many months.

She took a deep breath and pushed her feet into a pair of pumps. *I need to be open to whomever You place in my life.* As she spoke to the Lord, though, a slight uneasiness came over her spirit. Was she really trusting Him? Or was she using His will as an excuse to give way to her fears?

But, really, how far could her relationship – if she could call it that – with Kirk Haverland progress? The semester would finish in two weeks, and she'd not signed up for the summer touring choir, certain that Mama would like her home for the vacation months. So Grace would head home to Chetham, and new-in-town Kirk would find another eligible young woman while she was gone. Plenty of them buzzed around his pew every Sunday morning, eager to gather the nectar of his beautiful, sincere smile. He'd probably be engaged by the time she returned in the fall. He seemed eager enough for a romantic relationship, and he himself was certainly eligible: handsome, full of character, the nephew of the beloved reverend.

"Grace!" Violet's excited voice pounded through her musings. The door burst open, and the girl fluttered in, eyes wide. "There's a *man* waiting for you downstairs. A *man!*"

Grace shook her head. "Yes, I know. I have a date with him. I'll be down in a few minutes." She eyed herself in the mirror. Perhaps the gray dress would have been more suitable?

Violet came around the bed and looked over Grace's shoulder.

"You have a date, Grace?" she asked, as though Grace had just announced that she had sprouted wings. Beneath a gaudy silk scarf, one of Violet's pin-curls came undone. Violet scooped the disobedient lock into her hand and repinned it while exclaiming, "A date? With Kirk Haverland? For real?"

Grace realized that her friend must not have a date tonight. *No wonder she's taking such an eager interest in my business.* Giving up on changing her outfit, she faced Violet. "Mr. Haverland invited me to have coffee with him. We work together at the charity school."

Violet looked ready to swoon with a combination of envy and awe. Grace didn't wait for a verbal response. Snagging her coat and hat from the shared closet, she hurried downstairs.

CHAPTER FIFTEEN

They took a corner table, far from the noisy swirl of Conservatory students near the front of the café. He'd ordered black coffee for himself; Grace had asked for hers with cream and sugar.

"Sometimes, I miss coffee milk," she commented after the waitress had brought their drinks.

He paused mid-sip, the beverage's dark liquid reflected in his eyes. "If you'd prefer your coffee with milk instead of cream, I'm sure that it would not be a problem to replace it."

She couldn't help but smile. "No, coffee milk is *coffee-flavored* milk. Have you ever had it?"

He gave a mock shudder. "No. And it doesn't sound like something I'd like very much. Coffee-flavored? Why not just a coffee with milk?"

Grace shrugged. "It's a Rhode Island thing, I suppose. A diner in Providence started the fad a few years ago, and it's been all the rage ever since."

His dimple deepened. "I see. Have you lived in Rhode Island all of your life?"

"Yes." Talking about her home state reminded her of all the people and places she loved there. "Most of my family is there as well."

"A big family?"

She thought for a moment. How should she explain all the messy situations that had brought about the extensive list of people she could call *family* now? "I suppose so," she said at last, treading carefully. Kirk didn't need to look at all her family's dirty laundry, even if it was "under the blood," as Mrs. Kinner put it. "My mother remarried just two years ago, after my father died in an accident. I have five blood brothers and sisters, and – uh – one stepbrother." How strange to call Paulie that! She never thought of him that way. *But I guess that is how we will have to think of each other from now on. He will marry, and so will I, and we'll meet at Christmas and Easter and forget that anything ever happened between us—*

"How wonderful," Kirk's voice cut into her thoughts. "I only have one sister, younger than I by some years. You remind me of her quite a bit, you know. She's musical as well – plays the organ at our family's church. And she loves to read. Like you do."

Grace tilted her head. "How do you know that I like to read?"

Kirk chuckled. "I have my ways."

Grace shook her head. "I do like to read," she admitted.

He leaned forward. "And what do you read? Wait – let me guess."

Amusement lifted her eyebrows. "Alright."

Kirk traced the edge of his coffee cup and looked up at the ceiling in thought. After a long pause, he met her gaze. "Poetry," he announced. "But not the modern kind. Am I right?"

Perhaps he understood her better than she gave him credit for. She gave a small nod. "How did you know?"

He shrugged and then leaned back, satisfaction lighting his features.

"Are you trying to impress me?" Grace teased, surprising herself.

When Kirk grinned – as he did now – joy engaged his entire face. "Is it working?"

She narrowed her eyes. "Hmm. Guess which poet I read last," she challenged.

Closing his eyes, he breathed in deeply, as if he was putting all his concentration toward the task. Then a smile burst on his face again. Opening his eyes again, he leaned across the table. "You've been reading George Herbert. If I was a wagering man – which I'm not, so don't fear – I'd wager a week's pay that you've been reading Herbert's *The Temple.*"

Grace was dumbstruck. "How did you know that?" she asked, feeling a bit frightened. Was he privy to her library records?

"Just a guess, I assure you." Then, he took a slow sip of coffee. "Well," he allowed, grinning, "it helps that you've carried that book around with you for the past week to the charity school."

~ ~ ~

"You have the day off, Ben." The Doc smiled at him over his plate of toast and eggs. *As if he was some kinda king and could tell me when I can take a day off or not. I can take a day off whenever I darn well please. Don't need his permission.*

Mama's voice interrupted Ben's inward fuming at the Doc's obnoxious take-everything-over personality. "Are you helping at the clinic in Providence today, Sam?"

She sounded happy and content, sitting in her customary place near the window. The sunlight streaming through the panes gilded her gray-streaked brown hair and caressed her shoulders with a golden shawl. Ben grudgingly knew that he had the Doc to thank for the change in Mama. Ben could sense the peace that had taken hold of her – a peace totally foreign to him. *And I ain't responsible for bringing it about. He is, because he "saved" her after Papa died.*

And that rankled him as well. Why couldn't he have been the one to step in and save Mama? Why had she protested – albeit weakly – that night he'd given Papa what he had coming to him – yeah, and broke out the old cheater's tooth while he was at it? *I told her then – just pack up your stuff and leave him!* God knew – if there was a God in the heavens who cared one speck about them, which he doubted –

that he'd tried to save Mama. *I'd have worked my fingers to the bone to support her and the kids if she'd only have left Papa. Then I could've known that I brought about this goodness for her.*

"Yes," the Doc answered Mama, oblivious to the storm brewing inside Ben. "I thought I'd take Paulie with me. Give him some hands-on experience again. Are you up for it, son?"

Ben lifted his eyes from staring a hole in his laden china plate to see Paulie nod, a little sleepily. Huh. After two weeks on the job, the kid still wasn't used to heavy morning-til-night labor. What a wimp. Though even Ben had to admit that Paulie put everything he had into the work. *We'll be done with that old wreck before the end of July.*

Though, if they'd let him, he'd have burned it to the ground two weeks ago and saved the Doc the trouble of selling it. *With pleasure.*

"Good." The Doc wiped his mouth, took a last sip of orange juice, and rose from his seat. "Let's get an early start, Paulie. I just need to grab my bag from my office." He hurried from the room, his mind evidently already on the coming events of the day.

Paulie rose from the table, and a stream of hatred bubbled up through Ben as he watched the younger man. Paulie didn't realize what he had: a father who loved him, who wanted him to tag along and learn, who wanted Paulie's company. A father who wanted to be loved in return, not only feared.

From the foyer, the Doc called, "Ready, son?"

Ben resisted the longing that flooded him at that moment. *What would it be like for a man like Sam Giorgi to call you his son? Not just because he had to, since he married your mama, but because he wanted to? Because he loved you as his own flesh-and-blood?*

As he sat there watching Paulie scuttle into the foyer, his hatred reversed direction, heading back toward Papa. *Good thing he's already dead. If he wasn't, I'd kill him now if I could get away with it. I'd kill him and let his carcass rot in the sun. I hate him for everything he ever did.* Never before had he been so transparent with himself. Now, the admission made him feel free and brave. And alone. So deeply alone.

Cliff crammed the last half-slice of buttered toast into his mouth, chewed twice, and swallowed. "Mama, can I go up to Buddy's farm today? They got a new horse, and Buddy's dad said it'd be okay if we tried him."

Mama sipped her coffee. "Chores done?"

Cliff's head bobbed in a vigorous nod. "Yeah, did 'em early today."

"Homework?"

Cliff squirmed. "Don't got too much, Mama. Can I do it later?"

Mama's eyes went to the grandfather clock. "Be home by lunch, then. Church's tomorrow. I don't want you staying up late to finish your schoolwork and then nodding off during the service."

"Thanks, Mama!" With a quick kiss to Mama's cheek, Cliff dashed from the room.

With Cliff gone, Ben found himself alone at the table with Mama. He stirred his eggs around on his plate. There were so many things he wanted to say. So many things he felt but couldn't communicate. So much that would have to go unsaid forever because the pain dug too deep down in his soul to express it. Language fell short, flabby and inadequate as a picked-over roasted chicken.

"What will you do today?"

Mama's question caught him off-guard. He shrugged and shoveled in a mouthful of eggs. *Cold.* Oh, well. There were worse things in the world. *Don't I know it!* "Not sure yet. Maybe do some fishin' down at the stream out behind our old house."

Mama nodded and looked down into her tea. "Ben, the last time you came home…"

She stopped, and something in Ben wrenched. If he could go back! "Mama, I know I hurt ya." He pulled the words out of his throat as if by a tightened string. "I'm sorry. I – I didn't wanna do that. I ain't good around religious people – good people like the Doc. I – "

But she cut him off before he could continue. "No, Ben. You were hurting. Hurting bad. I know that. Sam knows that. And you came home to find things real different than you probably expected."

Ben shook his head. He couldn't let her think that lie. "Not really, Mama." He shoved the words out, hard as it was. "Grace wrote to me when Papa died. And when you married the Doc. I knew about it all before I came."

Mama's eyebrows furrowed. "Why were you so angry, son?" She said *were*, but Ben could hear the present tense in her voice.

Why? It was a question he'd struggled with for years now. "I don't know, Ma," he said finally, after a long pause. "I guess I'd always seen Papa as the thing in my way. As the reason behind why I always feel so angry – so angry sometimes it scares me, Mama." He swallowed, thinking through the feelings as he spoke. "I think I could kill someone at times. I think I would've killed Aldo if I hadn't been locked into a stall."

"Who's Aldo?"

"The bum who double-crossed me at Bousquet's."

"Oh."

He cleared his throat. "And so, I figured, with Papa gone, I'd return and feel good about things – about myself – about life in general for the first time in my life. But it didn't happen that way."

He looked up to find sorrow in Mama's eyes. And understanding. "I was still angry. And when I saw the way the Doc keeps control on things, it reminded me of Papa. And I can't stand that. I can't stand being under anybody's thumb anymore. If I have to be miserable for the rest of my life, then fine. I'll be miserable. But I ain't never gonna be under any man's control ever again. Nobody's ever gonna tell me what to do or how I ought to live ever again."

Mama sat silently for a moment. Then she rose and came to sit right beside him. He stiffened as he felt the plump warmth of her arm around his shoulders. He peeked at her from the corner of his eye. She was tentative, but determined. *And she still loves me, though I don't know why!*

And loved him more, if it was possible, than she'd loved him when he was a little boy who sat in her lap twenty years ago, rocking back-and-forth on the porch while she shelled peas and he ate the raw pods. *Where does that love come from? Why can't I have it? I sure don't care about her with the kind of love she has for me!*

Or the kind Grace had for him, either.

"May I tell you something? Something I've learned?" she asked.

Ben nodded, staring at the crusts of toast, tangled together on his plate.

"Most times, my anger comes from either fear or pride, and usually both."

His jaw hardened. Fear? He wasn't afraid of nothing. Though his gut told him otherwise.

"I was afraid of love for a long time, Ben."

Oh, so that was what this was about? Ben accepting Sam as the one who'd helped Mama? He turned a half-smile, brined in bitterness, toward Mama. "Yeah, then the old man came along."

Mama just looked at him for a long moment. "Yes. But it wasn't until I accepted the love of Another that I could accept Sam's love for me. It wasn't Sam's love that gave me peace. I had peace – at least in a small measure – even before your Papa died. I got that when I realized that Someone else loved me – Someone whose love would never wither up, like an autumn apple left too long in the root cellar."

Huh? He knew his puzzlement showed on his face. "What are ya talkin' about, Mama? You're usin' riddles."

"Jesus. It wasn't until I could accept His love for me—"

Enough. He shoved back his chair, threw her arm off his shoulder, and stood. "Not this again. Not this stupid Jesus stuff again. Where was Jesus when your cupboards were bare, Mama? Where was He when Papa brought his mistress home to live? Where was He? Where was He all the times...?" He couldn't continue. His head felt like it would explode and his chest blow up. He wished it would blow up and take the whole of Chetham with it.

Yet Mama didn't look shaken. She rose from her chair slowly, like a daffodil slipping from the winter soil. "He was there, Ben. I just couldn't see the Hand that held me. The love that had to drive me to Him through pain."

He turned burning eyes on Mama and felt something close to hatred for her for the first time in his life. The emotion surprised him, but he steamrolled on. "Yeah? Well, I don't want that kind of a God. I don't want that kind of love. The kind that hurts. That ain't love to me."

"He only hurts to heal, Ben."

"Oh, yeah? And how did He heal you when He took your baby from ya?" There. That would show her.

Mama's eyes opened in surprise. "But He didn't take the baby, Ben."

He sneered openly. "Oh, yeah?" he repeated. "Then where is it, Mama? Tucked away in a closet upstairs?"

"I gave the baby away."

"Ya what?" He stuttered out the words in disbelief. She'd given away Ben's baby brother like he was an unwanted kitten? "Why? Why'd you do that, Mama? Thought you loved that baby..." At least according to Grace's letters, she had! He couldn't keep the accusation he felt from showing in his eyes. What kind of a mother did he have, anyhow?

Mama's shoulders slumped as she let out a huge breath. "It's tough to explain exactly why, Ben."

"Money? Was it the money, Mama?" Here again, Papa was to blame! Even when they were getting along okay, he'd never given her enough to fill her cupboards, much less buy the stuff a baby would need. With a mistress on one hand and an estranged wife on the other, Ben could just guess how little Papa had put in Mama's piggy-bank, so to speak.

But to Ben's surprise, rather than immediately agree, Mama hesitated. "Well, yeah, partly. Things were terribly tight when your papa died. I had to take in washing. Grace worked, too. But there was more to it, Ben. More than just money problems, you know."

Uneasiness took hold of Ben's spirit and wouldn't let go. She was gonna go back into talking about... He swallowed. *Jesus.*

"I gave the baby away willingly, out of love for someone who gave me so much. Who introduced me to Jesus' love in a real, hands-on way. I'd heard of Jesus' love all my life, but it wasn't until someone acted like Jesus toward me that I understood with all my heart. And so I gave her a gift – a baby that she'd always wanted."

He raised his chin and snorted. "Oh, so a trade-off?" How was that kind of "love" different from the love Ben himself had experienced? Really just a barter system: you give me something I want; I'll give you something you want.

"No, it wasn't a payment. I gave the baby to her freely, as a part of my thanksgiving to God for making me free."

"What, free from Papa?" He'd calculated in his mind the time Mama would've had to give away the baby from the mentions Grace had made in her letters of Mama's delivery time and the newborn. Grace had stopped talking about the baby just after Papa died.

"No, free from my sin. Free from the fear that had enslaved me. He gave me the freedom of going to Him, my Father in heaven, through His Son." Mama looked at him with earnest eyes. "You see, Ben. Real love isn't satisfied with just taking; it has to keep pouring out what it's given. I had received so much that I had to pour out some to receive more."

A whole lotta nonsense if you ask me. The words rolled off his mind and heart like water from a raincoat. This notion of "love" had little to do with the hard world Ben had experienced, both growing up and after he'd left home. Still, let Mama think it was the answer to everything if it could make her happy. The last thing he wanted was for Mama to be unhappy.

But one thing nagged still. "Who'd ya give the baby to?" He shook his head. "Did you even give it a name before you handed it over?"

Mama looked away toward the window. "I can't tell you, Ben. You might find out one day. But when I gave the baby to… the woman, I wanted it to be finished. I didn't want the baby to grow up thinking of me as its mother or anything like that. Maybe it wasn't the smartest choice to do it that way, but that's how I wanted it. For the gift to be sealed shut."

"Ya didn't love it much to do that, did ya?" He heard the question lash out before he could stop it. If he'd wanted to.

Mama's eyes swung back toward him, the hurt glistening moistly in the blue-gray. "I loved that baby as much as I do any of my children – you, Grace, Lou… But a gift that doesn't cost anything isn't worth much, Ben. Is it?"

CHAPTER SIXTEEN

After Ben left to fish, Sarah climbed upstairs. Retrieving her Bible and journal from her bedside table, she headed straight for her sitting room. There, she sank into the cozy floral chair that cushioned her middle-aged bones and sat back. She closed her eyes and let out a deep, shuddering breath.

What she'd told Ben was true. Every last word of it. She wasn't sorry that she'd handed her baby to Emmeline two years ago. Each time she saw the little Kinner family at First Baptist, she realized afresh how glad she was that she'd gone through with the urging the Holy Spirit had pressed upon her heart.

Yet, at the time of the doing, the pain had been exquisite, boring into her heart. For months, every time she'd encountered Emmeline and baby David, the longing of her mother-heart had stretched out for him. She'd nearly had to tie her arms at her sides to prevent herself from taking him back. It had been on a particularly difficult day a few months after she'd married Sam, after she'd begun learning the hard, life-long lesson of her sufficiency in Christ, that God had brought her to a certain passage. She'd written it on the flyleaf of her Bible:

Come, and let us return unto the Lord: for He hath torn, and He will heal us; He hath smitten, and He will bind us up. Hosea 6:1

Now she traced her fingers over it and read her own note from that time as well: *He hurts me so that He will become the source of my healing. Anything God heals can't be broken. And He breaks only from the love that sent His Son to the cross for me.*

Sarah bowed her head. *Oh, Lord, heal my son. May Your love chase him down and bring him salvation. I long to see him whole and free from the sin that chains him, both his own and that which others have brought upon him. Free him, Lord. Whatever it takes.*

~ ~ ~

Grace pressed moist palms against her peach-hued silk dress and glanced one last time at the printed program Violet held on her lap. She breathed in, letting the oxygen shudder through her tense lungs.

"Nervous?" Violet whispered loudly enough to gain a glare from one of their classmates seated nearby.

Grace swallowed and nodded, unsure of whether she'd be able to reply aloud even if she wished to try. She'd attempted to pray, but the words kept mixing together. Finally, she'd decided to just rest in the Lord as best she could.

"I'm next." Violet rose from her folding chair, one of a hundred or so that filled the large recital room, and scooted by Grace, the hem of her deep mauve dress brushing against Grace's legs. "Wish me well."

Grace managed a smile. Now, if she could just take this end-of-the-year recital one moment at a time... She didn't worry about people disliking her voice; she worried about forgetting the words to her chosen piece!

Onstage, the soprano finished with a trill, and the audience broke into loud clapping. Grace joined in, letting her eyes travel to the most enthusiastic applauders, an older couple in the second row. Most likely the girl's parents. A touch of melancholy joined Grace's nervousness. If only the Conservatory wasn't located three hundred miles from Chetham, Mama and Dad would have come as well.

And perhaps Paulie, too…

She shook her head and forced herself to concentrate on Violet, who had taken her place onstage. The accompanist waited for Violet's cue, and, when he'd received it, took up the vocalist's piece. *Why would I want Paulie to come? He doesn't care about me. Not anymore.*

"May I sit beside you?" The soft masculine voice came near her ear.

Kirk. Eyes wide, she turned with a start. There, in his church suit and tie, he stood, waiting for her answer, a kind of entreaty in his expression. She sensed the other attendees' disapproval of his late arrival, and so she nodded quickly.

He took the empty seat on her right, leaving Violet's unoccupied. "I hope I haven't missed your performance," he murmured. "There were things that needed sorting out at the school, and I couldn't leave until ten minutes ago. I was so afraid that I would miss your piece, and I've been looking forward to it since my uncle told me of the recital a few days ago."

A slow thrill rippled through her. Kirk had come for her performance. Grace pressed her lips together, trying to keep the smile from overtaking her face. "No," she said, "you've come in time."

~ ~ ~

"Anything for me, Mrs. McCusker?" Sarah asked, injecting genuine friendliness in her voice as she descended the staircase. She would melt this woman yet. *By the grace of God.*

"Yes, madam." From her place in the entryway, the housekeeper maintained a smile colder than an after-Christmas snowman. Her thin-skinned hands held out two envelopes.

"Thank you." A glance told Sarah that one came from her sister Mary. Mary – who had held the guardianship of Sarah's youngest daughter, Evelyn. Years ago, during a time of intense discouragement, before she'd come to trust in Jesus Christ with all her heart and soul, Sarah had tried to keep Evelyn from having to endure the same difficulties as the rest of the family. She'd given her youngest daughter into Mary's care. Now *that* was something Sarah regretted doing, for Mary had made it all too clear that she had no intention of relinquishing Evelyn now that she had her, despite the change in Sarah's circumstances. And so, each day, Sarah prayed with fervency that God would work such losses together for good.

Sarah shuffled Mary's letter behind the next envelope. Her heart lifted when she saw it came from New York. *Grace.* Already, the day on which she expected Grace to return home for the summer was circled on her calendar. *One more week.* Sarah leaned against the bannister, threading a finger beneath the envelope flap to release the seal. *Paulie will be so glad.*

Her daughter's neat cursive filled both sides of two sheets. Sarah smiled as she read of Grace's new volunteer position teaching at the charity school. It seemed like a perfect fit for Grace. Sarah had never been overly comfortable with Grace pursuing a career onstage; it just didn't seem to be right for her. *Maybe she'll turn toward teaching for good.* Perhaps she might even teach music at one of the local schools in Chetham!

The smile dropped from Sarah's lips, however, when she came to the final paragraph of Grace's letter. Heart sinking, she read the lines twice, sure that she'd must have misunderstood:

> *The new headmaster, Mr. Kirk Haverland, has asked if I will stay for the summer term, and, if you'll allow me to, I'd like to do it. There's not much for me to do in Chetham over the summer, and I feel as though I am of real use here.*

Why would Grace want to stay in New York over the summer? Surely, if her family alone wasn't enough of a pull to come home, she'd want to spend this summer with Paulie! From what Sarah could tell – she wasn't in his confidence, but she had eyes – her stepson still wrote to Grace nearly every week. Grace had always been a close-mouthed girl, so Sarah hadn't expected to get any information from her about their romance, but she had assumed that, once the two were done with college…

And what about Ben? *I told her that he's come home!* When Sarah had mentioned Grace's fast-approaching return, Ben had merely tensed his jaw and shrugged, but still… Where was *Grace's* excitement, her eagerness to see her brother?

No, the distance she sensed in her daughter's tone certainly didn't make sense for someone whose heart was surely bound up with Paulie's – nor for a sister who had prayed for her big brother's return for years. None of it was like Grace.

"Mrs. Giorgi? Tabitha wishes to know if you have time to plan next week's menu with her." Mrs. McCusker's voice broke into Sarah's thoughts.

She tucked both Mary and Grace's letters deep into her dress pocket. "Yes, please let her know that I'm coming now."

One thing Sarah knew: She and Sam needed to have a discussion when he returned that evening.

~ ~ ~

Mama must've received my letter today. Grace paused with her toothbrush halfway into her mouth. Her stomach felt ready to sink to her toes. *She's going to be disappointed.* Every recent telephone call and letter from home had ended with Mama mentioning how few weeks remained before Grace would return to Chetham for the summer.

And every time Mama had reminded her, dread had washed over Grace's heart.

Oh, not because she didn't want to see Mama. Or Dad, or Cliff, or her married twin sisters, for that matter. And for sure, not because she didn't want to see Ben. Actually, the thought of Ben waiting at the other end of the railroad… well, that had *almost* changed her mind.

Almost, but not quite. Not when Kirk offered her such an easy excuse to avoid catching that train home – such a straightforward reason why she should stay in Crocksville through the long summer.

After her recital a few days ago, he'd given her a single white rose and asked if he could bring her for a celebratory soda. Riding on the joy of the occasion, she'd agreed without the slightest hesitation – even eagerly. They'd laughed and talked until the shop owner hinted that he needed to close up, and then Kirk had walked her back to her dormitory – where she knew that the other girls watched her arrive with "the catch of the century," as Violet Simmons so delicately phrased it.

At the stoop, he'd paused for a moment, gazing down into her eyes. A fear had taken hold of Grace; what if he kissed her? Did she want Kirk Haverland to kiss her? *No. Not yet.* She'd just prepared to say goodnight, firmly, and escape into the dormitory when he stepped back. He picked up her hand and kissed it. "Goodnight, Grace," he said, his voice soft in the warm spring air. "Sleep well."

When she'd climbed the stairs to her room, she found a tumbler in which to place her rose. Her hands trembled as she cut the thornless stem and touched the velvet softness of its pale petals. It was beautiful, and she couldn't help but feel her heart warm toward the giver. *He is a kind man. Truly.*

And then, the next day, he'd rung her on the telephone. Something to do with the Helen Higgins School, he said. Strictly business, she understood, he hoped? Would she consider staying to teach at the summer school – a paid position, of course?

"I hesitate to even ask, Grace. I know how much you love Rhode Island. How much you must miss your family. I'm prepared to hear you tell me no." Then he'd paused. "But I hope you'll say yes."

She'd told him that she'd pray about it – that she'd have to ask Mama and Dad, too. But in her heart, Grace had already known where she would spend her summer. Yes, spending it apart from her family would bring pain, both to her and to everyone awaiting her return: Ben, Mama, Dad, Cliff…

But not to Paulie.

And if she had to spend the summer apart from him to fully break her own love for him, then so be it. Grace would do just that.

~ ~ ~

"What do you mean, cold?" Sam unbuttoned his shirt, deliberate as the last inch of molasses dripping from the jar. Sarah knew that slowness for Sam meant that he was thinking something through.

She scanned the letter again and looked up at him, frowning. "I can't explain it. I know Grace. Well, I know her as well as anyone does. She's always been a closed book." She paused, trying to figure out how to explain her feeling that something just wasn't right. "I'm not sure what it is, but she says that she wants to stay away from Chetham this summer. Which I can't understand, Sam. Not at all. Ben is home now. Doesn't she want to see him? The Grace I know — that I thought I knew — would have been on the first train home to welcome him back. I actually hesitated to mention his coming to Chetham until she'd finished the schoolyear. I didn't want her to leave the Conservatory before classes finished."

Her shoulders lifted in a shrug. "But I guess I shouldn't have worried. She didn't care to come home, even with Ben here. Even though she and Paulie have been apart all year."

Sam stayed quiet, but Sarah could see that his face echoed the frown she wore. "I know he writes to her still," she continued.

"Every week," Sam confirmed. He tossed the soiled shirt into the hamper and pulled a crisp white one from the wardrobe. "I told him that I had no problem with them writing to one another. I just didn't want it becoming a formal engagement while they are away at school. I wanted Grace free to make her own choices."

"But what if he was her choice?" Where that question came from, Sarah couldn't say. Perhaps it had whispered in the corners of her heart for the past two years — the doubt that Sam had really done the right thing in forcing Paulie to postpone his courtship. Restless, Sarah turned toward the mirror, studying her eyes and the fresh lines around them.

Sam came up behind her, adjusting his tie around his collar. "Then, if the love is real, he'll still be her choice later. Right?"

Sarah hesitated. Sam didn't understand how a woman might question a man's love if she wasn't fully pursued. She faced him and began knotting the tie for him. "I hope so. He was good for Grace, you know, Sam."

"And she was for him. I wouldn't worry, darling." As she finished the tie, he pressed a kiss to her forehead. "Many waters cannot quench love, nor can the floods drown it. If their love is real, it won't disappear with the passage of a few semesters at school."

~ ~ ~

She wasn't coming home. It was over. Paulie's eyes felt like their cook, Tabitha, had taken a whisk to them, but it didn't matter. The sun had just peeked over the horizon, giving the barest outlines to the furniture in his bedroom, when Paulie threw back the sheet covering his body and rose from bed. He'd not slept at all – the first night in all his life when slumber had completely evaded him.

"Pray. Pray when you can't sleep. God keeping you awake may be His way of urging you to pray." Reverend Cloud's words from a sermon years ago had trickled through his weary but wide-awake brain. And, though his limbs wanted to remain glued to his mattress, Paulie had risen just after midnight and knelt beside his bed.

He'd stayed there for a solid hour, pouring out his heart one hurt at a time to his Heavenly Father, until he couldn't feel his knees anymore. Then, he'd risen and tried to sleep again. Yet once more, sleep refused her blessing. So Paulie had sat against his headboard and read the Book of Psalms, his own spirit echoing the grieved prayers of the shepherd-king of Israel.

And, through the night, his soul had calmed and quieted. He'd trusted the Lord again. Trusted more than he had in the past school year – those months since he'd never received an answer to his first letter.

I believe, Lord. I believe that I will see Your goodness in the land of the living. And whether that means that Grace will be mine here on this earth or that I'll be with her for eternity in heaven, praising You, You alone know. Oh, but Lord, I wish that she could've just told me straight-out that she didn't love me anymore.

The tears fell from his eyes to the sheet. *I will love her always. I can't take that back. No matter what, even if it means that I remain unmarried, I will remain faithful to what I vowed her.* It sounded so dramatic, he knew, but it rang true through the halls of his soul. *I can't stop loving her. And if she believes that I'm not the best one for her, then, well, I would rather that she marries someone else.*

A knife twisted inside his heart at the thought. Paulie closed his eyes, and though he couldn't picture her groom's face, he could see Grace walking down the aisle of First Baptist on Dad's arm, her smile so radiant. She walked by Paulie – standing alone in the second pew from the front – without a glance. *Oh, God, no. Please, if possible, let that not happen!* He drew the sheet up and held it over his mouth to suppress the emotion shaking his body. At last, the shuddering ebbed, and as another Son once told the Father, he mouthed, *But not my will, but Yours be done.*

Paulie came under another conviction that night, as the moonlight faded from his wallpaper and the dawn began. *I've been wrong about how I've been treating Ben. As if he's responsible for the pain in my own life. That's far from true. You are using this pain to bring beauty, Lord. Help me to see that. And help me to reach Ben. He needs You, even though he doesn't think he does.*

CHAPTER SEVENTEEN

Last night had been a mistake. The effects of it hammered through Ben's head, and he'd overslept. By the time his eyes finally struggled to open, the sun had fully risen. Launching himself out of bed with a groan, he fumbled for his shirt and pants. *Stay away from the booze on a weekday, Ben.* He'd done it for years on the track. Why couldn't he do it in Chetham?

But really, after the conversation Mama and he'd had yesterday, who could blame Ben for swimming in a sea of good, old-fashioned beer at Kingpin's? The boys had recognized him there, slapped him on the back, welcoming old Charlie's son back into their midst. And, as the swirl of alcohol drowned his disturbances, Ben had settled into the happy, comfortable misery to which he'd become accustomed over the years.

Now goody-two-shoes Paulie had made it out of the house before him. Was probably already whacking away at something in the old place. *Probably breaking it, too. I'll end up havin' to redo anything he's worked on, useless kid.*

That wasn't really fair, and Ben knew it, but who could censor his thoughts? They could control everything else, but not what he thought, right? And, sometimes, thinking nasty things was the only way to get revenge on a cruel world.

He pulled three-day-old socks and shoes over his already-sweating feet before stumbling down the stairs. He passed the old grouch of a housekeeper on his way down the staircase – nearly stumbled into her but caught himself on the railing.

"Mr. Picoletti," the old woman said. Golly, she couldn't be stiffer if she'd been a china doll. "Doctor Giorgi just asked me to knock on your door. He was afraid you were ill."

Her voice told him that she most certainly had her doubts about Doctor Giorgi's proposed diagnosis.

"I ain't sick," he grumbled and stumbled by her toward the front door. He'd have to skip breakfast this morning. He didn't think he'd be able to keep it down, anyhow.

"I didn't think so," Mrs. McCusker replied behind him.

He heard Paulie already at work before the house came within view. He tried to get his heavy feet to move faster, but his legs felt like pudding left out of the refrigerator too long. A few choice curses flipped off his tongue. At least that part of his body worked like it oughtta.

As Ben came through the final swath of trees, he saw that Paulie had clambered up to the roof of the barn and was using a crowbar to lift away the rotten wood. He'd stripped off his short-sleeved button-down and wore just his white undershirt with a pair of old trousers. As the bar lifted each board from its fastenings, Paulie grabbed one end with his now-hardening hands and tossed it into the overgrown grass. With chagrin, Ben realized that his stepbrother already had quite a pile waiting on the ground. He must've been at work for some time. Without calling out a hello, Ben slogged up the ladder and prepared himself for some wisecrack about how he was late.

But none came. Actually, Paulie looked kinda sick: pale, as if he'd not slept well. He paused in his work when Ben pulled himself onto the roof. "Good morning," he greeted him, but Paulie's face said that it was anything but good. "I thought we could start taking down the barn today. Maybe even finish doing it. That okay with you?"

Paulie had decided to talk civil to him? Now that was a surprise.

They'd not said anything beyond what was necessary for weeks – not since Paulie'd laid one on Ben for teasing that pretty Betty Cloud. In a way, it was a satisfying arrangement and seemed to prove what Ben had always thought: Paulie's Christianity was only skin-deep. But something unfamiliar colored Paulie's voice – a tone he'd really never heard from the kid, leastways, not toward him. *Humility.* "Yeah," Ben replied after a moment of absorbing this new state of things, "that'll be fine."

Paulie squinted at him in the bright sunlight. "We've only got one crowbar. You want to use it or...?"

Ben reached for the tool. As though he were gonna let that kid take control of the job! "I'll pry; you pull 'em off," he growled.

They settled into a rhythm, Ben using the crowbar to pry off the boards and Paulie pulling them out of their sockets and throwing them down. The steady banging of the boards hitting the ground sounded loud and foreign in the early morning, among the sounds of nesting birds in the woods surrounding the old Picoletti home.

"Did you go fishing yesterday? Your mama said that you planned to."

What in the world? Why the attempt at conversation all of a sudden? Ben eyed Paulie. What'd he want? "Yeah, I went," he carelessly lied.

"Catch anything?"

"Look, what's up with you?" Ben spit out, flinging the crowbar down. It spun out of his reach, but he didn't pay it any mind. Instead, he concentrated on spearing Paulie with a sharp glare of his eyes. "Why are you being nice all of a sudden?"

The young man's cheeks flooded with color. For a moment, Ben expected another attack to come his way. He readied himself. He wouldn't be caught off-guard this time.

"You're right, Ben. I'm awfully sorry. I've treated you terribly." At Paulie's words, Ben realized that his flush came from embarrassment, not anger. "I've been... been really upset about something I can't understand. Really upset for a long time. And I've been taking out my anger on you. I was wrong," Paulie repeated. "Please forgive me."

There was no room for haughtiness in Paulie's voice. Now the humility on his mug actually appeared authentic. *He really means it.* Ben didn't know whether to think the kid a fool for admitting to being a jerk or to admire him for his courage.

Unable to decide, he shrugged. "Forget it." He retrieved the crowbar and shoved its tapered end beneath a loose piece of wood, keeping his eyes down.

They worked in silence for a few minutes, and then, in between tosses, Paulie spoke again. "Will you stay in Chetham after we're finished?"

Ben barked out a laugh and felt the harshness of it like sandpaper in his throat. "That's a joke, right? Stay in Chetham? Why in the world would I ever do that?"

Paulie seemed surprised. "Well... your family's here. And I thought... I thought that your job with the racetrack was finished."

"My family? What family? You? You're my family? Oh, you mean Mama, Cliff, and Grace? They're *your* family now, aren't they? All of 'em. More yours than mine." He put muscle into his prying. "And what would I do in Chetham? You think people are gonna forget who my father was?" A chuckle jittered out. "The only guys who want me around are the ones at Kingpin's – who're just like the dear old man."

"We want you around."

Ben peered up at him. "Yeah, that's the joke of the year. Since when? This morning? You didn't want me here yesterday – or the day before – or the day before that."

Paulie was silent for a moment. "I was wrong, Ben," he said with the quietness of a May breeze. "I do want you here. You're my brother."

"Ha." That one didn't even deserve a real laugh. "Your brother, huh?" He let his arm fall to his side and stared. What he wouldn't give to crack this kid open and figure out what made him tick.

Paulie met his eyes. The kid's chest rose and fell more strongly now. *He's nervous. Worked up.* How much farther should he push him? Feeling like this, Ben really didn't want a fistfight – though it was tempting to see if Paulie really had meant his apology.

"Remember your nose, preacher-boy? Last time I come? Was that a brother that did that to you?"

Paulie's Adam's-apple bobbed beneath the stubble he'd neglected to shave. "You were hurting. You acted out. Just like I did with you these past couple of weeks. It was wrong. But we don't hold it against you, Ben."

Paulie's words caused awkwardness to creep up Ben's spine. "Hurting?" He swallowed. "I wasn't hurting." He put as much steady confidence in his voice as he could muster. No way on earth would he let Paulie Giorgi feel sorry for him!

Paulie hesitated, and then said, very quietly, "We want to help you, Ben. We love—"

"Help me?" Ben interrupted, punctuating the question with a hard shove of the crowbar. "You don't wanna *help* me. You wanna *change* me." A shell hardened over his heart as he spoke, protecting him from the likes of do-gooders like Paulie. What if they did succeed in *changing* him? All he knew was the way he now was; the way he had always been. The idea of changing from the inside-out brought cold sweat to Ben's forehead if he dwelt too long on it.

So he shook it off. It wasn't possible anyway. He was who he was. Nothing on God's green earth could alter that. "I'd like to see ya try to change me!" He spat a wad of saliva out on the rotten boards. And half of him meant it.

"I can't change you, Ben. Only Jesus Christ can do that."

Ben's nerves tingled. "Jesus Christ. Yeah," he laughed. A lot of luck Paulie'd have if he was counting on the Son of God to change Ben! "No wonder I ain't changed if you're waiting for that guy to fix me. He didn't fix my papa, did he?"

Paulie fingered the chunk of wood in his hand. "Your dad didn't want to change." He looked up. His brown eyes met Ben's stare, but, to Ben's surprise, they didn't wilt in the face of Ben's mockery. "Do you want to change? I guess a better way to say it is, do you want Jesus Christ to change you? Or do you want to settle for what you are? Like your dad did?"

"Oh, so ya think I'm like my father?" How dare he say that! "I ain't nothing like him." The idea made Ben's blood run hot.

Paulie didn't reply. Ben felt his frustration rise. "What? You ain't gonna defend what ya said?"

Paulie licked his lip. Anybody could tell he was nervous. *As he should be! Doesn't he realize that I've beat men to a pulp for saying less than that about me?* "I only mean," Paulie said at last, "that, if you're fed up with the way you are and you want to change, I know the One who can change you. Can give you a fresh start."

Ben raised his eyebrows, hoping that his disgust showed clear as dawn.

"Jesus is the only One who can get you out of the mess you find yourself in, Ben," Paulie said.

"What mess? I ain't in prison, am I? I'm getting by," Ben bit out. And it was true: As long as he didn't think too much; didn't remember; lived in the moment – yeah, then he felt okay. Not great, but okay most of the time. He drove the tool's end beneath more wood.

"There are prisons in men's souls, Ben. Not just the kind you get locked into by the police." Paulie reached out and placed a hand on Ben's crowbar to stop its motion.

Fury pulsed through Ben. Who did this kid think he was, to get in Ben's way, interrupting his work, just because he had something he wanted to say? Yet, when Ben stared into Paulie's face, the guy's earnestness frightened him. "There's the kind of prison sin has locked every last one of us into. It's the worst kind of jail. And only Jesus Christ holds the key to get us out. Because only He has paid for our release with His own blood."

Ben's jaw tightened. He flung off Paulie's grip on the crowbar, pried off another board, and tossed it down to the yard by himself. It clattered on the growing pile below. Did Paulie think Ben didn't know about Jesus dying on a cross for the sins of the world? What did Jesus dying have to do with Ben changing? And why should he change?

"I know that I don't have a right to speak, but –"

"You're right," Ben cut off Paulie. "You don't got no right to speak. Like you know me. Like you know what I've been through. Just shut your trap, okay?"

Paulie shut his trap.

CHAPTER EIGHTEEN

July, 1937

For Grace, the month of June had passed in a whirlwind of church activities, the beginning of the Helen Higgins School's summer session, and, of course, many dates with Kirk Haverland. Between preparing material for her classes – which she loved teaching – and seeing Kirk, she didn't have time to miss Chetham. Not much, at least. She lived in the dormitory, just as she did during the school year, and used her small weekly salary to pay for her room. She joined the summer choir at church. She wished that she had more time to pray and to study the Scriptures, seeking to know God's will for her, specifically, but, well, life just seemed to keep coming at such a terrific pace.

And one evening, sitting across from Kirk at a cozy diner near the center of Crocksville, Grace realized that she was happy. Not full of joy, maybe, but content. Able to go on with her life. Eager to see what the future held for her.

Without Paulie? Well…

Looking at the man before her, eating his tuna-fish sandwich, Grace thought that, yes, she could. *It's time to move on. Time to let Paulie go.*

And at that moment, Kirk glanced up. "Grace, I have a question to ask you, but I'm afraid it's going to sound terribly forward."

He paused, as if waiting for her reaction. Still thinking about moving on, Grace chose to smile in encouragement. "What is it?"

He set down the final bite of his sandwich and wiped his fingers on the napkin by his plate. "Well, you might recall me telling you about my sister, Delia? She keeps asking to meet you."

Grace's eyebrows shot up in surprise.

"I'm afraid that I talk about you quite a bit in our family letters and whenever I visit home on the odd weekend." He smiled a little sheepishly. "My parents are anxious to meet you as well."

Grace felt rather flattered but hesitant. Meeting his family was a big step in their relationship. "But doesn't your family live far away from Crocksville?" she asked in order to buy time to think everything through.

He tilted his head. "Not really. Our farm is located only an hour's drive or so away."

Grace knew that if she hesitated again, he would assume – rightly so – that she didn't want to encourage a more serious turn in their relationship. He might back off to give her space. *Is that what I want?* A slight desperation took hold of her and wouldn't let her go. She liked Kirk. She didn't want to be alone again with her fruitless dreams of a hometown young man with chocolate curls.

She twirled her fork in her mashed potatoes. "Yes," she heard herself say, "I'll meet your family, Kirk."

The grin he gave her washed away all her doubts. Surely, she'd done the right thing.

~ ~ ~

When Kirk pulled up to the modest white-washed farmhouse, anxiety tingled through all of Grace's limbs. She'd picked at her cuticles all the way here, not because she felt uncomfortable with

Kirk — quite the contrary! — but because she knew that she'd soon meet his mother, father, and sister. *They're just people, like you are.* But no matter how often she told herself that truth, it didn't seem to travel from her brain to her shaking hands. Meeting new people had never been her strong suit. She always wondered what they thought of her — a shy, pale girl with a tendency to suddenly speak her mind and a past which no one but those who had gone through similar situations could understand.

Kirk led the way straight through the wide-open picket gate to the side door. Its paint was peeling a little, and Grace resisted the urge to reach out and pull off a particularly detached piece. She tried to breathe deeply as Kirk turned the knob.

The side door opened into a very dirty mudroom. On either side of the tight space, two benches stretched from wall-to-wall. Cobwebs bloomed in the area beneath them, along with two pairs of apologetic rain boots, a hammer edged with rust, a widowed pink mitten, and a few small cracked flower pots. The smell of dampness permeated the air. Grace sneaked a glance at the pressed and pulled-together man beside her. How had scrupulous Kirk emerged from this kind of a home?

"Pardon the mess," Kirk apologized. His smile held a tinge of embarrassment. "It is a working farm." He pushed open the next door and entered the kitchen, calling out, "Mother! We're here." The room's heat lapped over the threshold, welcoming Grace with the over-zealousness of a plump Italian grandmother.

She stepped in behind him, glad to be able to hide behind his height. The room was spacious, with a bare-beamed ceiling and walls the color of fresh dandelions. Grace detected the scent of baking bread. This room, at least, was spic-and-span.

"Oh, Kirk! Whatever are you doing here so early? I told you—"

Kirk stepped to the side, and Grace could hide no longer. A short woman with the face of a happy basset hound burst into the room, wiping wet hands on an old-fashioned muslin apron that wore the creases of ironing with heavy starch. The woman waggled her eyebrows and looked at Kirk, expectation molding her features.

"Mother," Kirk said, and Grace blushed to hear the pride in his voice, "I'd like you to meet Grace Picoletti. Grace, this is my mother."

Grace swallowed and attempted a smile. "Hello, Mrs. Haverland." *Don't even think about picking at your cuticles.* She tucked her palms into the folds of her skirt to make certain that she'd follow her own admonition. "Thank you for having me."

"Well, it's very nice to meet you at last, Miss Picoletti – May I call you Grace?" Mrs. Haverland looked straight into her eyes with such kindheartedness that Grace felt the tension drain – mostly – from her.

"Oh, yes, please do," she replied, using all the oxygen she had left in her lungs.

Mrs. Haverland glanced at Kirk. "I'm afraid that supper won't be ready for another hour at least. I didn't expect you so soon."

Kirk shook his head. "That's alright, Mother. I brought Grace early so that she could get acquainted with Delia. Is she upstairs?"

"No, I think she's outside, putting the chickens in the coop."

"We'll head out there, then." He leaned over to kiss his mother's cheek. "It's good to come home on the weekend, Mother."

She reached up to pat his bony jaw with her plump, sun-spotted hand. "Go on."

Grace eyed the mixing bowl and various odds-and-ends of cookery still on the kitchen counter and table. "Would you like some help with getting dinner on the table?"

The older woman waved her hand toward the door. "No, no. I have it under control. Been cooking supper for the past forty years. Besides, Delia's already made the dessert: coconut cream pie. Go on and meet her. I think you'll like each other."

"Alright." Grace smiled and turned toward the mudroom door.

Behind her, Mrs. Haverland spoke low to Kirk – but not softly enough to prevent Grace from hearing. "Seems like a nice girl, son. And shame on you! You didn't mention how pretty she is," she added, a smile in her voice.

Feeling the blood rush to her face like a river flooded by the spring rains, Grace turned the knob and freed herself into the humid yard.

~ ~ ~

As Mrs. Haverland had guessed, Kirk and Grace did find Delia among the chickens.

"Delia, this is Miss Picoletti. Grace, my sister, Miss Haverland," Kirk introduced them through the wire fencing.

Delia's wide smile – very like her brother's – shone. After shooing the last chicken into the coop, she let herself out of the pen and fastened the gate behind her. "Call me Delia, Miss Picoletti," she said as she took Grace's hand in a ladylike shake. Around Delia's round face, wiry blond wisps had escaped from her faded blue head scarf, giving the young woman a slightly-frazzled appearance.

Grace couldn't help but respond with a generous smile of her own. "Then you'll have to call me Grace."

Delia gave Grace's hand another hearty shake before letting it go. "Alright, I will!" She turned to her brother. "Daddy's in the barn, Kirk, if you want to find him."

Kirk gave his sister's head a playful tousle. "Is that a hint that you want me to leave you two?"

Delia stepped away from his reach and crossed her arms across her chest, grinning. "Well, it would be nice to get to know Grace one-on-one. It's not every day that you bring a young lady to the farm, you know." She turned toward Grace with her eyebrows raised. "In fact, he never has. You're the first one."

Kirk looked from Delia to Grace and then back to Delia. "Is it safe for me to leave Grace in your hands? Should I be concerned with what you'll say about me?" he teased.

Delia raised her chin and snorted. "What nonsense. Everybody knows you're my favorite brother, Kirk."

He rolled his eyes, chuckling, and began to walk away toward the large barn that Grace could see at the far end of the yard. "And I'm your *only* brother, Delia."

She gave a good farm-porch laugh, and Grace laughed, too. What a delightful girl Delia Haverland was! Grace's eyes shifted toward Kirk's retreating figure.

"I think I'm going to like you very much, Grace." With that declaration, Delia looped her arm around Grace's waist. "Come and sit on the swing with me. I want to know all about you. I always like to know all about my friends."

To her own surprise, Grace realized that she didn't feel uncomfortable at all with Delia's forwardness, perhaps because it didn't have an underlying nosiness to it, just a genuine desire to love other people in the best way Delia knew how. So Grace responded by placing her own arm around Delia's somewhat-stout waist and walking up to the front porch with her. Around them, the lightning bugs had begun to appear, though the twilight hadn't yet fallen enough for the little creatures to appear to their best advantage.

They settled into a wide swing that creaked as Delia moved it back-and-forth with her foot in a slow, perpetual motion. "So where do you come from? And what's your family like?" Delia asked, her eyes fastened on Grace's face.

Grace told Delia all about her family back in Chetham, briefly detailing how Doctor Giorgi and Mama had married after all, despite their broken engagement of long ago. Cautiously, without giving details about Papa, she spoke of how God had brought first Mama and then Grace herself to know Christ personally, and Delia's hazel eyes filled with tears. She wiped them away with the back of her hand. "That is so beautiful to hear. I'm so thankful," she murmured, and Grace could tell that the young woman really meant it.

As Delia ran her hand down the chain holding up her side of the swing, Grace noticed a glimmer on the girl's suntanned fingers. "Pardon me if I'm speaking out-of-place, but are you engaged?" she asked, a little cautiously. Her strange relationship with Paulie had made her a bit gun-shy of putting others in the difficult predicament of having to explain their relationship status.

But she needn't have feared. Delia fairly beamed, her smile stretching her large mouth just like Kirk's did. "Yes. The wedding is set for October. Just a little affair, but it will be special."

"That sounds lovely. Is he someone you've known for a long time?"

Delia grinned. "I'll say I have. Lester and his family have lived down the road from us all my life. We went to school together from the time we were both missing our front teeth. And you..." She paused. For the first time since their conversation had begun, Delia appeared unsure of how to phrase something.

Grace felt a little twinge of nervousness but didn't let it show. She hated to spoil the closeness they'd experienced in their friendship so far. "What is it?" she invited, keeping her expression welcoming.

Delia twisted the engagement ring on her finger. "I just wondered if you and Kirk...?"

The words stuck in Grace's throat. She knew that, at this point, she should say that she and Kirk were seriously dating. That they were romantically involved with one another. Delia must know that. An honorable man didn't bring a girl to meet his family without serious intentions. She had a definite hunch that Kirk had a ring of his own in mind, eventually. But for some reason, she simply couldn't bring herself to finally say it aloud.

"You don't have to tell me," Delia assured her when the silence became a smidgeon awkward. "I just wondered because, well, I know my brother is pretty stuck on you. And that's saying something for Kirk. I don't think he's ever had a real girlfriend. Not long-term. He never can seem to find exactly who he's looking for. Until he found you, I mean. You're all he's talked about whenever he's come home these past few weeks."

Grace bit her lip. Had Kirk Haverland really fallen so hard for her? A virtuous, handsome man of purpose? Obviously, she should be flattered; she should reciprocate his feelings of regard. She'd realized that that was possible for her that night at the diner.

And she did. She respected his integrity and admired his already-competent manner of governing the Helen Higgins School. Maybe this was the start of love, the root from which it might grow, strong and embedded deep in the soil of a mutual regard for one another's solid character.

But could she further explore the possibility of falling in love with Kirk, while in her heart, thoughts of Paulie still lingered? *Heavenly Father, why won't you take away my love for Paulie? When I have a good man that I don't deserve right here, waiting for me to respond to him with more enthusiasm?*

"I once really loved someone," she admitted faintly, her eyes flickering to meet Delia's. "I'm not sure if I love him still." She held her breath. Would her new friend be angry that her brother – who, according to Delia, had never given his heart away before – chose to court a woman who had feelings for another? "Sometimes the memory of him – the young man I... loved – holds me back from Kirk."

But Delia only waited, her hazel eyes soft in the nearing twilight. "What happened?" Around them, the June-bugs began their nightly chorus.

"He fell out of love with me." The phrase, spoken aloud, sounded so common that Grace wondered why it had the power to rend her heart in two. The pain surged up in her chest, and she found herself babbling on, releasing all the misery of the past year of silence and the Christmas visit home in which Paulie acted like nothing was wrong between them – except that he had carefully distanced himself from her.

When she'd finished, the sun had sunk behind the hills that framed the Haverland farm. Dusk misted the earth. Delia sat silent, her gaze pinned to the ground, and embarrassment crept over Grace. Of course, she shouldn't have said all of that, especially to Kirk's sister!

"Paulie sounds like a wonderful young man," Delia interrupted

Grace's whirling thoughts. "You must be thankful that God put him in your life – used him to bring you nearer to Christ."

"I am." Grace's voice caught on tears she forced to stay at bay. "But his silence still hurts."

The next moment, she found herself gathered in a hug, surrounded by the strong farm girl's sun-browned arms. "I know." Delia hesitated, then spoke with a steady but gentle voice, "Sometimes, I think, it's best to not only appreciate the past but also to be prepared to move on to whatever God has for you in the future. To not limit your life to what God has done for you in the past."

Delia pulled back and held Grace by the shoulders, looking straight into her eyes. "You think that's what I'm doing?" Grace asked.

Delia's brow furrowed. "I think you might need to tuck away the happy memories of the past, kind of like I do with scrapbooks. I don't live in them. I live in the now. From what you're telling me, Paulie has removed himself from your life, Grace." She paused. "That sounds kind of harsh, doesn't it? Sometimes, I can be too blunt."

"No, not at all. I want to hear what you think," Grace assured her. And she did. Delia's words made sense. They even brought a numbing sensation to Grace's bruised heart. *My life with Paulie is over. She's right. It's time to move forward. I can't tread water forever.*

"Well, I just mean, that young man's not part of your *now*, like it or not. By his own choice," Delia continued.

"And Kirk is part of it." Grace realized too late that she'd spoken her answering thought aloud.

In the deepening twilight, she saw Delia's smile widen and her eyes brighten as though lit by fireflies. "Well, I didn't mean to push my brother on you, but if the shoe fits…" She laughed gently and tucked Grace's arm into her own. "Come on. Mother's probably got supper on the table."

But before they went inside, Grace stopped for a moment, fear taking hold of her. "Delia, you won't tell your brother about…?"

"About Paulie?" Delia shook her head. "No, Grace. I think that's between you and Kirk. It's not my place to get involved."

CHAPTER NINETEEN

B en eased to his feet, feeling every bone in his spine snap into place. Taking a long swig of water from the army canteen sitting atop Papa's old upturned barrel, he arched his back, easing the stiffness out of it. "We're almost done with this place," he said aloud, just for the satisfaction of hearing it himself. "Two more weeks, and it'll be finished. A lot earlier than I – or your old man, for that matter – figured."

"Are you still set on leaving Chetham when you're done?" Paulie asked. Sweat dripped from his scalp down his face. Ben felt the same salty moisture coating his own body. And no wonder. They were working outdoors in a humid Rhode Island summer. Back in late June, Paulie had finally succumbed to shedding his undershirt, and as both men worked side-by-side, their naked backs baked brown in the sun.

"Why're you askin'? Gonna miss me?" Ben made sure to lay on the sarcasm thick as butter on toast. No need for the Doc's son to realize how accustomed Ben had grown to his usually quiet but kind presence. Sure, the kid didn't always know how to hang a door or repair cupboards, but he meant well. *Actually, if he wasn't so full of his religion, he wouldn't be such a bad egg.*

Paulie just smiled in response. "We did good work, Ben, huh?"

Ben took a long look at the old place. With windows replaced, roof patched, and trim painted, among many other repairs, the Picoletti house did look good. It should've made him feel good, too, seeing his childhood home brought back to useful life. But Ben turned from it with a shudder. "Yeah. Hope whoever buys it from your papa will be real happy in it. We never were, but maybe they will be."

Paulie was quiet again, sadness painting shadows on his face. Ben raised his chin. The last thing he wanted was pity from the Giorgi boy.

~ ~ ~

Who would have thought that her little brother would turn out to be such a good correspondent? A letter a month. Smiling, Grace eased herself down on her bed and lay back against the pillows, holding Cliff's letter above her. She was thankful for the distraction from the torrid heat this week had brought. After smiling over Cliff's rhapsody on Tabitha's rhubarb pie and his complaint about the summer sports league, she read his last paragraphs:

Ben and Paulie are almost finished with the house. You should see it, sis. It looks really swell – not the way it was when we lived there at all. Barely looks like the same place. They've been working dawn to dusk on it for nearly two months, and Mama says it seems like they're finally getting along. Ben is... well, you know Ben. He's not changed. I've gotta give Paulie credit: He puts up with a lot of junk from Ben. Puts up with it with a smile!

Though maybe he's got a reason to smile. Keep it under your hat, Grace, but I think Paulie's got his eye on Betty. You know, Reverend Cloud's youngest daughter. She's come around the house a couple of times this summer already, and Ben told me that Paulie defended her something terrible when Ben poked fun at her when he first came here. She's a nice girl – not as nice as you, mind! If Paulie has got it in his head to marry someday, then I guess it'd be good for him to marry Betty. Especially if she cooks as good as her mama does for Youth Fellowship!

Grace let the letter drop to her chest. She stared up at the ceiling, unblinking. Was it true? Paulie really had forsaken her? In favor of prim Betty Cloud? *How long has he cared for her, while I held out hope that there was just some mistake – that he had a good reason for not writing?*

The tears burned up from their wells, wetting her eyes and mingling with the perspiration on her face. She didn't raise a hand to wipe her cheeks. Cliff had no reason to tell anything but the truth. She'd never spoken to her little brother about Paulie's declaration of love for her. *He's speaking only of what he sees.* And what he'd seen tore at her heart.

I never want to see Paulie again. Oh, Lord God, why?

~ ~ ~

Someone was shaking him, gently. Perhaps if he ignored it, the person would realize how tired he was from his long day of performing surgery and would stop bothering him...

The shaking persisted. Then, Sam heard a voice whispering, "Sam! Sam, love, wake up."

He recognized that the voice belonged to Sarah and swam to the surface of consciousness, despite the pull of sleep. Squinting into the darkness of their moonlit bedroom, he could barely discern her face leaning near him. He scrubbed at his eyes with the back of his hand. "What is it?" he mumbled, propping himself up on his elbows.

"It's Paulie," she said. "I went downstairs for a drink of water, and I heard him in his bedroom. He's crying, Sam."

His soul panged at her words. Sam pushed away any further desire to return to sleep and rose from bed. "I'll go to him."

He moved toward the door, praying as he went, wondering what had upset Paulie so. Had Ben done something awful today? Sam doubted it: From what he knew, Ben and Paulie seemed to have settled into a stiff but not unfriendly peace. What was this about, then? Perhaps Sarah, tiptoeing through the creaky sleeping house, had misheard, had misinterpreted...

But he himself heard the sniffles and muffled choking sobs as he neared Paulie's bedroom door. Sam's heart rose into his throat. What dragon was his son fighting in his spirit? His steps quickened. *For we wrestle not against flesh and blood, but against principalities, against powers, against the rulers of the darkness of this world, against spiritual wickedness in high places.*

Sam didn't bother to knock. He knew that Paulie's bedroom, though a place of privacy, had always been open to him. Turning the knob softly, he entered, his eyes adjusting to the lamplight.

Paulie knelt beside the bed, his Bible spread open on the rug next to him. Knelt – or more like sprawled in evident grief. He jerked his head around as Sam closed the door behind him.

Tears rose to Sam's own eyes. He knelt beside Paulie and opened his arms to him. Paulie didn't hesitate, collapsing against his father's chest. He shook with weeping, and Sam let his own tears fall into Paulie's dark curls.

At last, Paulie drew back. "I know it's for my best, Dad. Ultimately, I mean. I know God works everything out for good and all..." He sucked in a shuddering breath. "But I wish I'd never loved... No, I don't wish that. I'm a better man for having loved her. She would make any man better for having loved her."

Sam was stunned. That was what this was about? "Paulie, Grace will be home at the end of the summer for two solid weeks before classes begin again. I know that you miss her, but then it's only a few more years until..."

He trailed off, seeing Paulie violently shaking his head. "A few more years until what, Dad?" No bitterness lingered there, only sadness.

"Until you're both free to commit to one another. You know that my ban on your relationship holds only until you and Grace get your education under your belts. I wanted her to have choices, the same choices I would want for a daughter from my own body..."

"Well, it looks like she's made her choice." The words came out softly, broken as a reed in the wind. "And it's not me."

Sam frowned. "You can't know that, Paulie. If anything... Aren't you still writing to her?"

"Yeah, Dad." He smiled without joy. "Every single week. But she's not written to me." He drew in a breath. "And it hurts. It hurts to be rejected like that. I thought, when I gave Grace to God, completely, fully, that He'd give her back to me. But in the back of my mind, I always feared this – that she'd go away and never really return to me."

Wordlessly, Sam rubbed his son's broadened back. He hoped and prayed that Paulie was wrong, that this was just a misunderstanding between the two young people. But what if...? *Oh, Lord God, was I wrong to ask Paulie to ease off on his pursuit of Grace in years past? I always figured that their love would only be strengthened by this separation, if it was real, but it appears that I was wrong.*

And that his mistake had cost his son a great deal.

CHAPTER TWENTY

"Coming to church this morning, Ben?" Cliff poked his head around the corner of Ben's doorway.

Ben still lay sprawled across his bed, the covers flung to the floor. At Cliff's words, he opened one eye. Should he go and endure sitting among all them good religious folk through a boring sermon that racked his nerves... or should he stay home and watch the grass grow outside? *Nothing much else to be done in Chetham on a Sunday!* He heaved a sigh and lurched into sitting position, feeling lightheaded at the sudden change in position. "Yeah, kid. I'll go."

He swung his legs over the side of the bed and stood, stretching his arms out toward the ceiling. Maybe the pretty preacher's daughter would be playing the piano again.

~ ~ ~

There he was again: sitting right beside his mother in the seventh pew from the front, on the right side. *Slouching is more like it.* Betty shook her head and turned her attention back to the hymn-book opened before her. But, for some reason, the image of Ben Picoletti wouldn't let her go, even through three verses of "Be Still, My Soul." She dared a peek in his direction as she closed the hymnal and stood up from the bench.

He still slouched beside Mrs. Giorgi, but now his eyes had fastened onto Daddy, who had taken his place in the pulpit. His face wore a blank expression, like a white sheet of paper, though around the edges... Was it anger that she saw? Or just a bitter kind of hopelessness?

Mulling it over, Betty made her way to Mother's pew, sitting down and angling her body so that she could still see Ben out of the corner of one eye. Yes, anger definitely rested beneath his seemingly unruffled countenance. *What's beneath all of that toughness?*

Daddy's "amen" startled her. She'd missed the short prayer before his sermon. Embarrassment forced her mind to concentrate better, but from time-to-time, her thoughts wandered back to the scruffy man so obviously set in his ways of sin. What had made him so angry? So obstinate toward the Lord? Would his heart soften eventually?

Though why should it matter to you, Betty? He has plenty of people to witness to him in the Giorgi house, doesn't he?

That was true. All that her intellect told her was true. But something deep in her heart panged at the sight of Ben – so lost, so alone in the world. He reminded her of the puppy she'd rescued, years ago now, from a family that abused it. That puppy had been distrustful, too; angry and snappish. It had taken love – and patient time – to bring about a change in the dog.

But loving Ben Picoletti – in *any* sense of the word – wasn't Betty's responsibility, was it? Of course, she held Christian charity for him – wanted him to repent – but she could hold that for him from a distance.

Pretending to adjust her hat, Betty glanced across the aisle at him. At just that moment, Ben looked her way. Her eyes met his for a quarter of a moment, and her insides turned to gooseberry jam left out in the August heat.

One side of his mouth turned up and laughter entered his face. Betty whipped her gaze away from him, fixing it back on Daddy.

How humiliating! For a man – especially *that* man – to catch her looking at him! And that feeling that had run through her when her eyes had met his! How… how awkward it all was!

She wanted to forget that Ben Picoletti ever had set foot in Chetham and disturbed her neatly-organized life.

Didn't she?

~ ~ ~

Oh, dear. Betty slowed her steps and clutched her Bible to her chest more closely. Why did Ben Picoletti have to lurk at the end of the walk? Other departing congregants made their way around him, but he just stood there, shifting from foot to foot, squinting up at the hot sun.

Of course, he wasn't really lurking. She knew that. He was waiting for the rest of his family to be ready to go, and Betty had heard Mother ask Mrs. Giorgi if she wouldn't mind helping her in the church kitchen for a minute or two. She glanced over her shoulder. Ben's brother Cliff played tag with a group of boys on the lawn. She didn't see Paulie anywhere; knowing him, he was probably chatting with some older folks inside.

She should've stayed to help Mother wash the Communion cups. Then she wouldn't be in the predicament of having to stroll right past that… that man. Did he remember their eye contact during the service? *Of course he does, you ninny!* Betty's mouth dried as she approached him and he stopped his fidgeting. He met her eyes with a feral smile. She sucked in a breath.

"Hiya, Betty," he greeted her.

"Hello, Ben." She nodded her head and hurried her steps. Whew. She had passed him. The tension drained slightly from her.

"That's some dress you're wearing. You look as pretty as a rose."

Goodness gracious! He'd fallen into step with her! She peered out of the corner of her eye as she kept her pace. He matched his stride to hers! *He said I was pretty as a… as a rose.* She blinked hard, determined to turn her mind from the unexpected compliment. "T-Thank you," she stammered. Her steps slowed of their own accord. "And how did you like my father's sermon today?" There. That should put this handsome hooligan in his place!

Handsome?! Since when had she considered him *that?* Her insides began to turn back to warm jam.

"It was alright, I guess, for some people. Not for me."

She halted right there on the sidewalk between the church and her home and met his gaze, resolved to remain unmoved by the dark blue eyes that held the sparkle of the sun on the ocean. "How can a sermon about salvation be for *some people?* Salvation is for everybody. Everyone needs to be saved." Funny how such a one as Ben Picoletti – who, God knew, was in great need of salvation! – couldn't see that.

He raised his chin at her words, though, as if she'd challenged him to a duel. "Really? And just what do I need to be saved from?"

"From your sin." The phrase rolled out, smooth as butter, memorized from when Betty was a toddler.

"From my sin, huh?"

Was he laughing at her? Yes, she believed he was – with the bitterness of battery acid in his eyes. "Yes," she replied, unsteadied by his manner. "If you repent, God will forgive you and you will be saved and have a home in heaven with Him." The words worked when Daddy used them; why shouldn't they when Betty spoke now with Ben?

"And what do I got to repent of, Miss Cloud?" He took a step toward her, hands plunged deep into his pockets. "Wontcha tell me?"

She looked him over. Didn't he know? She herself didn't understand everything about the Picoletti family, but she'd heard enough. Enough whispered gossip to know that Ben had gone very wild – that he'd been with women, that he drank, that he swore... Who knew what else, too? *What kind of person is he, really?* And why, despite it all, did she find herself drawn toward him?

She swallowed, trying to think of a way to answer him. But before she could, he leaned in close to her face. She smelled the faint odor of tobacco on his breath and saw the stubble shadowing his jaw. Betty's heart picked up its beat. She looked from side-to-side. They stood on a public sidewalk. She had no need to fear him, did she?

"You listen to me, Betty. I'm sick of you churchy, goody-two-shoes people telling me I've got repenting to do. That I'm the one that's gotta say I'm sorry to God." His eyes narrowed. "In my opinion," he stated, jabbing his thumb at his chest, "*He's* the One that's got repenting to do."

"What?" She could only stare at him, not bothering to mask her incredulity. Was he really serious?

"You heard me. You people think you can just poke your face into a man's life and tell him the way he's livin' it is wrong. Well, I got news for you, tootsie. You don't know what I've been through! You don't know, and you can never know. You can never understand. So pack up your platitudes, got it? I don't got time for your baloney."

He stared at her with the ferocity of a terrier shaking a rat. Hands trembling on her Bible, she found herself nodding.

"Good," he growled and turned on his heel. Betty followed him with her eyes as he stalked back to the church. Something inside her shattered. It was not a romantic kind of heartbreak. Rather, the seal came free on a dam of compassion that she'd not been aware that she had within her soul.

~ ~ ~

Jesus, keep Grace safe. Keep her walking straight with You. As Paulie clung more intensely to Christ, he felt compelled to pray as he went about his day.

Why should he do it? Surely his parents prayed for Grace. Why should he torment himself with the vision of the woman who would never become his?

But praying for Grace had become as natural to Paulie as taking a breath of sweet morning air. And turning his desire for her into a prayer for her well-being brought peace to his soul. *You know what*

You are doing, Lord, though I don't understand.

~ ~ ~

"Grace, you're a natural at this."

How many times this summer had Kirk told her that? Grace smiled but otherwise ignored the man's presence in her empty classroom. *My classroom? I really must be getting used to teaching!* She stacked her music books and picked up her purse from the desk. Well, no matter. Summer school would end soon, and then she'd be heading for Chetham for two weeks of vacation before her second year at the conservatory began. Everything in her rejoiced that she would only spend two weeks in Chetham – only two weeks with the pain of seeing Paulie every day – before she could retreat to New York once more.

"I mean it. I don't flatter people." When she glanced up again, Grace saw that Kirk wore a completely serious expression. He stepped closer toward her. "I've been meaning to ask you this. I want you to consider staying on here permanently. As part of the full-time staff."

What? She frowned. How could he have forgotten? "I have three more years before I graduate, Kirk," she reminded him. "That's a long time to wait for me to join the staff." And whether or not she wanted to stay on at the Helen Higgins School permanently? Well, that was another question, too.

He smiled. "I know – You have three more years before you graduate with your bachelor's degree. But you could transfer to the certificate program and graduate next year."

Surprise numbed any other feeling. "But I'm completing the performance track. My scholarship agreement depends on that."

"What if I paid for your second year?"

"What? Why would you?" Within herself, she stepped back, away from him. Something didn't feel right...

I want to go home. I want to go back to Chetham. The thought pushed into her mind before she could stop it.

But she couldn't go back to Chetham. Not permanently anyway. Paulie was there.

Kirk reached for her hand. Too astonished and muddled to withdraw it, she let him grasp it. His eyes met hers, and she saw the earnestness deep-rooted there. "I don't want to lose you, Grace. You mean too much to me."

He loves me. She knew it then. *He wants me to marry him.* And perhaps that was what she needed, to take her mind off Paulie for good: to marry a good, godly man with whom she could minister to the poor. Surely love for him would follow. *I already care for him a great deal. Did Paulie ever pursue me with such keenness?*

Yes, he had. Until last September, when Paulie's love for her suddenly had ceased. And Shakespeare thought that a *woman's* love was frail!

Kirk gently squeezed her hands before releasing them. "Please don't answer now," he said, his words tumbling over each other like people competing for the last seat on a city trolley. "I'd like to take you to dinner tomorrow night. To Ciao Italia. Would you accompany me, please?"

Ciao Italia. That fancy-schmancy Mediterranean restaurant where the men wore tuxedos? Something in Grace's spirit tensed. Her breathing quickened as his blue eyes caught her own and held them. He was handsome. He loved both his God and her. He was steadfast. *But I don't love him. Not as I loved...* Tension gripped her. "I have a lot of packing to do. I'm leaving for Chetham at the end of next week." She clutched her purse against her body and moved toward the door. Oh, to put this off as long as possible. *For an eternity!* "Maybe when I return—"

"Please, Grace. It's very important to me." Kirk spoke low, earnestly, and Grace had never been much good at denying people their requests when she could fulfill them so easily.

"Alright," she agreed, swallowing down her doubt and forcing a smile. "I'll go with you."

Relief flooded his face. "Shall I pick you up at seven?"

"Yes." Why did she feel as though she teetered on the edge of a precipice, ready to fall to her doom? *That's silly, Grace.* Besides, she shouldn't walk by her feelings, should she?

CHAPTER TWENTY-ONE

B en spotted Betty Cloud the moment he entered the pharmacy. Who could miss that ruler-straight posture of hers or the brunette curls that hung down to her shoulders, bouncy as a filly's mane? She was sitting at the counter, straw deep in her drink. Looking at her caused the heaviness that always dragged on Ben's spirit to lift a little. He shook his head. For all her primness, Betty Cloud was something that could make a man – well, make a man feel like he oughtta do something with his life to deserve her.

The thought startled him. Since when hadn't he been good enough? *Always.* His inadequacy felt like a sack of rocks bouncing around in his soul all day, every day. A sack of rocks that he continually tried to ignore. Ben strode forward, not seeing anyone he knew well enough to sit down next to. He found himself standing just behind and to the right of Betty.

Ben cleared his throat. "Anybody sitting here?"

She started and turned toward him. Her brown eyes widened at the sight of him. After a second's hesitation, she shook her head. "No."

He smiled and plopped down in the empty seat. Mr. Culver, apron tied around his waist, bustled up, his scrawny legs like pipe cleaners. "What'll you have, Ben?"

Of course, Mr. Culver remembered him. Ben had come in here whenever he'd had a spare nickel as a kid – not that it had happened often. "'Member my usual, Mr. Culver?"

The elderly druggist squinted in thought, then recalled, "The chocolate cabinet?"

"You got it." As Mr. Culver stepped away, Ben turned to Betty, who quietly sipped her tan-colored drink. "What're you havin'?"

Without turning toward him again, she answered, "Coffee milk."

"What's that?" he asked, curiosity sincerely piqued. "New thing Mr. Culver thought up?"

She lifted her eyes to meet his, and he saw with surprise that hurt lingered in her gaze. Had he put that there? Something twanged inside him at the thought. It was one thing to hurt Paulie, but to hurt Betty Cloud... Well, Ben just didn't want to do that. Why was he the kind of guy who *did* do that kind of thing, even without trying?

Despite the distress he read in her expression, though, Betty answered his question in a very civil way. "No, one of the diners in Providence created it up a few years back. They mixed old coffee grinds into milk and sweetened it, then strained out the grinds."

"Must've been while I was away," Ben put in, trying to keep the conversation going, though he had no idea why. *Why do I suddenly crave Betty's approval?* Why did he feel like he wanted to make up for causing her pain? He really needed to get out of this town before...

"Yes," she said. Almost before Ben knew what she was doing, Betty had taken a nickel from her purse and laid it on the counter.

She's going. Panic spread through Ben's chest. He realized in that moment how much he regretted his words during his last exchange with Betty Cloud. "Please," he said, reaching out a hand to grasp her wrist. "Please don't go 'cause of me."

Her eyes dropped to where his hand held her wrist, and Ben saw the awkwardness parading across her face. He released her, noticing how very soft her skin felt against his calloused fingers.

Her gaze darted toward the door. "I have... Mother needs me to..." She stopped and took a breath, not looking him in the eyes.

Ben swallowed and spoke what he knew had to be said. "Betty, I was wrong with saying what I said on Sunday. I had no place telling you… I mean, you're a nice girl. A real nice girl. I'm the one who…" How to say this? "I made ya feel bad; I know I did, and I hate that. I don't ever want you to feel bad because of me. Because of somethin' I said."

Betty eased back onto the stool, not sitting on it completely. She pulled her lower lip into her mouth. She stayed silent so long that Ben was afraid she'd not reply. Not tell him everything was okay.

At last, she looked up, her eyes connecting with his. "Ben, you were *right* about what you said on Sunday." Her voice was the gentlest he'd ever heard it. "Maybe not about how you said it, but what you said was completely correct. I've never known the kind of pain you've had to go through. My daddy's never been anything but a kind, honorable man who walks with Jesus Christ, loves my mother and us children, and does his best by everyone in Chetham. The worst thing I've had to bear was probably the loneliness when my elder sister married and moved away. Like I said, nothing compared to your pain. So you're right when you say that I can't understand."

Ben felt that he had to say something to comfort her. She looked kinda forlorn, sitting there holding her purse so tightly that her knuckles whitened. "You meant well," he offered.

"Yes, but that doesn't excuse my insensitivity." She reached for her empty glass and poked the straw up and down a few times. "But Ben, even if you don't want to hear it, I have something I should say to you. That I want to say to you, I mean."

She seemed so nervous, he felt sorry for her. "Sure. Go ahead. Whatever you wanna say, I'll listen."

Mr. Culver chose that moment to arrive with Ben's chocolate cabinet. Ben stuck in the straw and offered the glass to Betty before slurping it. "Wanna sip?"

"No, thank you," she smiled, and Ben thought not for the first time what nice teeth the reverend's daughter had. Straight as a fence rail.

He took a deep suck at the straw, hardly tasting it what with Betty staring at him like that, and swallowed. "Shoot," he encouraged her.

Her shoulders rose with the deep breath she took. Wow, was she pretty. No wonder Paulie liked her. "It's only this, Ben. Like I said, I can't understand everything you've been through. But Jesus Christ can."

He stiffened at the Name. Why did she have to bring God into this? *You said you'd listen to her, so just keep your mouth shut and drink your cabinet.* He took a huge gulp and felt his brain turn numb.

"Why don't you try just bringing everything you struggle with to Him? Ask Him to change you – to transform you from the person you don't want to be into the person He wants you to become? Ask Him to help you give up whatever is stopping you from accepting Him as your Lord and Savior?"

His jaw pulsed. *Whatever is stopping you…* "How do you know I want to change?" he asked, to divert his mind from the troubling thought. "Maybe I'm happy the way I am."

Betty tilted her head, and, in her eyes, he saw earnestness overcoming her reserve. "Ben Picoletti, you may be able to hide it from yourself, but I see unhappiness written plainly on your face – every time you think no one is watching."

He gritted his teeth. Betty's probing held the same discomfort as the trip he'd once taken to the dentist. Maybe if he didn't answer her, she'd stop. She'd pick up her purse and leave.

He didn't want her to leave.

He didn't need to fear. His silence didn't quiet Betty Cloud. She hesitated only a fraction of a moment before adding, "You were made to be a lot more than what you're settling for, Ben. Can't you see that?"

He hated to admit it, but Betty's words stung. Stung because they held a barb of truth in them. Still, would he let her see that? He strapped on his armor, even as he realized how accurately she depicted his own feelings with her words. *People will hurt you. They will betray you.* The chant buzzed through his mind and heart. *As soon as you show them your weak spot, they'll dive in for the kill.*

Knowing that she waited for his response, Ben took his time, sucking up the last of the cabinet and purposely wiping his mouth on his sleeve. At last, he lifted his eyes to meet hers – gorgeous brown, the color of the fudge sauce Mama used to make when Ben was a little boy. "And if I don't wanna change? Am I still your friend?"

She kept his gaze locked in hers. "Yes, but real love doesn't settle for any less than the best for a friend. I wouldn't really love you if I didn't speak the truth, Ben."

"Love? You *love* me?" She'd walked right into that one! Of course, he knew that she loved one guy – and that wasn't him – but this was too good of an opportunity to tease her and take the attention off himself.

She winced but didn't flush like his sister Grace would've in such an embarrassing moment. After just a moment's hesitation, she said softly, "There are different kinds of love, Ben. Besides romantic." She pulled in her bottom lip and pushed herself off the stool. "I have to go. Have a good night, Ben."

She was two steps away from the open door when Ben called after her. "Actually, it's goodbye." Why did he feel the need to tell her that? What would she care? What did *he* care, for that matter?

She turned, head tilted expectantly, and Ben hopped off his own stool, leaving his empty glass on the counter. He strode toward her, half-grin in place to show that he looked forward to leaving crummy Chetham behind him forever.

"Yeah," he continued, "the old house is just about finished. I doubt I'll see you again before I leave."

She looked down at the polished, worn floor for a moment. When she raised her face again, a sweet but somewhat pained smile met his. "Well," she said, "goodbye. I wish you well, Ben."

"Thanks. You, too, Betty." He swallowed. "Goodbye." The word tasted like a ham sandwich left out in the sun too long.

With a bounce of her nutmeg hair, Betty exited the diner and his life.

CHAPTER TWENTY-TWO

They'd begun their dessert when Kirk asked the question. He didn't do it on bended knee or with trumpets blaring. Rather humbly, dignity molding his features with comeliness until he looked like one of the Greek gods Grace had read about in high school. *Apollo, for sure.*

"I don't expect you to say yes right away, Grace. I know that our relationship has not been a formal courtship." The words strode out of Kirk's mouth, well-thought-out. "If you are willing to marry me, to become my wife and serve the Lord with me at Helen Higgins and wherever else God leads us, I'd also like to ask your stepfather's blessing before we make the engagement official."

He paused. "I love you, Grace. You have captivated me as I thought no woman could. I'd planned to spend my life celibate. I never thought I wanted to marry. But then you and I collided... literally."

Kirk smiled, and Grace felt her own lips turn up in response, despite the tension rippling through her nerves. *I like him. I really do.*

He reached across the table and, for the first time, covered her hand with his own. His skin warmed hers. *I could be happy with him. I could make a difference in that school with him. I think that I could... learn to love him, even.*

"I want to be very clear, Grace. You marrying me is *not* a condition of you remaining at the school. That decision – You can make that independently of this. You are an excellent teacher, and I would hate to lose you, even if you decide that our relationship isn't going any farther. Isn't heading for marriage, I mean."

Pulling her hand back from his, Grace looked down at the melting slice of spumoni before her and tried to think. If she'd not been so busy over the past twenty-four hours, she would have taken time to pray about this proposal, which she'd known – in the corner of her heart – was fast approaching. *I think I made myself busy on purpose. I didn't want to think about it.* She let her eyes flit up and saw Kirk's gaze on her. *I didn't want to think about marrying anyone but Paulie.*

But she'd known that would never be. *He gave me up. He's going to marry Betty Cloud. What am I supposed to do, stay single all my life when I long to marry and have a husband and family of my own to love? Maybe God has sent this man...*

And when she *had* prayed over the past few weeks, bringing her relationship with Kirk before her Heavenly Father, she'd heard only silence. Not a yes. Not a no.

But she needed an answer now, didn't she? Before she went home and faced Paulie with Betty Cloud hanging on his arm. And Kirk was a good man. A godly man, who sought the Lord. And she did respect him...

As if he'd read her thoughts, Kirk leaned toward her, catching her eyes with his. "You don't need to answer me now." He cleared his throat slightly. "Is there someone else? Someone you're fond of?"

Awkwardness crept over her. How could she explain her relationship with Paulie to Kirk? Should she even try?

"I only presume to ask, Grace, because sometimes it seems as though you're holding back from our relationship. Even now – when I'm asking you to marry me. Perhaps an old beau?"

Grace twisted her napkin until it formed a rope in her lap. "I..."

His gaze held compassion. "I know that it can take a long time to get over such things."

Such things...

He pressed his perfect lips together. "But hear me on this, Grace. Sometimes, we have to make a decision to go forward even when our heart begs us to go back. Even when we might wish things had worked out differently. Sometimes the only way forward is through a well-reasoned decision, not through feelings or emotions."

He was right, wasn't he? Too long had she dwelt on what had once been rather than looking forward to what could be, hadn't she? *Oh, Lord, redirect my steps if I'm going down the wrong path!* Pushing away the thoughts of meadow walks with Paulie beside her, Grace drew a shuddering breath. "Yes, Kirk."

Joy began a slow dawn on the man's face, as if unsure that he'd heard correctly. "Yes? You mean...?"

She nodded and felt nothing but relief that the necessary word had been spoken. "Yes," she said, voice trembling. "You may write to my stepfather, Kirk."

~ ~ ~

"Paulie, would you mind seeing if your father has some extra stationary in his desk? I've run out and need some," Mother called as Paulie made his way past her small upstairs sitting room. "I would go myself, but my knees are bothering me and..."

"I'm glad to do it," he replied, stopping for just a second to smile at her. She sat at her little desk, a few letters already written and sealed before her. Looking at Mother, Paulie's heart warmed; how wonderful to have a mother again, even if he was already grown.

Downstairs in Dad's office, he shuffled through the contents of the desk's top drawer, looking for Dad's plain stationery. He knew that Mother probably wouldn't want to use the paper with Dad's office address embossed on it. The last few sheets of plain paper lay at the very bottom of the drawer. He pulled out half a dozen pieces and neatened the rest of the pile.

Paulie had just shut the drawer when a letter on the top of Dad's tidy but cluttered desk caught his attention. Normally, he wouldn't read Dad's mail without asking first, but one phrase arrested his eyes, seeming to leap off the page at him:

Your stepdaughter, Grace…

Almost without thinking, his hand moved toward the double sheets of neat and long-looped cursive. He picked up the letter with trembling fingers and, like a wolf gnawing his own bloody tongue, ate the words written there:

Frankly, sir, I am in love with Grace. I have made her aware of my intentions and feelings, and she has informed me that she is willing to engage herself to me if you and Mrs. Giorgi will provide your permission and blessing.

Paulie felt the cold beat of his heart crashing against his ribs. With measured breath, he placed the letter back on Dad's desk. *Alright, Lord.*

Who was this interloper? This man who had evidently stolen Grace's heart from Paulie? Paulie glanced down at the signature on the bottom of the second page, a signature that followed line after line detailing this man's plans for his and Paulie's beloved's life together. *Together.*

But it wasn't supposed to be this way. At the beginning of their last year of high school, he'd given up Grace in obedience to Dad's commands. In his heart, Paulie had been sure that God would give her back to him. Didn't God reward obedience? Didn't He give Abraham back Isaac when the patriarch had determined to offer the boy to God? *Why? Why? Why?*

Mother waited for him upstairs, but Paulie couldn't move. His knees locked in place; his feet stuck to the floor; his eyes stared down at the offending letter.

If this is My will for you, then it is good. The Lord is a strong tower; the righteous run to it and are safe.

And though he never heard a voice, Paulie knew that the presence of the Lord spoke to him that day when his soul cracked open and threatened to obliterate his faith.

Do you believe Me?

And he knew that, in that moment, he had a choice. He could flee to the strong tower, though he might weep as he did so. Or he could crumple to the ground and refuse to move, refuse to believe.

"I believe," he whispered aloud to the empty room, to the yellow finches twittering outside the half-open window. "I believe, my Savior and my God. I believe that I will see Your goodness in the land of the living."

The tears bubbled up, and he pressed the backs of his hands to his eyes. He knew that it was not wrong for him to grieve over what had been lost to him. Indeed, at that moment, it seemed that he might grieve over it for the rest of his life. And at that holy moment of grief, he knew the comfort of God. He knew that it truly would be *alright*.

CHAPTER TWENTY-THREE

O n the last Saturday in July, Ben knocked on Sam's office door. *I'm done with this place. Done at last.* But, though the thought did bring the hope of escape, it also made the cave in his soul even more unsettled, as if something rumbled there, unsatisfied with what these past two months had brought him.

What? You're not goin' to prison. Don't have to work for old Bousquet anymore. What else do you want?

I want to be free. The thought leapt into Ben's mind without warning. He shook it off, as a dog shakes water from its back after a swim in the lake. *Where had that come from?* He didn't want to know.

"Come in." Sam's voice broke through the thoughts flitting through Ben's brain. Relieved to not have to deal with them, he pushed open the door.

The Doc sat at his desk, some kind of medical supply catalogue in front of him. He looked very much at peace. Ben envied that. Envied it and hated himself for envying it. *What, you wanna be like him now?*

"We're just about finished with the house. Probably finish today, actually," he announced without prelude, not bothering to answer the Doc's smile with one of his own. Why should the Doc get a smile from him?

The Doc didn't look surprised. "You have done good work over there," he commented. "I stopped by a couple of weeks ago, and I was really impressed, Ben."

Why did the awkwardness have to creep into his chest at the praise? Ben pushed through the vulnerability that compliments always brought. "So, once I get that house done, I'm all set, right? There's nothin' else you…"

He trailed off as the Doc picked up his desk keys and opened one of the locked drawers. He lifted a heavy-looking, folded paper from the drawer and held it toward Ben. "This is for you."

Telling himself that he didn't need to feel nervous, Ben reached out a hand and grasped it, the paper smooth against his rough hands. He knew that there was dirt on his skin, too, and that it would probably imprint the creamy material. "What is it?" he mumbled, glancing up at the Doc.

But the older man only smiled, his expression serious and with a – a sense of almost beggary there. Suddenly, Ben's throat closed with nervousness. *Stop it! Just stop it! You can control this, no matter what it is.*

He unfolded the paper. It was a deed – the deed to Papa's house. Coldness blanketed Ben's shoulders, despite the hot breeze blowing through the open window. "What is this?" He held the opened paper lightly, as if it would scald him. His eyes darted up to confront the Doc's.

"It's the deed to your father's house."

Ben rolled his eyes – rolled them as hard as he could. "I know that, Doc. Why're you giving it to me?"

Suddenly, the reality of what he'd said rolled over him. *Giving it to me…* No, please, dear God, if there was a God: *No.*

"Because it's yours, Ben. Your mother and I discussed it before you ever came to Chetham. We never sold that house because we wanted you to have it. It's your inheritance."

Ben flung the paper down on the desk, rage pluming his lungs. "I don't want it! I don't want nothing from you," he heard the words racing from his mouth, as if another said them, as if he was watching a dream. "And I especially don't want that house. If I'd have known that's what you were up to, I'd have burned it to the ground the first day I got here. I'm leavin' Chetham, and you can't stop me. Not with a house, not with nothin'!"

He grabbed for the deed again, anger numbing his fingers. He leaned over the desk, so that he could be right in the good doctor's face. Grasping the paper in both hands, he held it straight in front of him. With the sound of the sparrows chittering in the bushes beyond the window, he tore the deed in two and then again in four. Satisfaction rippled the pool of bitterness in his soul. "There. You can keep your lousy deed. I don't want it." He enunciated each word to make sure that they lodged in the Doc's brain and let the torn pieces of paper float down to the desktop. "Got it, old man? I don't need you. I don't need you to be my father. I don't need you to give me nothin'. I hate you. And I hate that house." The last sentence ground out with such intensity that it left Ben breathless. Embodied before him, he saw, rather than one man, a trinity of men: the Doc, Papa, and God, all blurred together. *All equally rotten in their own way!*

He gave the Doc one final glare, turned on his heels, and stalked out of the office, making sure to slam the door good and hard behind him. The pictures shook on the wall in the foyer.

Looking up, he came face-to-face with Mrs. McCusker, her arms full of clean laundry. He brushed by her, not caring that he'd made her drop her pile of folded clothing, and stormed out the door, rage fueling each step. He'd finish that stupid house today if he had to work twenty-four hours straight and get out of here. He wasn't spending one more night in the Doc's house.

~ ~ ~

Sam sank into his desk chair. He'd thought that he was prepared for any reaction. But he hadn't been. And Ben's – well, it gutted him like a rusty fishing knife. Though there wasn't the closeness he felt with Paulie, obviously, he had long ago acknowledged Ben's sonship in his heart and mind. His own father-heart stood with its door wide open, ready for Ben to walk in and make himself at home.

But it wasn't going to be. *Ben is going to leave Chetham. Permanently.* As the realization crushed him, the beauty of that Wednesday morning lost its shine. The song of the birds outside his windows jarred on his ears. With quiet steps, he moved to shut the windows, despite the heat. His eyes lifted to the clock on the mantle. He was due in his office in an hour.

Right where he stood, he dropped to his knees, bowed his head over them until his forehead touched the floor. *Oh, God above, You are mighty to save. You are strong to deliver. This boy – my son – will You not save Him? Will You not restore what sin has crushed and mutilated?*

Sweat trickling down his neck, Sam went on praying for a long while, pouring out his heart to his own Father. And then, when his vessel of words seemed empty, he stopped and listened to the Silence.

Was something required of him? He opened his wet eyes, unseeing. *Oh, God, if there is anything in the way – anything stopping Your work – remove it. Give me life for Ben, as You promise You will give in Your Word. No matter what it costs…*

Here Sam paused. What could it cost? Was he really willing to pay *anything?*

He set his face like flint. *Yes, Lord, whatever it takes.*

CHAPTER TWENTY-FOUR

B en could hear Paulie hammering away as he stalked up the dry path through the wood. Only one more day to work with that stupid kid – that kid who'd played Grace – that son of the man who'd betrayed Mama all those years ago.

As he came out of the humid dimness of the pine trees, he saw Paulie up on the roof. Ben wondered what on earth he was doing up there. *I wish he'd fall off the roof. It'd serve him right.* No, on second thought, that would be too good for Paulie.

"Whatcha doin'?" he yelled out, cupping his hands around his mouth.

Paulie started. Then, squinting against the strong early morning sunlight, he held up the hammer. "That storm last night knocked a few shingles off. Getting them back on."

Hitching his own tool belt around his waist, Ben hoisted himself up the ladder, two steps at a time. Anger proved itself a wonderful fuel for energy. Finding other places where the shingles had come off in the storm, he set to work putting them back in order. Two minutes later, he hit his thumb with the hammer so hard he looked twice to see if he'd smashed it off. A string of expletives flew out of his lips. Feeling utterly out-of-control, he stripped off his tool belt with one motion and threw it down on the roof. Nails flew in every direction.

176

Paulie stopped hammering and stared at him. Ben's chest heaved. What did he care what this kid thought of him? *I don't care one iota. It's his fault – his old man's fault, at least – that I'm even here.* His teeth ground. Why hadn't the Doc left him to rot in prison? *I would've been happier.* He sucked in the hot air, the scent of dry grass filling his lungs. He hated this house. He eyed Paulie. He hated that kid. That good, helpful, loving kid. Rage poured over him.

"You angry about something, Ben?"

He narrowed his eyes. "Whadaya care?" Like he was about to peel back his armor for Paulie to pick at his tender skin!

Paulie raised himself up from his crouching position and squinted into the sunlight. "I do care about you, Ben."

How unbelievable was that! "Yeah, I'll bet." The laughter snorted out. He couldn't stop it – and didn't want to. Let the boy know how idiotic he sounded. "Nobody cares about me. Not the real me, anyways."

Paulie stayed quiet for a long time. *See, told ya so, kid. Even you can't say you care about the real Ben Picoletti. You only care about the guy you want me to be.*

Then he spoke. "Who's the real Ben Picoletti?"

"Huh?" Ben scrunched his face. "The real Ben?" He snickered without a single drop of joy. "I'd think you'd know by now. That'd be the one and only standing before ya now – the guy who threw up all over your old man, the one who bets at the races, who can swear the spots off a cow, who's gone out with every pretty dame that'll let him. The one who would've killed his papa with his bare hands – if only the goon hadn't up and died first."

"That's not the real Ben, though, is it?"

He bristled. Who did this kid think he was? He let his eyes burn into Paulie's, but a different kind of fire blazed in his stepbrother's gaze.

"Just think about it. When you were growing up, is this who you wanted to become? Is this how you want Cliff to think of you – the same way you thought of your dad?"

The same as Papa. The thought repulsed Ben – filled his mouth with slime. His chest heaved; his arms shook. He knew that it was true. True... and yet he could do nothing about it, could he? As he'd once told Grace, he'd been born in the gutter.

"The way you're living – that's not who you were created to be, Ben. That's not who you have to be. Your choices–"

"What do you know about it, anyway, huh?" The words splattered out of his mouth, bringing a short-lived satisfaction. "My choices? Was it my choice to have a father who went out on my ma? Was it my choice to go to school hungry day after day? Was it my choice to have to do anything – anything at all – just to bring in a little money?" He glowered. "Don't talk to me about choices, kid. Not 'til you've walked in my shoes."

Compassion shone in Paulie's face now. Ben hated him for it. To be pitied – pitied! – by the likes of Paulie Giorgi! "You need to know Jesus, Ben. You're right; I can't ever understand what you've been through. But Jesus does. I know that for sure. And He wants you to come to Him and get the rest you're looking for, Ben. I know that you're weary."

And he was. Oh, he was so tired that the legs of his soul felt ready to fall off. How much longer could he go? At Paulie's words, something foreign stirred in Ben's heart, mingling delight and terror: delight at the promise his words seemed to bring, terror at the vulnerability they required. "What can He do for me?" He heard his own voice come out husky, without permission. To cover up the nakedness of his soul, he sarcastically added, "Can He change the past?" No one could do that. The bitterness of it burned him.

"He can forgive you," Paulie stated simply.

Forgiveness... Despite all the times he'd told himself differently, Ben knew that he needed that. Oh, how he needed that!

"He can help you forgive your father," Paulie added.

Something explosive caught fire in Ben at Paulie's suggestion. Forgive Papa? How dare he even say such a thing? Didn't Paulie know what Papa had done to Mama, to his kids... *to me?*

"Nobody ain't gonna tell me what to do!" Ben spit out. Fury so filled him that he felt out of control of his words, of his body even. His arm stretched back and swung with force he'd not known he had. His fist connected with the underside of Paulie's jaw. The younger man's head snapped up and to the side. He stumbled and fell to his knees, scrambling for a foothold on the shingling while at the same time trying to clutch his jaw with one hand.

"Come on!" Ben heard his voice shout, hoarse as a crow's. "You wanted to fight. Get up and fight."

The coward couldn't even rise to his knees; he just sat there, holding onto his jawbone.

"Put up your dukes, kid! It's showtime." The rage exhilarated Ben, adding the energy of a kite in a full-on storm.

Paulie tried to open his mouth to speak, but the pain must have exceeded his ability. Instead, he twisted his body down like a roly-poly bug.

"Did I break your jaw?" Ben asked, though he seriously doubted it. He'd broken a bone in someone's face in a fight once; he'd felt the snap when the bone fractured beneath his fist. He leaned over Paulie. "I hope I did. Then maybe you'll think twice next time before you tell somebody to do something that you know nothing about!" he snarled, saliva spewing and landing among the tangle of Paulie's sweaty curls.

Paulie mumbled something, rocking against the pain. Good. *I hurt him bad.* The satisfaction slid through Ben's heart. He spat, this time on purpose, straight onto Paulie's head, and turned to go.

He was leaving this crummy town and the memories it held behind him. He would never return. *Never.* They would never hear from him again. "I'm done," he stated aloud, making his way across the roof. Too bad if a little work still remained to be done on the house. Let the dear old Doc do it himself. *I should've burned it when I had the chance back in May.*

Ben had come near the edge of the roof when he tripped – over what, he didn't know – maybe over a stray tool – maybe over his anger. He fell, scrambling for a foothold on the hot shingles. His feet couldn't find anywhere to grip, though. He kept slipping, splinters biting his hands. Fear entered his heart. He was nearly at the peak. If he fell...

Then he felt a hand grab him around the wrist. He darted a glance up. Paulie! The young man had clambered over the roof to him. Paulie's face had already begun to swell where Ben had slugged him, and blood dribbled down the corner of his mouth and chin.

The rage Ben had felt moments before poured over him again and mingled with the fear that had possessed him when he realized that he couldn't maintain a grip. The last thing he wanted right now was a weak, cowardly do-gooder messing up his ability to help himself! *Get away from me!* The thought pulsed through his brain. Ben clutched at the shingling with one hand and flung away Paulie's grasp with the other.

Paulie let out a girlish yelp, and something heavy slid alongside him as the shingling Ben himself held onto gave way. Splintered wood dug into his flesh as he fought for a new grip, every muscle taut.

A half-second later, he found it and took a moment to breathe. That'd been close. He sucked in air and looked to see where his enemy had gone.

But the roof was empty, burning dark in the morning sun. Had the kid hightailed it down the ladder already? *Probably heading home to cry to his daddy.* No matter; by the time Paulie returned with the enraged doctor, Ben would be long gone.

Scuffling into sitting position, he grabbed his tool belt from where it had fallen and flung it off the roof. The Doc had purchased it for him; let him collect it now! He clambered over to the ladder and swung down, making each step more firm than necessary, pressing past the pain in his torn-up hands.

At the bottom, he turned, and his heart nearly stopped.

There, in the dry grass, Paulie lay, one arm awkwardly twisted beneath his body, his head at a funny angle. *Is he dead?* The thought raced through Ben's mind and turned his legs into jellyfish. He stumbled over to the body and fell to his knees beside it. He touched the shoulder, gently at first, then jiggled it a bit harder. "Paulie! Hey, kid. Kid, are you okay?"

Was he even breathing? Ben turned Paulie over and put his hand over the kid's bloody mouth. The worst of his fear fell back just a little when he felt the shallow, unsteady air coming from Paulie's parted lips. Or nose. He couldn't really tell where the air was coming from; but at least it was coming.

For now. The kid was hurt bad. Panic raced through Ben, filling him with a surge of adrenaline. He pushed his arms beneath Paulie's broken form and heaved to his feet. "It's okay, kid. You're gonna be okay," he murmured, his voice shaking out the words compulsively. *You gotta be okay, Paulie!*

The very sky darkened as Ben stumbled back to the Giorgi home, taking the shortcut through the woods. The birds quieted as he pushed past the brambles, heedless of the noise he made with his trampling. *Keep breathing, kid. Keep breathing!* Paulie's head and shoulders hung over Ben's arm on one side; his legs dangled like unwound yo-yos on the other. And all the time, Ben's heart spun and crashed in his chest. What would the Doc do to him when he found out that Ben was responsible? *It's prison for sure this time…*

And looking down at the battered body in his arms, Ben knew that he richly deserved it.

CHAPTER TWENTY-FIVE

S am came home for lunch to find Sarah on her hands and knees in the flower garden out front. She hadn't noticed his presence, and he stood just a few feet behind her, delighting in the sight of his wife. She'd given herself fully over to her task, pulling weeds from among the cone-flowers with her garden-gloved hands and tossing them into a basket kept for that purpose. Her hair had come partially down from its usually-neat French twist; his eyes traveled down the slight streams of gray running through the brunette pieces.

Stepping closer, the strains of a song met Sam's ears. In her slightly-out-of-breath voice, Sarah sang the third verse to one of her favorite hymns, "It Is Well with My Soul." Sam stood, marveling in his wife, soaking in the joy she brought to him. As much as he'd loved this woman in their youth, he couldn't quite believe how much Sarah filled his heart now.

She rose then, picking up her nearly-filled basket, and jumped when she saw him. A smile touched her lips, drawing attention to the dirt smudges filling the entire area between her nose and her mouth.

"Hello," Sam greeted her and stepped forward, cupping the back of her head with his hands. He looked down into her ocean-colored eyes and saw the love and trust she held for him swimming there. Thanksgiving filled him. How had he been given this second chance with Sarah? Why was this grace given to him?

He touched his lips to hers, gladdened when she answered with a kiss of her own before drawing back. "Sam! Mrs. McCusker might be watching." Sarah glanced over her shoulder toward the house.

He winked. "Let her watch."

Sam pulled her back for another peck, but she wriggled away, smiling. "Lunch will be on the table in a few minutes. We should clean up." Sarah drew off her gloves and tucked them into her apron pocket. "We're having cold ham and potato salad," she said, her fingers moving to adjust the pins in her hair.

He leaned toward her and stole another kiss. "Who needs lunch when I have you?" How he loved to tease her!

Sarah's face turned five shades of red successively. "Samuel Giorgi! I think you just said that out loud. What if Taylor heard or... or..."

"Then he'd think his employer was very much in love with Mrs. Giorgi," Samuel informed her. "Which he is, I might add." He leaned close again. "But I will do my utmost to keep my voice lower, madam."

Sarah raised her eyebrows, but he could tell that she was more happy than upset at his indiscretion. They had begun strolling toward the house when a man's yell from the direction of River Avenue stopped Sam in his tracks. His arm dropping from its place around Sarah's waist, he jerked around to find the source of that voice, rank with terror.

He didn't need to wait long. From far down the long driveway, Sam saw and recognized the auburn-haired man, half-running, half-staggering toward them. Ben carried something – or someone – in his arms...

"Help! Doc! Doc, help!"

"Oh, Lord help us," Sarah gasped. Her basket dropped to the ground, spilling weeds around their feet. "It's Paulie, Sam."

His mind took in what she said, but he didn't believe it. *Couldn't* believe it. He stood immobile even as Sarah dashed toward Ben, her apron fluttering out, her sandals kicking up the dust of the driveway. Sam simply could not move. The muscles in his legs became pudding. His eyes stared deathlike at the spectacle of Sarah meeting Ben halfway up the drive and then turning to come back toward him.

And then they approached him. Ben's shirt wore a stain of fresh blood – *Paulie's blood.* Sam feared to look at his son. What would he see? But drop his eyes he must. And when he did, the breath in his lungs crumbled and turned to powder.

"Oh, Lord, Lord, have mercy on us," he heard himself say. Paulie appeared dead: unconscious, his jaw ballooning in his paper-white face, his arms dangling awkwardly at his sides. But that meant nothing, right? *A lot of hurt people appear that way.* He told himself what he told every injured person's family at the hospital. *Unconsciousness is the body's way of trying to handle an injury.*

A severe injury.

"What happened?" Sarah asked. Then, without waiting for an explanation, she directed, "Here, bring him into the house," and began hurrying toward the door.

Sam found his voice. "No, he needs to get to the hospital," he croaked. "Now." Regaining all appearance of restraint but feeling so utterly out-of-control, he took his son's body from Ben. The younger man's arms shook from the effort of carrying the fully-grown Paulie from... "Where did this happen? At the house?"

Ben hesitated, but then gave a single nod. He kept silent but looked as innocent as a criminal locked away for life, breathing heavily through his open mouth.

Sam bent his head over Paulie. Relief washed through him as he felt his son's warm though shuddering breaths exhale from his mouth. If he was breathing, he was, at the very least, alive.

"Taylor!" Sarah called toward the garage for the driver and groundsman.

But Sam already strode toward the car he'd left parked in the driveway. Energy pulsed through him, causing his son's 160-pound body to feel as though it weighed half of that. Each second saved meant another fraction of a chance that Paulie might live. "We don't have time to wait for Taylor. Get in the car, Sarah. Ben, come with us."

~ ~ ~

The Doc leaned forward in the driver's seat. Ben could see the sweat traveling down the sides of his face. None of the windows were even cracked; Mama and the Doc hadn't thought to open them and Ben didn't dare.

Didn't care to, either. Who cared if he sweated to death? The realization that the young man who lay across the backseat with his head in Ben's lap might die – very well might *die* – pounded through his brain. Paulie was innocent. And now he lay broken across Ben's lap. *And I'm the one responsible.* Sweat dripped along his temples. His hand shook like a shot-up horse as he rubbed away the moisture.

The Doc hit a pothole. Ben winced, thinking of the tire, hoping that it hadn't popped. A glance down at Paulie told him that the kid hadn't even felt it. Unfortunately. If he had, it would've meant that he'd regained consciousness. Ben had encountered plenty of head injuries in his time at the racing stables – other injuries too, but the ones in which people slipped into a deep sleep had always brought terror to him. He'd often tried to escape getting involved in helping the injured fellow to the hospital or whatever. Because that kind of injury most often resulted in death.

He swallowed hard. Death. That scared him more than anything else. You couldn't control death... couldn't run away from it... couldn't beat it...

And what lay beyond? After the final race had played out? After you'd spent all your cards? Staring down at Paulie, Ben felt very sure – deep in the marrow of his bones – that there might be a God after all. An angry One. And the thought terrified him.

Unable to look at Paulie's swollen, bloody face any longer, Ben turned his gaze out the window, where the sun rippled across the roadside grass, cheerfully as if a young man wasn't dying in his arms. *Why'd ya try to help me, stupid kid? I would've gotten a grip on that roof without you!*

Up ahead, he saw a policeman seated on a bicycle. He grimaced. The Doc was most certainly going above the speed limit. But as they approached, the policeman looked at the Doc and just waved them on. *He must be used to the Doc speeding toward the hospital for emergencies.*

"How'd this happen, Ben?" From her seat beside the Doc up front, Mama repeated her earlier question, craning her neck toward him.

Ben's mind went blank. What should he say? He couldn't tell the truth. If the kid died, they'd lock him up for murder. He glanced back down at Paulie's face to avoid meeting Mama's searching gaze. Intense discomfort threaded through his spirit. Was it guilt? It'd been so long since he'd felt it. Anger and bitterness had always overpowered that sense, and, by them, he'd justified whatever action he'd taken. But he knew that *this* could not be blamed on Paulie or on Mama or on the Doc. Yeah, maybe Paulie'd got what he had coming to him with the punch to the jaw...

Though, remembering it now, Ben wondered how he could have swung so hard as to fracture the kid's jawbone. Surely, he hadn't meant to. Had he?

The uneasiness grew worse. The body across his legs grew heavy. "Uh," he mumbled. "I guess he fell off the roof."

The Doc's knuckles whitened on the steering wheel. He stayed silent and accelerated.

"What do you mean, you guess?" asked Mama, not harshly. "Didn't you see it?"

"Uh, no." And here, at least, Ben was honest. He *hadn't* seen Paulie's actual fall. "I found him layin' on the ground when, uh, when I came back from town. Went to buy more nails."

Mama closed her eyes and turned back around. "All summer long, they've been working on that place," Ben heard her murmur. "All summer, and now he falls off the roof."

"God knows," the Doc mumbled beside her, his eyes tight on the road.

God knows... Ben knew now what a guilty conscience felt like.

CHAPTER TWENTY-SIX

"Sam, you're too close to this. It's better if—"

"No." Sam grabbed Skippy's shoulder. "I'm coming with you. This is my *son,* Skippy. I *will* be there." There was no way on God's green earth that Skippy Fortunati would keep him from attending his son. *No way.*

Skippy's mouth turned down, dour beneath his salt-and-pepper mustache. "What about your wife?"

"Sarah's fine. She's waiting for our pastor and his wife to arrive." With Ben sitting beside her. He looked as guilty as a dog who'd stolen a bone from the butcher shop.

Skippy hesitated, his eyes searching Sam's face. Sam kept the worry and pain from showing there. It was critical that he remain able to act calmly. If he didn't, Skippy wouldn't let him into the examination room.

"Alright," his colleague relented. "But it doesn't look pretty, Sam. The nurses are cutting off his clothes now. You know, if he fell from a roof, the internal injuries could be significant. And he's not regained consciousness, even once." Skippy licked his lips. "He's in a deep sleep, Sam."

The words sliced into Sam's hearing with the hurt of glass shards against bare skin. He closed his eyes, then opened them to the bright lights of the hospital corridor. "I know that," he replied, voice quiet. *Oh, Lord, if... You know... Help me...* His spirit cried out in half-coherent phrases even as he followed Skippy's hurried feet into the private room.

Light flooded the white room. Several nurses, their competence and seriousness evident in every neat, quick movement, buzzed about the wheeled cot on which Paulie lay. In the few minutes of Sam's consultation with Skippy, they'd scissored away his son's clothing. A thin white sheet covered Paulie's body up to his shoulders. Sam's skin chilled at the sight. *Draw the sheet another foot up and it would be as they do for...*

Sam shut his eyes. Swallowed, feeling his Adam's apple go up and down. No, he wouldn't think that. He opened his eyes. Surely, surely, his firstborn, the only son of his body, would not...

"We're bringing him in for x-rays now, Sam," Skippy spoke at his side. "Then we'll have a better idea of how things stand."

Sam forced himself alert. "Alright." He edged his way to the cot. The nurses made way for him, knowing him by sight, at least, as the eminent Doctor Giorgi.

Whose son is dying.

No. *Oh, dear Father in Heaven, no!* He barely touched Paulie's chilled hand, unwilling to further cause pain or harm by picking it up just to bring a bit of solace to himself. Who knew how much damage carrying him home and then in the car to the hospital had caused already? "We're taking you into x-rays now, son," he informed him, keeping his voice as steady as he could. Better that he know that his father was with him if there was any possibility of his comprehension.

The orderlies stood ready to push the cart toward the door. Sam stepped back and murmured aloud the only Scripture that came to mind when all other thoughts scrambled:

"The Lord is my Shepherd;
I shall not want
He maketh me to lie down in green pastures: He leadeth me beside the still

waters.

He restoreth my soul: He leadeth me in the paths of righteousness for His name's sake."

His jaw hardened. Teeth clenched, he continued:

"Yea, though I walk through the valley of the shadow of death, I will fear no evil:

For Thou art with me; Thy rod and Thy staff they comfort me."

He couldn't continue. His eyes full, Sam bit back the sob that rose in his throat.

~ ~ ~

Sarah wished that the nurse would leave. *It's not as if I'm going to steal the telephone!* Sweat soaked through her gloves as she stared at the receiver and waited for the operator's returning call, which would let her know that the long-distance connection had been made. Through the glass window of the nurse's station, she could see Ben hunched over on the couch, a paper cup of coffee cooling beside him.

Even in her own distress, Sarah's heart went out to her eldest son. He'd seemed so distraught all the way to the hospital that she had finally concluded that the appearance of things must have deceived her: Ben must truly have come to care for Paulie as a brother. She'd never seen him so upset.

She let out a frustrated breath. Nearly ten minutes had passed since she'd requested the connection. The operator was taking a long time to call her back. Her heart sank, knowing that this could mean that the operator was having trouble getting ahold of Grace. *Answer. Oh, let one of the girls answer the telephone!*

~ ~ ~

Grace bounded down the stairs, hoping to get to the telephone before it stopped ringing. She'd been in the middle of taking down her pin-curls when she'd heard its first trill.

Reaching the entryway, she snatched up the receiver. "Hello?"

"Chetham Memorial Hospital, Chetham, Rhode Island calling."

Surprise turned to fear at the operator's words. Chetham Hospital? Though Dad worked part-time at the hospital, her parents had never called her from there. *Something must be wrong...*

Her stomach clenching, she accepted the call and waited for the operator to let Mama – or Dad – whichever was calling – know that they'd been connected.

"Grace, is that you?"

She could hear the worry stretching Mama's voice thin. Grace swallowed hard. "Yes, it's me, Mama."

Silence held for just a moment, and then she heard Mama release a shuddering breath. "There's been an accident."

CHAPTER TWENTY-SEVEN

In ten minutes, she had her bag packed. At least Grace thought she had everything she needed in it. She'd done the packing automatically, her mind numb, her heart pulsing hard with prayer. Mama's words kept running in circles in her brain. *Paulie's hurt... The doctors say it doesn't look good... I thought that you should come...*

And she had heard, too, the thing that Mama was afraid to say, the shadow that lurked behind her words: Paulie might not make it. Mama was afraid that Paulie was going to die.

Grace couldn't entertain that thought. When it pressed itself too hard into the edges of her consciousness, the horror cut off her breathing. Oh, not because she feared for Paulie. He would live better in the hands of the Lord Jesus; she knew that.

No, because she couldn't imagine her own life without Paulie in it, somehow, someway. Even just as a stepbrother. Even just as Betty Cloud's husband.

She left a note for her summer roommate, explaining the situation, and lugged her suitcase downstairs. After she'd called for a taxi, Grace realized that needed to explain the situation to Kirk. He deserved to know why she'd left early and where she could be reached. She turned back to the telephone and called the school office, glad that no operator was necessary for the across-town call.

The part-time secretary answered on the second ring. "Hello. Helen Higgins School."

"Hello, Sandy." Grace didn't even attempt to sound normal. "May I speak with Kirk – uh, Mr. Haverland, please?" Though she knew that some of the staff and volunteers suspected that she and Kirk had formed a strong attachment, it was not officially public knowledge. Something in Grace's heart wanted to keep it that way as long as she could. Making it public seemed to make it more… final – seemed to lock the door labeled *Paulie* forever.

"I think Mr. Haverland might have left already. He was headed…" Sandy broke off. "Oh, no, no. I was wrong. Here he comes right now. I know he'll want to take *your* call." Her voice held a teasing tone. Grace grimaced but didn't reply.

Grace heard a scuffle as Sandy put the receiver down on her desk. "Yoo-hoo, Mr. Haverland. Miss Picoletti is on the telephone for you."

Another scuffle, and then Kirk's voice came over the wire. "Hello, Gra – er, Miss Picoletti?"

Grace could imagine the inward giggling in which Sandy currently must be indulging, but that mattered little now. Who cared if a secretary laughed when Paulie lay unconscious in a hospital bed? "Yes, it's me," she answered. "Listen, Kirk. I have to speak quickly. My taxi will be here any moment now." She took a breath to organize her thoughts a bit.

"Taxi? Where are you off to?"

"Home. Back to Rhode Island." The words came out in gasps. "My stepbrother has been in a terrible accident. He's not… not…" *He's not expected to live.* As the thought slithered through her mind, Grace couldn't hold back a choking sob. She clapped her hand over her mouth to stifle any further outbursts. She didn't want Kirk to know how great her distress was at the news of Paulie's accident. Why, she didn't understand. Kirk was her fiancé, nearly. Why should it matter if he knew that this upset her? Shouldn't she want his comforting arm around her shoulders? Regardless of the *should,* though, she knew that she didn't. Not now. Not when Paulie was...

Kirk had heard the sob, however, as well as the distress in every syllable she'd spoken. "Grace! Grace, listen to me. I'm coming over right now. Don't leave with that taxi yet."

She heard the horn toot in front of the dorm. "It's here, Kirk. The taxi's here. I've gotta go. I'm going to try to catch a train."

"Which one?"

"I don't know yet. Any train. I have to get home." She paused to suck in a breath. "Can you find coverage for my classes for the rest of the summer?" She asked merely as a formality. Even if he couldn't find anyone to take over for her, Grace was still going to Rhode Island. Nothing on God's green earth was going to stop her.

"Yes, yes, of course. Don't worry about all that."

Kirk lapsed into silence for a moment. Grace opened her mouth to tell him she needed to go when he spoke again. "Grace, I'm coming with you."

"What?" Surprise squashed any other emotion. "But you have classes..."

"There's only one week left before summer school ends. The other teachers can handle a few days without me. I need to be with you, Grace. With your stepbrother." He paused. "What's his name again?"

She swallowed hard. "Paulie." At the feel of his name on her lips, the dam holding back the reservoir of her tears broke. Against her will, her face crumpled and her hand refused to hold the receiver to her ear any longer. She hugged it against her shaking chest as the tears rolled down her cheeks.

"Grace?"

Putting the receiver back to her ear, she opened her mouth and forced her tongue to work. "Yes?" she gasped.

"I'll be over in a half-hour. We can drive down. Tell the taxi you don't need him."

"Drive? But I can take the train. You don't need to trouble yourself–"

"Grace, let me do this for you. I love you." Kirk's earnest voice came to her ears. But it could not touch her grief.

The taxi gave a longer blast. *He wants me to tell him that I love him, too.* But in the face of Paulie's injury, Grace could not do it. She drew a breath that shuddered her shoulders and forced the receiver back to her ear, the speaker back to her mouth. "Alright. I'll tell the taxi driver," she managed before hanging up.

~ ~ ~

How long they'd been sitting, waiting for news, Ben didn't know. What he did know was that the guilt that had clenched his stomach earlier had spread, shadowing his every thought and movement with the understanding that Paulie – that innocent guy – lay broken on a hospital bed because of him. *For* him, in a way. Paulie had been trying to reach Ben, help *him* avoid falling off the roof when Ben had flung aside his help... throwing Paulie down in his stead.

Across from him, Mama sat, the small waiting room chair hugging her plump body. She held a little book open on her lap, the title saying something about God's promises, but she wasn't reading it. Her eyes stared ahead of her, barely blinking, her lips moving slightly.

"Mama," Ben whispered. They were alone in the room, but it still didn't seem right to speak aloud in a place where people might be dying ten steps down the hallway.

She didn't respond.

Tentatively, Ben stretched out his hand and laid it on hers. "You okay, Mama?"

Mama blinked, as if coming out of a trance or something, and gave him a weak smile. "Yeah, I'm fine, Ben. I was just praying."

Praying... Something he should've probably done long ago. But it was way too late for Ben now, wasn't it? Paulie lay busted up on an x-ray or an operating table, probably too far gone for them to do anything. And Paulie's accident was just one thing in the long line of Ben's offenses, wasn't it?

Protest welled up in his heart. *I've tried to do the best I could in life, haven't I?*

But his best wasn't good enough. Not good enough to even make him return good-for-good.

Why did I shove the kid? Why?

Because he'd hated him. *I hated Paulie because he does right and I don't. Because I'm filled up with bitterness... and he's not. Because he has... forgiveness for his sins... and peace... and I don't. And I can't while I keep on the path I want to go.*

Damnation settled into every crevice of Ben's soul as he sat glued to his seat in the waiting room, beneath the searching lights. And God would be right to damn him. Ben knew it now. So would the Doc, for Ben killing his only son. *If he knew...*

But maybe it would be better if the Doc did know. Maybe it would be better if Ben took the punishment he deserved – maybe it would provide a salve for his conscience – the conscience that would give him no relief. Going to prison for manslaughter – maybe that would atone at least for *this...*

The door opened. The Doc came in slowly, his surgical coat unbuttoned. *He must have been with them when they operated. I don't know if I could've done that, if I was him.*

Ben and Mama rose, both waiting intently to hear what news he brought. The Doc's face wore lines of fatigue, deepened by worry. "Well," he said after a moment. "It's not looking good. His jaw is fractured; he's broken several ribs and one arm. There was some internal bleeding; if he hemorrhages..." He trailed off, his Adam's apple bobbing with the emotion he suppressed.

Mama slipped both arms around the Doc's waist. Ben looked away, discomfort tensing his limbs. "I'm praying," Ben heard her murmur in the Doc's ear.

"Thanks." It came out as a choke. The Doc's Adam's-apple bobbed. "Is Grace coming?"

Mama nodded. "Tonight, hopefully. The Clouds will be here soon. And Geoff and Emmeline will keep Cliff overnight."

"Good." The Doc raked his fingers through his graying waves. "Skippy keeps saying that he wonders how Paulie broke his jaw like that, falling from the roof. Seemed more like a boxing injury, he said. Still, nobody knows how far he fell. He could've hit the side of the chimney or…" The Doc trailed off.

The pain stood naked on the older man's face. Ben turned away, desperate to escape from the shadow of it. How this man loved his son! *And I took him from him.* The guilt rose, a hurricane wave on the beach of Ben's soul.

"I did it." He realized only after he'd spoken that he'd gone through with it. "I killed him."

Mama swiveled from her place at the Doc's side. The surprise in her eyes mingled with sorrow, and the disappointment there knifed Ben. *Rightly so.* "What?" she said, as if she couldn't have heard him right.

"I did it." He couldn't look straight at the Doc now, though God knew that's who he'd offended. He met Mama's eyes instead. "I punched him in the jaw. So hard that… Well, that's how it broke. I wanted to kill him. Then I slipped on a loose shingle or somethin'. Started to fall. He – He grabbed me. Tried to help me, though I'd just…" Ben let out a puffing laugh, thinking of the horrible absurdity of it all. "I flung him off the roof. I didn't think about killing him then – not just then, you know – I wanted to hurt him was all. But then I found him on the ground…" Remembering it forced his eyes closed. *As if closing them could scrap what I seen!*

Silence fell over the room with the sudden coldness of a winter's night. He was shut out. As it should be. He knew what came next. A call to the police. Handcuffs. Jail.

All of it richly deserved – and more. For Paulie would never see the light of day again. From the look on the Doc's face a few minutes ago, Ben knew that by this time tomorrow, Paulie would be on a shelf in the hospital morgue.

"I'm sorry. I'm so, so sorry." The apology choked out. Worthless words. Only words. No matter how much Ben might mean them. A man's son – a man's righteous son – lay dying by Ben's hand. Nothing could settle this situation in the right. Nothing but just punishment dealt by the Doc. He couldn't meet the man's eyes – couldn't bear to see the hate that must swirl there now. *I've done this.*

But the shock came when warm arms encircled him, drawing him into a firm embrace. Ben felt his head pressed against the Doc's white-coated shoulder. Instinctively, he tensed. But then, he heard the man speak, in a strong but broken voice. "You're my son, Ben. All is forgiven. *All* is forgiven," he repeated, as if to make sure that Ben had received the unbelievable message. He released him but still held Ben at arms' length, eyes meeting eyes.

And Ben saw there that it was true. "But, why?" he asked. "Why would you forgive me? You know what I've done to you – to him. Why would you still call me your son?"

The Doc spoke to Mama, though he kept his gaze on Ben. "Sarah, would you go and sit with Paulie? He's in room 218, down the hall to the left. I don't like to leave him alone so long."

Mama slipped out, the door clicking shut behind her. Through his tears, Doctor Giorgi smiled – a smile rooted in joy. "Ben, sit with me. Let me tell you how Jesus Christ forgave me."

And there, in the hospital waiting room, with his son Paulie physically dying, another son was born spiritually to Doctor Giorgi: Ben Picoletti, who was given the right to become a child of the living God.

CHAPTER TWENTY-EIGHT

Sarah opened the taxi cab's door before its wheels stopped spinning. "Please wait for me. I'll only be a few minutes," she requested as she slid from the backseat. "I'll pay extra."

"Okay, lady," the driver replied, apparently only too happy to collect money for idling in her driveway.

In the midsummer twilight, she dashed up to the front door of their home with a speed she'd not exercised in more than a decade, slowing down only when she nearly lost her shoe. She stopped and pulled them both off. She had to hurry – had to get back to the hospital. She hoped that Grace would arrive any time now, and Sarah wanted to be there to meet her when she did. The Lord knew that Ben wasn't fit to greet his sister by himself; she'd left him still weeping intermittently but assuring her that he would be alright. Sam had returned to Paulie's bedside, of course.

Mentally, she mapped out exactly where she needed to head toward in the house. Ben's room – to grab a fresh set of clothes to replace his blood-stained ones. Her and Sam's bedroom – to find another shirt for her husband as well. *And more sensible shoes for me.*

In her bedroom, she found an overnight bag into which she tucked the clothing. Within five minutes, she was heading toward the front door again, having seen neither Mrs. McCusker nor Taylor.

Maybe I should bring one of Tabitha's breads. Just in case someone gets hungry. The cook, who had turned part-time, didn't work on Tuesdays, but she usually left a few quick breads on the counter to help cover her day-off.

Leaving the overnight bag with her shoes beside the door, Sarah hurried toward the kitchen, her still-bare feet silent. She rounded the corner and entered the brightly-lit room without pausing.

Then she saw Mrs. McCusker. In the split-second before the older woman reacted to Sarah's entrance, Sarah noticed that the housekeeper held one of the burner-covers off the lit stove. In her other hand, she held a square envelope. *She's going to burn that.* The thought flitted through Sarah's mind just as Mrs. McCusker jerked around to face her, apparently having heard someone come into the room.

At the sight of Sarah, the gray-haired woman froze. Fear mixed with bald anger on her narrow face. The next moment, she dropped the lid back on the stove. Straightening her shoulders, Mrs. McCusker moved to push past Sarah. *The kind of attitude she hasn't taken toward me in a long time.*

Sarah's veins throbbed with nervous excitement. "What are you doing?" she heard herself ask. She blocked the doorway with her body, not sure what she'd do if the housekeeper insisted on getting by. She couldn't force the woman to tell her what she was hiding, could she? *She's in my house. In my employ. I have a right to know what she was going to burn in my stove, don't I?*

The housekeeper avoided Sarah's eyes but kept her chin pertly raised. "I'm not sure what you mean, madam. I was just preparing the stove – going to make myself a little supper."

Sarah licked her lips. *God, give me guidance.* "Then what is in your hand?"

The woman's hand tightened on the envelope. Mouth twitching, she shook her head as if in disdain. "What? Oh, this. This is only something I needed to dispose of."

A boldness came over Sarah – bringing with it a calm that she knew came from God above. "Then let me throw it away for you."

"What?" Mrs. McCusker repeated. Her swallow went down hard. Her skin appeared to drain of what little color she had.

Sarah held out her numb hand. "Give me the envelope, please. I will take care of it."

The housekeeper met Sarah's gaze with eyes like sharpened steak knives, and Sarah saw the revulsion and scorn the woman had held for her – and hidden well – emerge hungrily again after a two-year hibernation. A few heartbeats of silence passed, accompanied only by the faint *drip-drip* of a faucet not properly turned off in the bathroom down the hall.

Sarah wanted to drop her hand back down to her side and let Mrs. McCusker pass – let things continue as they always had. But she knew that the housekeeper was testing her with this silence; if Sarah backed down now, she would not regain her authority again with the woman. *And who knows what she is hiding?*

Sarah kept her hand out, waiting to receive the envelope.

At last, Mrs. McCusker placed the square packet in her hand.

"Thank you," Sarah acknowledged, expecting the woman to leave the kitchen. When Mrs. McCusker didn't move, standing there with all the rigidity of Lot's wife, Sarah let her gaze run down to the envelope. Her heart rose into her throat at what she read.

It was addressed to Grace at school. Paulie's name and address marked the upper-left-hand corner. A stamp – not processed yet by the post office – clung to the upper-right.

Sarah didn't understand. Didn't want to understand. The puzzle pieces, though, began to swarm in her mind: Grace not wanting to return for the summer; Paulie's increased pensiveness over the past academic year; the few times her daughter had asked after Paulie during telephone conversations, as if she hadn't heard from him personally....

"You were going to throw this into the stove," she voiced the realization aloud. The housekeeper was the one in charge of getting the mail to the post-office.

Mrs. McCusker hesitated just a fraction of a second before giving the smallest nod of her head. Pride bloomed on her thin face as she admitted to her intention.

Slow anger kindled in Sarah's blood. "Have you – Have you done this before?" Even as she asked the question, Sarah knew the answer: *Yes.*

With the acidity of an unrepentant man about to be hung, Mrs. McCusker smiled. "Oh, yes, madam. Every time he wrote to her this year, in fact."

Sarah's throat dried. "Every time?" she repeated. "Why?" The housekeeper had always disliked Sarah; from Sarah's first day as Sam's wife, Mrs. McCusker had thought Sarah an upstart who didn't deserve to be her beloved employer's wife. As long as the housekeeper showed respect, Sarah had let that pass. But Paulie? Why should Mrs. McCusker hurt him? Of all people, Paulie was her treasure.

"Why? To keep him from your daughter, of course." Mrs. McCusker narrowed her eyes as if Sarah was daft. "That seemed to be the only way to do it – seeing as the doctor's eyes have been blinded. He thinks the world of her, the doctor does, as you well know." She said it as if Grace had committed a crime… and as if Sam should be committed to Butler Hospital for the Insane as a result of his regard for her. "The good Lord knows that *he* would do nothing to stop them from marrying. Nothing to stop his only son from stooping so low."

So you took it into your own hands to make sure it didn't happen. Remaining silent for a long moment, Sarah prayed that God would pour His wisdom through her. He knew for sure that she could hardly see through the red tide of fury that washed over her.

With a clarity outside her own ability, Sarah took a deep breath spiritually. "Gather your things and leave, Mrs. McCusker. There's a taxi outside. He will take you wherever you need to go."

"What?" Incredulity seeped through the pride masking the housekeeper's face. "You can't do that."

Sarah swallowed. "I am doing it. As of this minute, you are t-t-ter…" Why did the word have to escape her now?

The stiff smile that had stayed on Mrs. McCusker's face throughout the exchange curled into a sneer. "I believe that the word you're searching for is *terminated*, madam. Yet, just as you can't remember how to pronounce it, you also do not have the power to enact it." She drew her gray-clad shoulders up with the rigidity of a drill sergeant. "Only Doctor Giorgi has the ability to terminate me."

Did she speak the truth? Sarah paused, licked her lips, and forged ahead, knowing that there was no way back. "I am his wife," she stated, inwardly cringing at the shake in her voice, "and I'm telling you that your time here is finished. Get your things and go."

The housekeeper's chin rose another fraction. "And if I refuse? If I wish to wait to appeal your decision with the doctor himself?"

Here Sarah was sure of herself… and of Sam. So much so that she nearly laughed. "Mrs. McCusker, I'm showing you mercy. God knows we all need it, and I've surely had my fair share of it over the years. But I can't say what the doctor will do when he finds out that you've tried your best to damage Paulie's happiness… and Grace's… by stealing and lying for the past year. So, if I were you, I'd hurry up out of here *before* my husband finds out what you've done. It would be a shame to get the police involved, you know."

At the word *police*, some of the starch fell out of Mrs. McCusker. Indecision flitted over her face for just a moment before she gave a fractured nod. "I'll be ready to go in an hour," she bit out.

Sarah watched as, shoulders buckled, the older woman moved from the kitchen with quiet steps. She waited until she heard footsteps ascending the staircase toward the housekeeper's suite on the third floor before she let the breath whoosh out of her lungs. "Thank You, Lord," she murmured as she walked on shaky legs toward the stove. She knew that she needed to stay until Mrs. McCusker left, and she might as well have a cup of tea while she did so. *Maybe the taxi driver would like some, too. Goodness knows, he'll be waiting longer than expected now!*

CHAPTER TWENTY-NINE

"Y ou really didn't need to come with me." As she and Kirk passed through the glass doors of the hospital, Grace heard the words leave her mouth for perhaps the fourth time since they'd left Crocksville, eight hours ago. In her heart, she meant, *I really wish you hadn't come with me.* She yearned to be alone to grieve Paulie in all the ways she needed to do it. But Grace knew that she couldn't tell Kirk that. *He wouldn't understand.*

Or he would. And that might be worse.

At the front desk, Kirk took over, asking for directions to Paulie Giorgi's room.

The receptionist rubbed tired wrinkles from her forehead as she looked through her files. "Ah, Paulie Giorgi. That's Doctor Giorgi's son, isn't it? Heard he came in here hurt badly." She grimaced as she said it, and Grace wondered just how much the receptionist had heard.

Shuffling through the files, she found the one belonging to Paulie's case quickly. "Here it is. But he's not being permitted visitors. Family only." She peered over her small reading glasses.

"I'm his stepsister." Thankful now for the title, despite it being the only claim she had to him, Grace kept her eyes locked with those of the receptionist. This woman would not prevent her from seeing

Paulie. *Her* Paulie. "And this is my fiancé." Or he would be, as soon as Dad gave the okay.

The receptionist smiled at Kirk. Who could help smiling at Kirk, with his Hollywood-handsome face and sparkling eyes? "You can go ahead," she relented. "It's room 218 on the second floor. But," she added, looking at Kirk, "you'll have to stay in the waiting room. Only family is allowed into the patient's room." She turned her gaze to Grace, the smile turning sympathetic. "Your stepbrother is very badly injured."

Grace swallowed the cold lump of saliva that had risen in her throat. "Thank you," she managed, her hands dropping off the edge of the reception desk.

"Come along, sweetheart." His hand on her back, Kirk urged her toward the staircase that curved up to the second floor.

Resentment at his presence flexed in Grace's spirit again, but she refused to let it gain strength. *He has every right to be here. His motives are right. He wants to support me. He wants to be part of my family. He's my fiancé.*

She mounted the wide marble steps at his side. He kept his arm around her waist as they climbed. She resisted the desire to twist away, run up the staircase ahead of him, and rush straight to Paulie's side. *I don't want you here, Kirk. Oh, why couldn't I have gone through this alone?*

For a split second, she closed her eyes. This wasn't about her, though, was it? She was here to comfort Mama and Dad, to give stability to Cliff if he needed it. And to say goodbye to Paulie, almost certainly.

Help me, Lord. Help me to do Your will, not my own.

They arrived at the top of the stairs, and the entrance to the second-floor opened its gaping, white mouth. Without hesitating, Grace walked through, unable to keep herself right by Kirk's side. He hastened his steps but dropped his hand from its place on her back. Their shoes clicked on the well-cleaned floor. At nearly nine o'clock, formal visiting hours had ended, and the hospital halls drowsed, the only sound coming from the occasional murmurs of a doctor or nurse from within the rooms, the groan of a patient, or the hum of a softly-played radio.

Grace tracked the room numbers. 212. 214. 216...

"Here it is." Kirk stopped at the door crested with two-one-eight. He hesitated. "Are you sure I can't come in with you?"

She shook her head violently. Her teeth had begun to chatter ever-so-slightly; her fingers felt cool as milk fresh from the dairy truck. "No, I'll be fine. Besides, it's family only. And Dad and Mama are probably in there. Ben, too." For the first time since Mama had called, her thoughts traveled to her eldest brother. Mama had said that Ben had been the one to bring Paulie home.

Kirk's eyes sought hers. She forced a smile to convince him that everything was just peachy. "If you're sure." He drew her hand up to meet his lips. "I'll find the waiting room."

She wasn't able to bring herself to speak again. Nodding, she turned and eased open the door. It made no sound as it turned on well-oiled hinges, and she slipped into the dimly-lit room.

She blinked a few times as her vision adjusted to the lamplight. The scent of ammonia, bleach, and other chemicals she couldn't identify but knew as belonging to a hospital lingered in the air. A sink stood to her left. She stepped past it slowly, toward the thick curtain that partially concealed the bed and the area immediately surrounding it. Mama and Dad – maybe Ben, too – would sit within that curtain, perhaps lovingly stroking Paulie's hand or silently praying...

Wait. Someone sang, very softly, in a whisper nearly. A woman's voice. *Not Mama.* Her thoughts flashed to Mrs. Kinner, but no, just as quickly she discarded that possibility. She knew Mrs. Kinner's voice as well as Mama's; she'd heard her sing so many times with her piano over the past few years. An icy stream froze her heart as she realized the truth.

On her tiptoes, Grace took the final steps toward the curtain. The tears rose and brimmed in her eyes, hot and full, as she gazed at the scene.

Betty Cloud, her fluffy nutmeg curls tied back with a green ribbon, sat with her back to Grace. Paulie lay unconscious and heavily bandaged beneath the soft lamplight. An I.V. stood sentinel at his side, dripping fluid into his broken body. *Oh, Paulie.*

Why was Betty here? The receptionist had said that the hospital was permitting only *family*. Betty wasn't...

She was engaged to Paulie, then. She must be. The hospital wouldn't have allowed Betty into his room if she wasn't. Grace couldn't stop the tears from overflowing, running down her cheeks in rills, as she watched another girl do what she wished with all her heart she could do: comfort Paulie in his last hour.

Where's Mama? And Dad? And Ben? Had they all just left him? Left him to Betty Cloud?

She couldn't stay. Couldn't trust herself to maintain her composure. Though she'd known that Betty and Paulie were close from Cliff's letters, to see their relationship in person and in this context taxed Grace's self-possession beyond ability. *And he's going to die.* She pressed a flattened palm against her mouth, not minding that her lipstick must be staining her glove.

Turning, Grace tiptoed out, careful lest her heels betray her presence. She nearly collapsed against the hallway side of the door and sucked in lungfuls of air. *Mama. Mama, where are you?*

She glanced around, half-bewildered by the brighter lights of the hall, wiping tears from her eyes. Where was the waiting area? At least Kirk would sit waiting for her there, his arms open to hold her close. She felt at a loss for direction until a nurse swept toward her from the other end, her arms full of precisely-folded linens.

"Can I help you, miss? Visiting hours are over, you know." The squint-eyed older woman came to an abrupt halt before Grace.

"Uh, yes. I need to find the waiting room. I'm looking for my mother. And for my dad. He's Doctor Giorgi."

The nurse visibly relaxed. "You're Doctor Giorgi's daughter?"

"Yes." Weariness pulled at Grace's shoulders.

"Follow me. I'll bring you to the waiting room." With the same suddenness with which she'd stopped, the nurse turned on her heel and strode away down the bleached corridor.

Grace scurried to keep up with her. She was glad when the woman stopped at a door only a few yards away. "In here." The nurse pushed the door open but didn't enter.

"Thanks," Grace managed. She paused before walking over the threshold, squeezing her eyelids with her fingertips in a futile effort to stop crying. Another deep breath filled her chest.

The small waiting room wore the same stark-white as the rest of the hospital. Kirk rose as soon as she walked into the room, his arms opening to receive her in a loving hug. But, even as her fiancé's arms encircled her, Grace's attention jumped toward Ben, who had also stood when she'd entered but hadn't approached. *My brother.*

The last time she'd seen him, he'd worn the leftovers of his own alcohol-induced vomit, Paulie's blood across his knuckles, and an expression that held the bitterness of three-day-old coffee. That'd been two years ago.

Now, her eyes still saw a rough-looking fellow, with dried blood splattered across his shirt, and yet... yet something had changed. A light had dawned on his darkly-tanned face. He held an open book in his hands. *A Bible.* One of the hospital Bibles, left in the waiting room for anxious relatives of the sick. "Ben."

She left the shelter of Kirk's embrace and fell into her brother's, feeling his brawny forearms wrap around her body with the fierceness of grief and pain. She leaned her face into his chest, unmindful of the sweaty stench. Thankfulness for him threatened to burst her heart.

His hand stroked her hair, hesitantly at first, then more surely. She knew that he was trying to soothe her. After a few moments, she eased back, her gaze going from the bloodstains on his shirt to his face. She gulped. "Did... Did you find him?" How awful for Ben!

Pain swept across Ben's face. "I... Yeah." He licked his sun-chapped lips. "It's a long story, Canary. One I gotta tell ya, but not now."

Her stomach clenched. She met his eyes with her own and saw

peace mingling with the sorrow there. Her hand rose to touch his cheek. "Alright."

"I met your fiancé." Ben shifted to take Kirk into their conversation.

"Oh. Good." Grace had forgotten that he was present. Wiping her cheeks again, she turned toward him. "I... I went to Paulie's room. He wasn't conscious. And... And someone else was there." She darted a glance toward Ben.

He nodded. "Yeah. Betty Cloud's sittin' with him."

"Where's Mama? And Dad?" The questions tumbled out, snarled with the indignation that rose again at the mention of Betty. Even if she was his fiancé, they shouldn't just up and leave him in her care!

"The Doc – I mean, Sam – went to talk to some other docs about Paulie's x-rays or somethin'. And Mama went home just to grab some fresh duds for me and the – uh, Sam." He hesitated. "I would've gone in and sat with Paulie, Grace, but, honestly, I was a mess for a while here. I was afraid I'd blub all over him."

She could see that. His face had swollen like a melon; his eyes strained with redness. "It's okay. Don't worry about it. He's fine with Betty."

A dull throb took over her spirit. She turned to Kirk. "I need to go home. There's nothing I can do here right now." Home to Mama. Mama would comfort her, would tell her the tale of Betty and Paulie and make it seem quite right, would make her understand that God would work it out in the end. *I can't face Betty Cloud, the grieving fiancée, alone, without Mama.*

Surprise entered Kirk's eyes, but he nodded without questioning Grace. "Alright."

CHAPTER THIRTY

She's here. My Grace is home. At the sound of a car door slamming shut, Sarah rose from her chair beside the unlit fireplace. Thank goodness that Mrs. McCusker had just left. Sarah didn't want to consider whether the former employee would have found more choice words to spew at her daughter.

Hurrying into the entryway, Sarah couldn't wait for Grace to open the door. Her fingers shook as she turned the knob and flung wide the door. There, just coming up the front steps, Grace climbed with the weariness of an old woman. At her side... *That must be Kirk Haverland. The one who wrote to Sam.* Sarah tried not to grimace. Well, at least, she couldn't fault the young man with being inattentive. He strode right at Grace's side, one hand to her elbow as a support and the other carrying her small suitcase. Behind him, she saw what must be his own car. So he'd driven them all the way from Lake Champlain.

When Sarah opened the door, Grace looked up. Relief flooded her daughter's tired face. "Mama," she said. Her steps quickening, she climbed the steps ahead of her escort. She threw her arms around Sarah without hesitation. Sarah forced herself to unstiffen and hug her daughter back, relishing in the closer relationship God had given them in recent years.

Grace pulled back after a moment. "How did you know I'd come here?"

She touched her daughter's face, shadowed in the deep evening. "I called the hospital, and your brother told me you'd left for home." Sarah didn't bother to add that she'd needed to stay to ensure Mrs. McCusker's uneventful departure. The housekeeper had only left moments before Grace had arrived.

Taking a deep breath, Sarah looked from her daughter to the man. "And you're Mr. Haverland, I'd guess?" She tried hard to keep the coolness she felt toward him out of her voice. After all, it was hardly Mr. Haverland's fault that Mrs. McCusker had succeeded in her plotting. He seemed like a nice young fellow, after all. Though he wasn't Paulie, of course...

"Yes." The golden-haired man gave her a respectful nod. "I'm Kirk Haverland, ma'am. Please, call me Kirk. I'm very glad to meet you."

Sarah nodded, unable to reply in kind. She turned and led the way into the house. "I'm headed back to the hospital soon. I just needed to, uh, take care of some things here." The unopened letter weighed heavily in her dress pocket. Should she tell Grace about it? Or would it be better to wait – to see what happened with Paulie? Perhaps she should talk to Sam – see what he thought about it all before she set any potential dominoes into motion. Covering her worry with a tight smile, she faced the couple again, beneath the entryway chandelier. "Would you two like to return to the hospital with me?"

"I don't think so, Mama. Not tonight." Grace's voice held the flatness of a bottle of Coca-Cola, opened three weeks past. "I saw him already. Betty Cloud... seems to be taking good care of him."

Sarah eyed her daughter. No bitterness had tinged her words. *Just the loss of hope*. There was a difference between bitterness and hopelessness; Sarah knew that oh-so-well. Only those unacquainted with grief believed them to be the same. She chose her own next words carefully. "Reverend and Mrs. Cloud came earlier in the evening with Betty, but then word came that Mr. Tascotti had another heart attack. He'd been rushed to the hospital as well. The Clouds felt that they had to go to him."

"Quite understandable," Kirk voiced.

She looked at Kirk. His face held deep concern. "Mr. Tascotti has no immediate family in the area. He's a member of our church, you see," she explained to Kirk before turning her attention back to Grace. "I ran home to find a change of clothes for the men, and I wanted your father to feel free to leave the room if he needed to speak with the other doctors about Paulie's treatment while I was gone. Ben – Well, it wasn't possible to leave Ben with Paulie right then. So Betty volunteered to sit with him if your father couldn't."

"And she's his fiancé after all," Grace stated in a thin tone. "Of course she should be with him."

With the clarity that dawn brings, Sarah finally understood. "His fiancé? Where would you get an idea like that?"

Confusion masked Grace's face. "Well, she's in his room, and the hospital said that only family were permitted. Besides, Cliff wrote to me..."

Sarah shook her head. "Grace, first of all, your father is Doctor Giorgi. The hospital isn't going to tell him who is and isn't going into his son's room. Second, I don't know what in the world your little brother wrote to you, but Paulie and Betty Cloud are most definitely *not* engaged."

Shock covered her daughter's face. "But I thought..." Her eyes went to Kirk, who stood as if curious why all this mattered. But Sarah saw the fear in her daughter's gaze and recognized it. *It's the fear that covers you when you realize what you have done out of unbelief.*

The grandfather clock bonged in the dining room. Ten o'clock. Her pocket felt as though it carried a chunk of lead. Sarah made her decision. *If I were her, I would want to know.* "Grace, I have to get back to the hospital soon. But before I do, I need to speak with you."

Kirk smiled, openness in his expression. His arm went around Grace's waist, and she stiffened. He didn't seem to notice. "Certainly,

Mrs. Giorgi. Where shall we sit?"

Well, there was no way around it when a man couldn't take a hint. "Alone," Sarah specified. "I need to speak with my daughter alone, Mr. Haverland." She wouldn't call this intruder by his first name – as if he'd already won his prize!

Kirk hesitated. "Certainly," he repeated after a moment. He looked down at Grace, but she didn't return his gaze. Her eyes stayed locked on Sarah's.

"We'll just be a few minutes." Sarah moved toward the staircase. There was no way she was going to have anyone hearing this but Grace. Halfway up the stairs, she admitted to herself that she should at least provide the man with a place to sit while he waited. "If you'd like, you can wait for us in the sitting room."

~ ~ ~

"I didn't open it." Mama held out the envelope, creased and dirtied by Mrs. McCusker's handling. *As if it was worthless.* When it contained a treasure beyond vocal expression.

Taking the letter, Grace swallowed hard. *Help me to forgive that woman, Lord.* Good thing that the housekeeper had left; Grace didn't know what she would've said to her if she'd stayed longer. But her anger burned even more strongly toward her own self. She thought of Kirk waiting downstairs for her. Of Paulie, dying in a hospital bed, his letters unread, his character maligned. *All this time... All this time, he was writing to me. He did remain true to his promises. Why, Lord, did I not believe You? Why did I so quickly give in to fear, rather than cling to the hope that I have in You?*

She glanced up to find Mama looking at her with expectation. Grace felt her heart sink from her chest straight to the rug covering the floor of Mama's upstairs sitting room. "I thought so much less of him than he deserved." Her voice cracked like cheap glassware overheated. Her finger ran up and down the side of the envelope, finding the ridges of the stamp. Why couldn't this letter have reached her before she'd...?

Mama shook her head. "But you know better now."

She ground her teeth to stop the tears that brimmed in her eyes anyway. "But it doesn't matter now, does it?" Finally, she knew what the heroine in *Tess of the D'urbervilles* felt when her Angel Clare finally came around – too late for a happy ending.

Mama's eyebrows came together. "What do you mean?"

"I gave my word to Kirk – that I'd marry him." Tears filled her eyes. She pushed them back, so tired of weeping! "We were only waiting for Dad to give his blessing. How can I go back on my promise?"

Mama lifted her chin, as if she'd disagree. Grace's spirit stretched out, longing for Mama to say that she thought otherwise, that Grace was free to change her mind, break up with Kirk, and take her place at Paulie's side. But then sorrow replaced the defiance in Mama's expression as quickly as it had come. "Well." She turned her words over with the gentleness of waves on Crescent Park beach. "To be honest, I don't think you need to worry about that, Grace. I don't think – that is, the doctors say that, well, Paulie may not make it."

Hearing Mama say that so clearly, without reservation, broke the vessel in Grace's heart. The tears ran over the edges of her eyes, washing her cheeks with their saltiness. She didn't sob; that wasn't her way. But she knew deeply what the psalmist meant when he spoke of the brokenhearted!

Mama pushed a handkerchief into her fingers. Her hand came to rest on Grace's shoulder with a comforting touch. "You didn't do anything wrong. Paulie's letters never reached you. How could you have known? You needn't feel upset with yourself."

But Grace did feel upset with herself. Not only had she believed less of Paulie than her experience with him justified, but she'd also gone ahead with her own wisdom, led by fear. *Oh, Lord, when will I learn to trust You? To listen to Your voice when You check me in my spirit? To trust that You will make all things plain?*

And then frustration joined the grief. Why had the Lord not

stopped her before she had gone this far? Did He not care that her heart would be broken? That Paulie would perhaps die without ever knowing that she'd loved him to the end? Or that, if Paulie lived, it might be to see her married to another man? *Lord! Don't punish me according to my sins, but in Your mercy redeem this. Please. For the honor of Your Name.*

CHAPTER THIRTY-ONE

Ben sat in the first row of the tiny hospital chapel. His eyes stayed fixed on the cross, suspended against the front wall. *He did it for me. He gave His life so that I could be free – so that I could live.* Hard to believe as it was, it was impossible to *not* believe. A Voice inside Ben whispered the truth: He had been born again, born from above.

His ears alerted to the sound of the clunky door opening behind him. Was Paulie worse? Had the Doc – Sam – come to tell him…? Tensed, Ben hesitated to turn to face Paulie's dad but then steeled himself. He had never feared before – not in that way at least. He wouldn't start now.

He stood and turned all at the same time. And found, not Sam, but Betty Cloud letting the door shut behind her with a decided clank. Betty… What would she think of him now? Had she heard that his foolish anger had caused all this? And had she heard that he was sorry – sorry for it all – and had asked for forgiveness? Shyness overcame him, a new sensation when it came to girls. His hands found his pockets. At least there they wouldn't fidget.

Despite the dim light of the chapel, Ben could tell that Betty wasn't surprised to find him there. *She came looking for me.* Had Sam sent her? He wet his lips. "Is Paulie…?"

Shaking her head, Betty moved down the aisle toward him, her steps quiet but sure. "No, he's the same. Your mother came back with Grace. They're with him now."

He nodded, watching her flowing descent as she took a seat in the front pew. Her eyes sought out and focused on the cross, as his had a few moments before. "Doctor Giorgi told me. About you getting saved."

So she had heard that part at least. "Yeah. Ain't that something? Guess nobody expected that. 'Specially not me."

The corner of her mouth tilted up, giving courage to Ben's heart. Should he tell her the rest? The silent moment between them stretched like saltwater taffy as his nerves jangled worse than any telephone. But really, what did he have to hide? *God knows it all anyway.* And had forgiven him. Didn't he want her to know, too? Better, after all, to see what she'd do with their friendship when she knew what he was capable of: nearly murdering a man.

He swallowed hard and slid onto the rigid bench beside her. The blood thundering through his veins, Ben plunged forward. "Betty, I was the one who pushed him, ya know."

Her smiling mouth sobered. She stiffened and turned toward him, but he couldn't read her eyes as they scanned his face. "Why'd you do it?"

Ben gulped. Might as well be thorough now. "I was angry. So angry I could kill him. And I… And it looks like…" He trailed off, unable to get the words out of his throat. He let his head fall into his hands, unable to face the young woman beside him. The girl who must hate him now. *And I deserve it.*

He waited for her to lash him with her words or to rise from the bench and leave, unable to linger in a near-murderer's presence any longer. But, instead, he felt a gentle hand rest on his bowed-over back. At her kindness, a sob broke free from Ben's heart.

"Poor Paulie. Why'd it take me nearly killing him for God to save my soul? I was so stupid. *Am* so stupid." His nose ran now, mixing with his tears. He turned his face to the side to wipe his nose on his shirt-sleeve.

"Here." Betty interrupted his action by rummaging in her dress pocket. She pulled out a lacy hanky and offered it to him.

"Thanks," he managed, taking the delicate scrap with his calloused fingers. He wiped his cheeks and snuffled his nose into it.

"God knows best, Ben." She spoke quietly, sincerely.

Could it be? He stole a watery glance at Betty. There was no judgment there.

And since it felt so good to get his sin against Paulie out in the open, Ben kept going, the cooling wave of repentance washing over his spirit. "I'm sorry for how I've treated you, Betty. I was awful."

"Yes, you were." Straight-faced, she gazed at him for a few seconds, then let her lips turn up in a half-smile. "But that's okay. I forgive you, Ben."

"And I'm sorry, too, that you'll lose Paulie." Anybody could see how much that kid meant to her. Causing her this pain, too... well, it came close to crushing him until he remembered Betty's own words from moments earlier: *God knows best.*

Ben would believe that. He wouldn't understand, but he would believe, by God's grace.

"We'll all lose him." She cocked her head to the side as if not understanding why he'd singled her out as the victim of suffering.

Ben frowned. Had he been mistaken? "But you and him... I was sure that you liked him." It sounded so brazen, even for him, stating out-loud that she'd held romantic feelings for his stepbrother.

Betty blinked several times, her long lashes sweeping the rose of her cheeks. She seemed to struggle for the right words. "Ben... Paulie wasn't the one for me. Once, I thought that maybe... But not anymore." She bit her lip and then released it, not meeting Ben's gaze. "Sure, I admire Paulie. What girl wouldn't? But I think his heart belongs to your sister. And has for a long time."

She glanced over at him, as if to see if he agreed. Remembering all the conversations he'd had with Paulie over the summer, Ben could only nod. Had his own jealousy – twisted and not even recognizing itself for what it was – made him believe that Paulie had taken up with Betty?

Betty kept eye contact with him. "I've realized in the past few weeks that I have to stop planning out my own life – trying to walk in just the right way so that God gives me what I want. I – I need to walk with Jesus Christ because I love Him. Not so that He'll give me something. And I need to open up my heart to whatever – or whoever – He gives to me. Even if that thing or person doesn't fit my original plan for my life."

A faint hope struggled to rise in his heart, with the wobbliness of a newborn colt striving to stand on its infant legs. "C-C-Could you care for anyone in that way, Betty? The way you thought you cared for Paulie?"

The moment he said it, Ben dropped his eyes to the floor. What a fool he was! How brash, to think that this girl, utterly admirable in every way, would look his way – would find him worthy of anything but her contempt? Even forgiven by God, he still knew that he was a dog – or worse.

The silence stretched for so long that, at last, he dared to look up. Her solemn brown eyes shone – shone toward him. A smile brushed her lips. "Well," she murmured, rising from the pew. "We'll have to wait and see."

CHAPTER THIRTY-TWO

Grace took a quiet seat. Only a lamp lit the private room, removed from the glare and hushed bustle of the hospital. In vain, she struggled to swallow down the lump that had fixed itself in her throat as soon as she'd seen Paulie's dear face, swathed in bandages. One of his curls had escaped the gauze prison, dark against the bruised, pale skin.

If only he would wake. Her soul swelled with grief as the moments passed. She strove to pray but couldn't find the words. Slowly but without hesitation once she had made up her mind, Grace reached for his hand, seemingly the only part of his body that hadn't suffered damage. She needed a connection to him. If he could not wake and speak, then she would communicate in this way, with the touch of her hand on his.

It was cool – too cool. *He's lost too much blood.* Since Dad's blood matched Paulie's, the doctors had even tried transfusions, but Dad had said something about internal bleeding as well. *'We've attempted to stop it, but…'* She'd seen the hesitation in Dad. He didn't want to say it, but Grace knew that he believed that Paulie's time was limited. *'Go to him now, Grace,'* he'd said, emphasizing the *now.*

And so she'd come here into his room alone, leaving Kirk in the waiting area with Mama. It had been difficult to shake off the man, but, to Kirk's obvious surprise, she'd insisted and stood her ground. *I need time alone with Paulie before Kirk barges in.*

Dismayed, she shook her head. It wasn't right to think of poor Kirk that way. He didn't deserve it. *I was the one who encouraged him. I was the one who didn't listen to the Holy Spirit.* She should be chastening herself, not Kirk.

Now, she rested their joined hands on the cold white sheet, and the tears rose, brimming to the edges of her lower lids. Why should she try to stop them? They poured out freely as the widow's oil, tracking down her cheeks and moistening the bedclothes. His breathing shallowed; Dad said it might. Her heart sank. She must say it now, lump or no lump clogging her throat.

"I got your last letter, Paulie. I wanted you to know," she spoke softly, for his ears alone. If only he could hear her! Then he would know that she had not forsaken him, not truly. And he would know, too, that she believed him faithful as well. Her voice broken, she continued, "Your love has been what you promised all those years ago: enduring, persevering even when you must have thought there was no hope."

His hand was so cold. She raised it to her lips and tasted the salt from her tears when she kissed it. Then she nestled their joined hands beneath the blanket, willing the warmth from hers to pass to his. "I never answered you that summer before our last year of high school, Paulie. You told me that you loved me. Two years ago. Do you remember?"

The tears blurred her voice, and she struggled against them. This must be said. He must hear this from her before the door of death opened and he found himself in the Everlasting Arms. "Of course you remember," she went on lightly, as if he'd replied, as if they now sat together in the tall meadow grass behind the Picoletti house, as they'd done in the summer of 1935. "So, I'd like to answer you properly at long last. Better late than never, right?" Her hand tightened on his. If she could hold him here by strength alone, she'd do it. *But I can't.* Her grip loosened. *Only You can bring the dead back to life and make the lame to walk. Only You know what is best, oh my Savior and my God. Our times are in Your hands.*

Grace tucked the messy chunks of hair behind her ears and fixed her eyes on Paulie's expressionless, swollen face. "I love you, Paulie Giorgi. I wish that I could've told you before, but I couldn't. Not as a stepsister loves a stepbrother, but as you said you love me."

For long moments, she couldn't speak. Her chest felt weighted as if with concrete blocks. It was done. She'd said what needed saying. A supernatural Comforter settled His wings over her anguished heart. Then she whispered, "I'm praying for God to heal you, Paulie. But even if He doesn't answer me in this life, I know that you go to Him to be healed completely."

Someone cleared her throat at the cracked-open door. Grace slid her hand from Paulie's and turned to see Mama at the door, understanding on her face.

"The doctors need to come in for a few minutes," Mama explained.

Nodding, Grace rose to her feet. She wiped away the tears that continued to start and stop without warning and moved to Mama's side. Mama's arm came up strong and warm around her, tightening Grace to her body.

"Should I talk to Kirk?" she asked Mama quietly. "Should I tell him how things are between Paulie and me? Or is that foolish? If Paulie is going to..." She couldn't finish the sentence but met Mama's eyes instead, searching for wisdom.

Mama reached out and tucked a stray chunk of hair behind Grace's ear. Her hand rested on Grace's face, comforting and warm. Her face wore sympathy but not answers.

Grace stepped close to Mama, not willing for anyone to hear. "I love Paulie, Mama. I know that. And, if he woke up from this, if God spares him longer in this world, of course I'd want to marry him. And I'm certain he feels the same way about me." The thought of Paulie – dear, sincere Paulie – continuing to love her whether or not she loved him back flooded Grace with joy in the midst of her grief. He had affirmed that much in his last letter, the one Mrs. McCusker had almost succeeded in destroying. *He still loves me.* And it seemed to be with a purer, stronger love than ever before.

Mama released a deep breath. "I guess, then, that you have to make a decision, Grace. If you tell Mr. Haverland that you still love Paulie and then Paulie... doesn't make it, Mr. Haverland may not want to marry you any longer. It's hard to marry a woman who loves someone else."

"I know, Mama. But I wonder, is it right for me to keep that from Kirk?" She ran her fingernails over her cuticles. "And yet, if I do tell him and Paulie lives, can I take back my promise to marry him? In God's eyes, I mean. Though I gave my word in haste." *In disobedience.* The bitterness of it – to have Paulie's love within reach but to be unable to take it – struck her heart a bloody blow. She forced her voice to stay steady. "The Scriptures say that the righteous keep their vows." She closed her eyes against the pain. "Even to their own hurt."

Mama thought for a long moment before she said, very quietly, "I think it's always better to tell the truth. And then trust that God will work it out for good."

A calm settled over the sea of her wind-tossed spirit. Grace touched her lips to Mama's round cheek. "Thanks, Mama." The words came out cracked as flea-market china. She knew what she would do.

~ ~ ~

When Grace entered the waiting room, heart trembling, she found Kirk sitting in a corner chair, a thoughtful expression on his face. She knew that she looked a mess, what with her hair pushed behind her ears, her cheeks smeared with tear-tracks, her eyes swollen nearly shut from crying. When she took a seat beside him, he jumped, as though he hadn't seen her coming.

"I'm sorry. I didn't mean to startle you," she apologized, her voice quiet so that she wouldn't wake Ben, who slumbered across the room, his head resting in his hands.

He took a long look at her, as if trying to figure out the depth of a lake in which he'd never swam. "That's alright."

Grace hesitated, but before she could speak again, Kirk took her hand in his. He ran his index finger over her knuckles for a long minute. What was he thinking?

"Grace," he said at last with the care of one using a clothes-wringer, wary of catching his hand in the rollers, "I heard you talking to your stepbrother. To Paulie, I mean."

Her breath caught. He'd heard… how much? Her skin burned hot with embarrassment. What must he think of her now? What kind of conclusions had he drawn? Heart pounding, she opened her mouth to explain.

But he held up his other hand. "Please. Let me say this first. I had come to bring you a cup of water – I didn't know how long you'd stay in there, and I thought that you might become thirsty." He nodded toward the still-full paper cup beside him. "But when I heard you tell him that you loved him… Well, let it suffice to say that I understand now why you couldn't tell me you loved me back in New York, before you came home to Chetham. I had no idea that you and he – that your relationship went beyond that of stepbrother and stepsister."

Grace looked down at their joined hands. "Kirk, I thought that Paulie had given me up. My mother just found out today that our housekeeper had taken his letters. It was a misunderstanding. He never did stop… stop loving me, you see." *Nor I, him.*

He gave her hand one last squeeze and let go. "I do understand, Grace. And I'm not angry at all. You never deceived me; I don't believe so, anyway. I never asked you about Paulie. Not directly, at any rate."

Pausing, Kirk caught her eyes with his. "And I hope that you believe me when I say that I do still love you and would like to marry you." He spoke low, his voice rough with emotion. "I believe that you may come to love me over time just as much as you love Paulie now."

He stopped and seemed to wait for a response from her. Grace couldn't give it, other than to nod, keeping her face calm. *He wants to keep the engagement then.*

"But," continued Kirk, "real love isn't forced, Grace. I want you to choose me. I'm releasing you from our engagement because I know that, as long as Paulie lives, your heart isn't in it. Not now." He took a deep breath. "And if he comes through this, I'll gladly give your marriage my blessing. But also know that if he doesn't come through, my promise to you still stands: I love you and would like you to be my wife."

Her soul quieted, Grace nodded. "Thank you," she murmured. Was it for his commitment to keeping their engagement or for his release of her own obligation to it? *For both.* Looking at him, Grace knew that – if Paulie did not come through this peril – she would be a blessed woman to place her hand in Kirk's. Surely, God would give her love for him as well. Wouldn't He?

"But let's not think of that all now." He leaned forward. "Will you pray with me? For Paulie?"

She looked up at him, unable to mask her surprise.

"I want him to live as much as you do," Kirk said, his eyes serious. Then he added with a half-smile, "Well, perhaps not *quite* as much."

CHAPTER THIRTY-THREE

She sat with Paulie that night – all that long, dark night. She sang hymns softly, the ones she knew he loved, the ones he'd sung so joyfully at her side in church all during their last high school year of 1936.

Others came, too, of course. Dad came in and out, often with another doctor or nurse at his side. They prodded Paulie, gave him injections and adjusted his I.V. – things Grace didn't understand – didn't want to understand. Grace couldn't meet Dad's eyes; the pain bled too raw there. Was that how the Father God felt when He saw His Only Son ripped and scarlet on a cross so long ago? Yet the Father had endured the loss of His Son – He had gone through with the sacrifice. *For such a one as I. For such a one as Paulie and Ben and Mama and… and all of us.*

Mama came, too, staying and sitting in the corner chair. Around midnight, Grace saw that she'd fallen into the sleep of the exhausted and grieved. Ben and Kirk stayed together in the waiting room.

Her spirit drained, Grace continued to pray, asking for a quiet heart, pleading for Paulie's life to be given to him. *Turn the tide, Lord. You calmed the waves of the sea. You are able to do this. You are able to heal him, if You wish. Do good for us. You are good, and You always do good. Help my unbelief.*

Around five in the morning, the call of the robin woke her. A crick twinging her neck, Grace lifted her head from where it rested on Paulie's bedcovers. She shook herself to clear the fuzziness from her mind. How could she have fallen asleep when Paulie needed her to stay awake, needed her to pray and sing him through the night?

The gray dawn gleamed faintly at the window. Again, the robin called out. Inexplicably, hope lifted its delicate fronds in Grace's heart. She stood up on stiff legs and moved toward the light.

The harbinger of spring. That was what Emmeline Kinner had called the robin. Weariness in her every motion, Grace pushed aside the white curtain. Pale streams tiptoed into the room. She clicked off the lamp, tired of its artificial glare, before finally turning toward her beloved. If only he would wake! If only he would even flutter his eyes.

But he lay just the same as he had last night. If anything, his breathing sounded more shallow and his color appeared more ashen. The worn-out tears rose to her eyes again. The robin's voice clattered against her ears. It seemed like a cruel joke, to let the robin sing of life and joy, and then to allow her to turn and see the boy whose kindness had once illuminated the cheerlessness of her days, sprawled nearly dead.

Yet there is a spring beyond the grave.

Where had that thought come from? She ground her teeth to stop the sob from crawling out of her chest. *It's true.* She knew that it was. She had staked her life on it. Would she turn from the truth so soon because hardship and loss had come?

On shaking legs, Grace crossed to Paulie's side again. Lowering herself to the chair, she picked up Dad's Bible lying on the table beside his bed. Mama must've gotten it when she'd returned home last evening. Its gilt-edged pages felt velvety with use as Grace's trembling hands found the passage that tapped at the door of her heart:

Then Martha, as soon as she heard that Jesus was coming, went and met

Him: but Mary sat still in the house. Then said Martha unto Jesus, Lord, if Thou hadst been here, my brother had not died. But I know, that even now, whatsoever Thou wilt ask of God, God will give it Thee. Jesus saith unto her, Thy brother shall rise again. Martha saith unto Him, I know that he shall rise again in the resurrection at the last day. Jesus said unto her, I am the resurrection, and the life: he that believeth in Me, though he were dead, yet shall he live: And whosoever liveth and believeth in Me shall never die. Believest thou this? She saith unto Him, Yea, Lord: I believe that Thou art the Christ, the Son of God, which should come into the world.

Grace rested the Bible on her knees. "Lord, I believe." The words sounded loud in the silent room. "You are with me, even through this." She picked up Paulie's hand – very cool – and made the decision to trust in Christ, her Beloved. *Even in this.*

A little later, Mama stirred on her chair in the corner of Paulie's room. Rubbing the sleep from her eyes, she rose quickly. "I'm going to get your brother from the Kinners," she murmured, touching Grace's shoulder. "It's nearly six. Cliff should be here if…"

Grace knew what Mama meant. She, too, must have seen Paulie's gray pallor and guessed what might come soon. "Okay." A peace had settled over her heart – a peace not without deep grief, but a peace nonetheless. A hope that went beyond the life this world had to offer.

"I'll tell your dad that I'm heading over there. Will you be alright if I leave?" The concern shone openly in Mama's eyes.

"Yes." And as Mama closed the door behind her, Grace knew that it was true. She kept looking into Paulie's face and thinking, *Soon he will be with Jesus. Soon all his pain and sorrow will be gone forever.*

Once, not too long ago, she'd thought that life without Paulie would be barren. Still, she'd been willing to give him up. She'd done it when she'd gone to the Conservatory a year ago, hadn't she? But in her heart, she'd always hoped that the rubber wouldn't have to meet the road – that she wouldn't be put to the test in the end. Because, in truth, Paulie did mean so much to her!

228

But Jesus meant more. She knew it now. If God asked for Paulie to be utterly, finally laid on the altar, who was she to withhold him? Who was she to put terms of service on her faith or her love for the One who had died for her? *I cannot forsake Him now. Oh, Lord, do not forsake me!*

And so she stayed on by Paulie's side as the grayness of the shadow of death descended over the room. She huddled close to her Shepherd, though, because of the heartrending mist, she could not always feel His presence. When would He usher her beloved beyond the valley, to the green pastures where death could no longer reach him? For his sake, she prayed that it would be soon.

CHAPTER THIRTY-FOUR

Words didn't exist to describe the pain that splintered his body into more pieces than he could count. If he could count. Which, considering the headache that trampled through his brain, he thought unlikely. He tried to wonder where he was – what had happened to cause the agony that reverberated through every limb and tendon and vein – but his mind couldn't find the energy to do it. After a moment of half-hearted fighting, he surrendered his body to the anguish, unable to do anything but breathe and merely absorb his surroundings.

Darkness spread before him, and at first, he thought that he lay outside – that it was night. Then he realized that his eyes were closed. *Too much effort to open them.* They felt as though the lids had rusted shut. *What else?*

A voice, familiar and yet one that he hadn't heard for a long, long time, touched his hearing. It reminded him of the earth shimmering after a hard spring rain, of sunlight illuminating the white-crested waves, of a song sparrow singing in the midst of a forest of white birch trees. Was it an angel? *Am I dying?* The thought filled him with a fearful delight.

The voice continued:

There lies beneath its shadow
But on the other side
The darkness of an awful grave
That gapes both deep and wide;
And there between us stands the cross
Two arms outstretched to save
A watchman set to guard the way
From that eternal grave.

Perhaps he was in heaven, but he needed to open his eyes to rid himself of the dreadful pain that clutched at his body, holding it prisoner. *Lord, help me open my eyes.* He struggled but couldn't do it. Exhausted, he mentally fell back. The voice had stopped singing.

Whispering. Scuffling, as of a chair being pushed back. The squeak of someone sitting down. A door shutting with the quietness of a tiptoeing kitten.

Again, he struggled against the heaviness. *I have… I have to open… Please, Lord my Savior.* What held his lids down? Pain pummeled him. His eyes slipped open at last.

He was in a white room. *A hospital.* So he wasn't dead. Or dying, for that matter. Not yet, at least. The pale light made his head throb even worse. He let his eyelids close again, unable to think of anything but the pain radiating through his face, neck, sides, arms. *Everywhere. Everything hurts so badly.*

Where was Dad? Anxiety rushed through his chest, tensing what few muscles were not already cramped into rigidity. Yet the pull of weariness overcame even that; it was a ripe-tide, and he couldn't swim against it…

~ ~ ~

A chair creaked into the fuzzy blackness of his dream, shaking him out of sleep. This time, he didn't wait for the waves of pain to overtake him. *Help me, Lord. Help me.* Someone groaned, and he realized it was he himself. With his eyes cracked open, he blearily stared up at the far-off white ceiling.

Someone sucked in his breath nearby. If every fiber of his body didn't ache, he would've whipped his head to the side to see who was there with him, but he found that, when he tried to move his head even a fraction, pocket-knives of agony stabbed his skull.

Whoever it was shoved back his chair and stumbled away. The door opened and shut. Paulie gave into the pressure of the pain and weariness. He slept.

~ ~ ~

When the white room came into blurry focus again, a chair creaked immediately. He'd barely had time to blink before the wonderful face of his father came into view right above him. He tried to lick his lips but found that he couldn't even do that.

Dad's throat bobbed. "Son." The single word held the many-colored shades of an autumn sunset, juxtaposing pathos with joy. Tears flooded Dad's reddened eyes and spilled down his unshaven cheeks. He touched a finger to Paulie's cheek as if it was made of English bone-china.

Dad.

"Ben said that you had opened your eyes. I couldn't – didn't want to get my hopes up."

Ben. The accident returned to Paulie's mind. This was the result of Ben pushing him. *I could've died.* He remembered how he'd thought he was a goner as he plunged the few dozen feet off the roof. *God was gracious.*

Where was Ben? He had to be here; Dad had said that the person in the room had been his stepbrother. And that voice. Had he imagined it? The singing that had drawn him out of his deep sleep? That had given him impulse to try to open his eyes? Had it been Mama? *No.* If he hadn't known better, he'd have thought...

It was too much of a struggle. The throbbing in his head

increased, and he let his eyes close in relief.

CHAPTER THIRTY-FIVE

I *heard the voice of Jesus say,*
Come unto Me and rest…

It was her voice. He knew it now. *Grace came. She came.* The bliss of that thought overcame the clawing pain. He let her finish the hymn, soaking it into his soul. Even though she cared for another man, his own love for her had not diminished. He realized that, as she sang, she cradled his hand in hers. *She came. For me.*

As the last word dissolved, he opened his eyes. Again, the swift creak of a chair. Without moving his head, he peered toward the right. There she stood, a smile feather-light on her lips. Her hair had come out of its stylish waves and hung messily tucked behind her ears, as it had when he'd first asked if he could carry her books home for her, years ago. Her dress wore the creases of one who has sat in vigil for a loved one without thought of appearance.

And her eyes… They held his steadily, though the red of sleeplessness tinged their whites and the nearly black circles underscored the skin beneath them. In them, such depth of emotion and will shimmered.

He waited for her to speak. How long had he wished to hear her voice?

But, instead, she bent. Her lips just barely touched his cheek. When she straightened again, her hair brushing his skin as she rose, he saw clearly the confident love that dwelt in her gaze. *For me.* The thought overtook him as his eyes slipped shut again.

Something had changed while he'd slept. He didn't know what had happened to bring Grace back to him, so fully, so completely. Whatever it was would have to wait until he woke again.

~ ~ ~

Grace lifted her hand in farewell as the car rumbled away from the hospital. Regret put small wrinkles in the overall joy that clothed her heart. *If only I had trusted You, Lord. If only I had waited, as You told me. Kirk would not have been hurt.*

But she had made the mistakes. Had done the wrong. She drew in a breath. And had repented. *Oh, Lord, that You would work all of the hurt out for our good.* The story of a man she'd read about in the Old Testament pulled at her mind. *May I not have caused irreparable pain. Be gracious to me, Heavenly Father.*

She would believe that He would. For didn't He want good for His children? Would not the Judge of all the earth do right?

As soon as Dad had announced that he'd witnessed Paulie waking, Kirk had met Grace's hope-filled gaze with a determined though sorrowful one of his own. A man of honor, he had released her from the engagement immediately. Now, the following day, he'd gotten into his car to make the long journey back to Crocksville.

Alone.

It would not be the last she'd see of Kirk, though. Conservatory classes began in less than a month, and, unless God directed her otherwise, Grace knew that she needed to return and finish out her degree program. *Three more years.* God had opened the door for her there; who knew what plan He had for the musical education He was giving her?

I will trust in You. As Kirk's automobile disappeared into the distance, Grace turned and entered the hospital once more. She climbed to the second floor with unhurried steps, letting other visitors pass her. She was just about to knock on Paulie's door when it opened and Ben emerged.

Her heart glowed at the freedom written plainly there. She had never seen him like this. Even as a boy, Ben had always been a fighter. Sensitive, yes, but reacting with his fists up rather than his knees on the ground. It had nearly taken Paulie's life to bring Ben to liberty. Grace thought of Paulie, lying bandaged, barely able to speak, in the room just beyond them. The cost of Ben's release had been high. She thought of Calvary and her own day of repentance, of turning away from her own sufficiency and turning to Christ. *The cost always has been high.*

Tears in his eyes, Ben drew her into a tight hug, the scent of his hardworking skin filling her nostrils. "He forgave me," he murmured into her ear. He drew away and held her at arm's-length. Childlike wonder filled his voice and illuminated his eyes. "He forgave me, Canary."

EPILOGUE

Her hair whipped her eyes. Grace closed them shut against the sting but smiled all the same. How could she help it on such a day as this? The wind gusted away as suddenly as it had come, and she opened her eyes to take in the scene before her.

Far off down the beach, Mama and Dad strolled, her mother's hand tucked into the crook of his arm. Their steps took them half in and half out of the salty water as it rolled incessantly back-and-forth. Nearby, Ben led Cliff up a rocky outcropping, their bare feet scrambling up the rocks with the agility of crabs. Their endeavor was made a little more difficult by Cliff's clutching a greasy bag containing the remnants of their clamcakes.

Grace sucked in a deep breath, letting the briny air fill her lungs. Could more joy fill her than she felt at this moment?

"You can join them. I don't mind." Paulie's words slurred out, blurry as she knew that his vision had been for a while after he'd woken.

She turned to look at him, Paulie, by her side, alive, safe. God had given him back to her, as He had given Lazarus back to Martha and Mary. Shaking her head, Grace smiled. "No. I'll stay with you."

He shifted on the sand, a grimace shadowing his face as he moved. Six weeks after the injury, a cast still encased his arm and he tired easily. His jawbone had healed well overall, though lingering soreness caused him to keep his mouth as immobile as he could. Dad had insisted that he rest while the rest of the family walked on the shore.

"You're leaving Monday." It was a statement, not a question.

Grace nodded. She'd already taken an excused absence of nearly a month from the Conservatory. If she planned to continue there this term, she needed to return later this week. And, when she'd prayed, she'd not felt at liberty to walk away from the education God had opened to her. A large part of her yearned to stay in Chetham, but she knew that obedience to her Savior had to come first and only.

A comfortable silence spread over them. Beyond the waves, the sun began his descent.

"Before you go," Paulie spoke into the quiet, "may I give you a gift?"

A gift? When had he had an opportunity to shop for a gift? Paulie yet couldn't hobble around the house without exhaustion and pain overtaking him, never mind go into town to do some shopping. "You don't have to give me a gift, Paulie." Having him, knowing that he loved her faithfully, that was a gift large enough to last her lifetime. Pulling her knees up to her chest, Grace wrapped her arms around her lower legs and buried her bare toes deep into the sun-warmed sand.

"This is for you, if you'll accept it."

She turned her head. In his hand, he held out a blue velvet box, identical to the one in which her pearl earrings had lain when he'd given them to her years ago. Her heart jittered, but she told herself to keep still. *Grace, it's jewelry. He knows that you wear the other earrings a lot, so he's bought you another pair.*

But something small and bright inside her soul hoped it was something quite different. She swallowed and dared to meet his eyes.

They gleamed with eagerness. "I can't open it myself because of this silly thing," he explained, grimacing at his bound arm. "But I hope that you know that I wish I could."

He still held the box in his open palm. With steady fingers, she reached out and took it. The lid opened smoothly on its brass hinge. Inside, a ring glittered on its bed of velvet: a creamy pearl surrounded by clusters of tiny diamonds. She lifted her gaze to meet his.

He was going to propose to her. Paulie was going to ask her to marry him.

"Grace Picoletti, I love you. I think I have since the day you charged me a dime to help me with my mathematics homework. You are a pearl of great price, sweet Grace – not to take the Scriptures out of context." He smiled. "A man would be a fool – I would be a fool – to give you up for anything in this world, outside the Gospel."

Tears rose in her eyes. Was it possible to feel *more* joy? She'd wondered that a few minutes earlier, and now wondered it again. Perhaps God expanded your capacity for taking in joy as He gave more to you...

"But what about your father?" The thought drew her thundering emotions to a halt. Two years ago, her stepfather had been very clear that he thought that Paulie and Grace should remain unattached to one another until they'd finished college.

"He's changed his mind. He told me that, if I'm willing to wait for you and you want to marry me, then he'll give us his blessing to become engaged. Just after I was released from the hospital, Dad brought me to the jeweler's to have your ring created." He paused. "The diamonds around the pearl are from my mother's engagement ring."

She tucked her errant hair behind her ears and let her smile fill her face. "And the pearl?"

Paulie touched her chin with his forefinger. "The pearl, sweet Grace, is for you. It's one-of-a-kind, uniquely beautiful in every way. It has known adversity and has come out of it shining and pure in heart. And, by God's grace, so have you."

The tears brimmed and overflowed.

"Will you marry me?"

~ ~ ~

The dog-days of September brought back all his childhood memories, heavy on his heart as the humidity was on his body. Emerging from the woods that hedged Chetham on three of its four sides, Ben tramped down the thick grassy slope toward the Catholic church he'd attended as a boy. The dry straw crunched as his bare feet crushed it, but his stone-hard soles couldn't be pierced by the sharp blades. As he approached the church, he heard the bell pealing from the steeple. *Calling all the faithful to assemble.*

He stopped half-way down the hill, shading his eyes against the setting sun. Below, on Main Street, groups of communicants ambled toward the open church doors. Father Frederick stood on the threshold, welcoming them. Ben had to give it to the old priest; he'd looked the other way – even privately encouraged Mama – when she'd married Samuel two years ago, a decision that effectively ended her relationship with the Catholic church. *Maybe Father Frederick felt sorry that he'd not helped her when Papa…*

He shook his head. Who knew, really? The best thing he could do was forgive the old priest for any wrong he'd done, knowingly or not. *God knows I have my own sins to remember.*

Though He has cast them into the depths of the sea.

At the thought, a burst of joy bloomed in Ben's heart, like a spring crocus unfolding from the dark soil of winter. *He has made all things new.* Grace's words to him in a long-ago letter had borne fruit in the largest way of all: He was a new creation with a future and a hope hidden in the Man who had loved him from all eternity past.

In smaller ways, as well, God had given Ben a new start: with Sam and Paulie, with Mama and Grace and Cliff and the twins, even. And with other citizens of Chetham, besides. Having finished work on the old Picoletti house, Ben had found paying carpentry jobs all over town, more than enough to support himself… and, God willing, a family of his own one day.

He had a fresh beginning with Betty Cloud, too. In an hour or so, he'd arrive at her doorstep, spit-shiny clean, ready to spend an evening at her folks' house. Ben couldn't keep the grin from his face at the thought… nor at the fact that she'd told him that she was looking forward to it. With the most beautiful smile on her face, too, when she'd said it – a smile for him, of all people.

He waited until the heavy door closed behind the priest and the last note rang from the bells. Then Ben drew a breath deep into his lungs, feeling the oxygen invigorate him for what lay ahead, and descended down the slope.

He didn't pause when his path took him nearly to the steps of the church itself. His destination didn't lie there. Instead, Ben continued down the cobbled walk that curved around the side of the towering stone building. Mass had commenced; he would not be disturbed in the shadowy yard nestling behind the church.

His heart began to thrum more intently as he came close to the marked graves, many with candles lit at their bases, some with wilting meadow flowers. Eyes straight ahead, Ben headed directly for the more recent tombstones. He knew that it wasn't a case of losing his nerve, but rather of doing immediately what ought to have been done so long ago.

There it was. A simple marker, with only one line besides a name and the date of birth and death to indicate that a body – with a history, with a soul – lay moldering beneath the sod. It said: *Gone, but not forgotten.* Probably, Papa's brother had arranged for the inscription. The grass had never re-grown correctly over the dug grave; it sprouted here-and-there on the rectangular earth with the sparsity of a man who was rapidly balding.

He knelt, feeling his knees gut into the soft spots in the dusty ground, and set down the small ceramic pot he'd carried from the Kinners' house. Knowing that Emmeline had given Grace that geranium plant from her own cuttings and that the older woman was a generous sort, he'd made bold this morning – gone to the Kinners' house and asked her for a small pot – if she could spare it. Emmeline had given it to him without hesitation. Little David had peeked out from behind her legs at him, and Ben hadn't been able to help but feel once more that the kid reminded him so much of his own brothers and sisters. In those moments, standing in Emmeline's shining kitchen, Ben's true relationship to David had emerged in his heart and mind with the slow beauty of a springtime dawn. He'd looked from David's shy grin to Emmeline's tense but peaceful smile, and Ben could tell that she knew that he had guessed.

He'd smiled back and nodded to let her know that it was alright. He believed – truly believed with a quiet in his soul that passed understanding – that God would work it all together for the good – the great good. He didn't need to strive. Didn't need to fret and fight against it. For once in his life, he would trust his Heavenly Father and believe that God was indeed good.

And here, on the cracked, moldy surface of Papa's grave, Ben would stake his claim in that goodness – and would, once and for all, let go of the past in the only way possible.

From his back pocket, Ben pulled out a trowel and dug a hole several inches deep right beside Papa's marker. He filled the bottom of it with water from his pocket flask. Then, with the gentleness he'd used on the horses back at Bousquet's stable, he loosened the geranium from its pot and set it into the hole, pushing the soil around the plant and pressing down until he knew that it would grow straight.

He looked up to the blue sky, brushed by the spreading branches of the willow trees that stood sentinel over the graveyard. How had he not seen it for so long? He'd spent so much time being angry at others for the wrongs they'd done to him that he'd not thought about the One whom *he* had offended – the One who stood ready to forgive him because He had given Himself in Ben's place. Knowing that, believing that, how could he yet hold Papa's wrongs against him?

He couldn't.

Settling back on his haunches, Ben let his fingers trace Papa's name, bitten deep into the stone. "I forgive you, Papa." The words came out softly, like a ghost floating away at the advent of sunrise. "I don't hold it against you – any of it. I ain't gonna lie to you; you didn't do the best you could, like some folks say. You threw us to the side like we was trash you didn't need. You let us fend for ourselves – your own kids, half-starving. You hurt Mama–"

His voice cracked. He swallowed, waiting, waiting until he could continue. He had to continue. And he had to do it well. It was important, this first step into the future. His heart beat, slow and steady in his chest. From the church behind him, he could hear the drone of the communicants responding during the service. A beetle crawled onto his knee. Brushing it off, he felt himself steadied enough to go on.

"But all of that, Papa – I don't hold it against you," he repeated. "And I wish I could do it over – wish I could've been a better son to you and Mama, 'stead of getting angry and bitter. I'm sorry for breaking your tooth out, Papa. I should've treated ya with respect even if you weren't right."

He stayed there for a long while, beside the red flower, at peace, the bitter fragrance of the plant mingling with the perpetual salt-scent in the Rhode Island air. He let his heart and mind rest quiet before his God. He didn't feel any different from the moment before he'd entered the graveyard. Yet, at the same time, he knew there *was* a difference – a freedom in his soul whose bounds he would know more and more as time went on.

The crickets had begun to chirp their ancient twilight ballad when Ben rose from kneeling, stiff-kneed and full of grace, and retraced his steps back up the slope toward the Giorgi home. Behind him, the geranium still bowed her scarlet head.

A Note to Readers

Thank you from the bottom of my heart for coming along to Chetham, Rhode Island, with me. I hope that you've had a beautiful, worthwhile journey and that you've enjoyed getting to know Grace, Paulie, Sam, Sarah, Ben, and all the rest of the folks whose lives have been chronicled through this *A Time of Grace Trilogy*.

For those of you who are curious, you'll not find Chetham on maps of Rhode Island. I've based Chetham on several 1930s-era towns in the Ocean State and have located it north of the capitol city, Providence. Likewise, the town of Crocksville and the Conservatory there, as well as the Helen Higgins School, while based on era-appropriate models, are ultimately products of my imagination.

If you'd like to learn more about this time period and the research that undergirds this series, I'd love to have you visit my website at www.aliciagruggieri.com. You'll find some resources and links there that I think you might find interesting.

Finally, if you've enjoyed reading *A Love to Come Home To*, would you consider leaving a short review for it on Amazon, Goodreads, or any other place where booklovers gather? That will help other readers discover the story of the Picolettis and Giorgis as well. Thank you!

I'd love to hear from you! Please contact me through my website (www.aliciagruggieri.com) or through any of my social media links.

Thanks again for reading! I pray that the words have been a blessing to you.

Grace and peace,

Alicia G. Ruggieri

2 Corinthians 4:7

Acknowledgments

There are so many people who go into the making of a book. I'm thankful for each one whose encouragement, prayers, suggestions, and loving criticism have made *A Love to Come Home To* possible. You are each a gift from the Lord God to me!

Thanks to my wonderful critique team – Rebekah, Londie, and Anita. What would I do without your sharp eyes, sensitive hearts, and tactful tongues? You've each made the story of Ben's redemption stronger.

To the many author-friends whose wisdom and advice have fortified my steps: What a provision of the Lord you each are! Thank you.

A big thank-you to my street team – Ladies, what a joy to work with you to let others know about the *A Time of Grace Trilogy*! Thanks for your encouragement, effort, and prayers.

Once again, thanks to the Rhode Island libraries and their employees. What a blessing it was to have so much material on Depression-era Rhode Island right there on the shelves! Thank you for making Rhode Island history a priority, helping writers like me.

Thanks also to my dear husband, Alex, who reads drafts of my books and fuels my writing with the occasional latte. Mama-Bee, my thanks go to you, too, whose encouragement always inspires me to press on in the truth. Thanks to all of my family – both those to whom I was born and those to whom I'm bonded through marriage – for your loving, kind support of my writing endeavors.

To readers who purchase, read, and enjoy my books: Thank you! May the Lord bless you with the grace and peace that comes from knowing Jesus Christ.

Made in the USA
Charleston, SC
21 July 2016